Samuel French Acting Edition

Let's Mur

by Monk Ferris

SAMUELFRENCH.COM   SAMUELFRENCH.CO.UK

FOR PRODUCTION ENQUIRIES

UNITED STATES AND CANADA
Info@SamuelFrench.com
1-866-598-8449

UNITED KINGDOM AND EUROPE
Plays@SamuelFrench.co.uk
020-7255-4302

Each title is subject to availability from Samuel French, depending upon country of performance. Please be aware that *LET'S MURDER MARSHA* may not be licensed by Samuel French in your territory. Professional and amateur producers should contact the nearest Samuel French office or licensing partner to verify availability.

Please refer to page 98 for further copyright information.

For
MADELINE KAHN
in thanks for
my primal
Broadway credit

CAST OF CHARACTERS

TOBIAS GILMORE — a Wall Street broker
MARSHA GILMORE — his wife
VIRGIL BAXTER — a friend and neighbor
PERSIS DEVORE — a lady with a secret
BIANCA — the Gilmores' maid
LYNETTE THOREN — Marsha's mother
BEN QUADE — Bianca's boy friend

Time: The Present, mid-October
Locale: The Gilmore's posh Manhattan apartment

ACT ONE: Late afternoon, Monday
ACT TWO: Immediately following
ACT THREE: Immediately following

Let's Murder Marsha

ACT ONE

Curtain rises on the living room of the GILMORE apartment in Manhattan [see Set Design]. It is late afternoon on a Monday in mid-October. The first thing we see is MARSHA GILMORE's rump; she is seated on footstool, leaning forward into — and mostly hidden by — the gap beneath the seat-cushion of the wingback chair, searching for something. She straightens to a more decorous sitting position and lets the cushion fall back into place, and we see that she is an attractive and well groomed woman in her middle thirties. She looks left and right, frowning, then stands, goes to sofa, drops to a sitting position on the coffeetable, and proceeds to search — in vain — under each of its two seat-cushions. She stands, slams the cushions back into place, and speaks.

MARSHA. Damn. (*looks about uncertainly, then moves to desk, and is systematically searching inside drawer after drawer as BIANCA, the GILMORES' maid, a young lady barely more than 20 years of age, enters from kitchen and pauses just inside upstage archway*)

BIANCA. Did you call, Mrs. Gilmore?

MARSHA. (*glances to ascertain identity of speaker, then resumes her search before replying*) No. I said "damn".

BIANCA. (*politely*) Damn what?

MARSHA. (*slams final drawer, moves toward tall cabinet that serves as a coat closet*) Damn book. (*opens cab-*

inet, in which we see normal closet paraphernalia—top-coats, jackets, etc.—and rummages)
BIANCA. Damn what book?
MARSHA. (*still rummaging*) *The Creeping Slasher.* It's being true to its title. (*will give up on closet, shut doors*) Not the slasher part, the creeping part. I can't figure where it's got to—(*crosses past BIANCA and will go behind bar*)—and it's driving me beserk.
BIANCA. The plot or the disappearance?
MARSHA. *Both!* (*vanishes from view as she searches behind bar*) And it was due back at the library yesterday! Bad enough not finding the book or learning the identity of the killer—(*will rise into view again, bookless, as she finishes*)—without getting fined ten cents a day besides! (*moves from behind bar to spot midway between bar and wingback chair, and stands there uncertainly*)
BIANCA. (*frowns*) The library wasn't *open* yesterday.
MARSHA. It wasn't? Why not?
BIANCA. It's *never* open on Sunday.
MARSHA. (*had taken two steps toward fireplace, but now stops and faces her*) Sunday? Yesterday was Sunday? But that means—
BIANCA. Means what, mum?
MARSHA. Today must be Monday. And it can't be.
BIANCA. I don't see why not, mum. Monday has a way of following Sunday.
MARSHA. But Bianca—it's impossible. Firstly, if it's Monday, then the damn book is at least *two* days overdue, and I'm just not that slow a reader; but secondly, if it's Monday, Mister Gilmore would be at his office, and I've called him there twice today and he's not!
BIANCA. Perhaps he stepped out.
MARSHA. Bianca, Mister Gilmore is a broker. Mon-

days are busy days for him. No one on Wall Street steps out on a Monday.

BIANCA. Nevertheless, mum—

MARSHA. Oh, all right, all right, have it your way. Monday it is! (*looks left and right, frowns shakes head*) I don't suppose *you've* seen *The Creeping Slasher* lying about?

BIANCA. Sorry, mum, no. Where did you see it last?

MARSHA. (*points at wingback chair*) I always read right there, before the fire. October tends to be chilly. It's cozier that way.

BIANCA. (*moves from archway, will move down to fireplace via route that takes her below wingback chair*) It is rather chilly, now that you mention it. I'll just start up the fire.

MARSHA. (*sighs*) For all the good it will do.

BIANCA. Mum?

MARSHA. Well, I mean, what's the point in having a cozy chair before the fire and no *Creeping Slasher?*

BIANCA. (*at fireplace, now, going about starting it up*) That's true enough. Still—if you *do* find it, the fire will be cozy and ready for you.

MARSHA. (*fondly*) Oh, Bianca. You *are* a treasure!

BIANCA. (*demurely*) Mum . . . if I might ask a question—? (*sees from MARSHA's shift to an interested curiosity that this is permissible, and so continues*) Why do you always *hide* your mystery thrillers?

MARSHA. I'm not sure I follow you, Bianca.

BIANCA. (*busy finishing off the fire-starting*) Well— you *do* read *everything* by Anton Dupré—I'm surprised you don't simply have them all on a nice bookshelf in your room.

MARSHA. All? But Bianca, how could I? Think of the library fines!

BIANCA. I mean, *buy* them, mum. If you enjoy them so much—(*The fire is now glowing, and she straightens from her work and moves toward MARSHA.*)—I should think you'd want to own them.

MARSHA. Oh, I would, I truly would. But be reasonable, Bianca: If I bought them all, I'd soon run out of hiding-places. There are only so many chair-cushions and drawers.

BIANCA. But why hide them in the first place?

MARSHA. Oh! Oh, now I see! Well, it's very simple. Mister Gilmore doesn't approve of mystery novels. He says they rot the mind. He thinks people should read nothing but the classics, like *War and Peace.* I tried that once. Everybody is named Ivan Ivanovitch, or some such impossible name. Never again. I couldn't keep the characters straight. Now *there's* a book could *really* rot one's mind!

BIANCA. I see. Yes, I quite understand now. But mum —if you *must* hide your thrillers, why not have just *one* hiding-place? You know, a special spot where the book will always be when you want it.

MARSHA. Because I never know where I'll *be* when Tobias pops up. I have to ditch the book in the quickest place that's handy.

BIANCA. Well, then—try to remember—where were you the *last* time he popped up and you had to ditch *The Creeping Slasher?*

MARSHA. I wish I knew. Tobias pops up everywhere in this apartment. Still, why shouldn't he? I mean, it *is* his *home,* after all. Which reminds me—(*frowns, looks at wristwatch*) Shouldn't he *be* here by now? It's nearly six o'clock.

BIANCA. He *is* a bit later than usual, mum. Perhaps he stopped off to buy you a birthday present?

MARSHA. A what? Birthday present? Oh, dear, is it

that time of year *already?* I *can't* be *another* year older
. . . *can* I?

BIANCA. Not quite, mum. Your birthday isn't till
tomorrow.

MARSHA. Well, that's a mercy.

BIANCA. And, if I may say so, mum, you don't look
your age at all. However do you do it!

MARSHA. Work, Bianca. Hard work. Watching my
diet, getting plenty of exercise, and of course avoiding
late hours whenever possible. A woman needs her
beauty rest. (*abruptly, snaps her fingers, eyes wide with
delight*) Beautyrest! Of course! That's *it!* (*starts for
bedroom, fast*) My missing thriller is under the mat-
tress! Oh, *thank* you, Bianca! (*exits*)

BIANCA. (*more a comment to herself than a reply*)
For what? (*shrugs, starts for archway, but is barely
there when MARSHA re-enters, book in hand*)

MARSHA. Bianca, would you be a dear and get my
coat? I simply *must* get this back to the library today!

BIANCA. (*will get topcoat from cabinet, during:*) But
aren't you going to finish it, mum?

MARSHA. There's plenty of time to finish it on the bus.
I only have two chapters to go.

BIANCA. You're not taking your car? (*business of
helping MARSHA on with her coat*)

MARSHA. (*clumsily shifting the book from hand to
hand so she can get her arms into the sleeves*) No. Tried
that once. Never again. The only time I could read was
at stop-signals, and then I'd get engrossed in the plot,
and people would honk their horns at me something
dreadful, and I'd lose my place, and try to find it at the
next stoplight, and—

BIANCA. (*has the coat on her now*) There you are,
mum.

MARSHA. Oh, thank you, Bianca. You *are* a treasure!

(*moves to front door, opens it*)

BIANCA. What shall I tell Mister Gilmore?

MARSHA. About what?

BIANCA. If he should return home and ask where you are—?

MARSHA. Um . . . say I'm out for a stroll.

BIANCA. In October?

MARSHA. Why not? I mean—after all—it *is* October, isn't it? (*exits, shutting door after her*)

(*The moment she is gone, BIANCA goes behind bar, gets gin, vermouth and a cocktail shaker, and starts mixing a batch of martinis; she is just in the process of stirring the mixture when DOOR CHIMES sound; she hesitates, shrugs, sets shaker on bar and answers door; MARSHA enters.*)

BIANCA. Oh! Back so soon, mum?

MARSHA. (*moving to cabinet without a pause*) Forgot my purse. They won't let you on the bus without money.

BIANCA. (*as MARSHA rummages, moves back to bar, where she will pour a martini into a stem glass*) Not necessarily, mum.

MARSHA. (*ceases rummaging briefly*) Hmmm?

BIANCA. (*will drop an olive into drink, during:*) Well, they *do* let you *on* without it. They just won't let you *stay* on if you don't pay your *fare*. (*She will taste martini, frown, and set it down, during:*)

MARSHA. Do you know—I never thought of that. They'd put you off at the next stop, wouldn't they! (*BIANCA will remove olive from glass, dump drink back into shaker, and add more gin to the mixture, during:*) Then, if you did the same thing on the next bus, and the next—you could eventually get downtown for nothing!

BIANCA. (*will stir and pour drink again, during:*) The only problem is, the way the buses run, it could take you half a day for a trip of any length.

MARSHA. (*resumes rummaging*) Still, it's worth remembering. In case one ever gets stuck without busfare. (*finds purse*) Ah! Success! (*will close cabinet, move to desk, set book down on it, and start looking in purse, during:*) I hope my library card's in here. I'd hate to have to come home empty-handed . . . (*finds card, brings it into view*) Oh, good! (*replaces card in purse, glances barward just as BIANCA is replacing olive in drink*) Bianca! I hope you haven't taken to drinking on duty?!

BIANCA. What, mum? . . . Oh! Oh, no, mum. This is for Mister Gilmore. He likes it ready and waiting when he comes through the door. Working on Wall Street must be something of a strain.

MARSHA. No, not really. Tobias just likes martinis. Now I really must dash! (*exits with purse, but neglects to take book*)

BIANCA. (*the moment door closes, picks up martini, takes a sip, sighs with pleasure*) Perfect! (*drinks rest of martini in one swallow, picks out olive and chews it happily while pouring second drink, and is just adding new olive to this drink when DOOR CHIMES sound again*) *Now* what's she forgotten?! (*starts for door, spies book on desk*) Oh, the silly goose! (*picks up book, opens door on:*) Here you are, mum!

(*Extends book, then takes backstep as PERSIS DE-VORE—a 30ish, very svelte lady [blond hair in upsweep, sleek black trenchcoat and matching boots, dark sunglasses with harlequin frames and jeweled tips]—steps into room.*)

PERSIS. (*takes book*) Thank you. (*looks at title*) I've read it. (*sets book on desk*)

BIANCA. (*flustered*) I beg your pardon, mum, but—?

PERSIS. (*sensing unspoken question*) Persis Devore. Is Mister Gilmore in?

BIANCA. Why—no, mum . . . but he's expected momentarily. Would you—um—care to have a seat? (*gestures sofaward*)

PERSIS. (*will move that way and sit*) Thank you, my dear. (*As she goes, BIANCA glances at book, abruptly hurries over and hides it in nearest desk drawer, shutting drawer just as PERSIS seats herself on sofa.*)

BIANCA. May I take your coat?

PERSIS. No, thank you, my dear. I won't be staying long.

BIANCA. Um . . . would you like a martini while you're waiting?

PERSIS. (*pleased and surprised*) Why, thank you, yes.

BIANCA. (*hurries to bar, gets martini, brings it to her*) Here you are!

PERSIS. Thank you. (*takes sip*) Mmmm, this is delicious!

BIANCA. Yes, I know! (*instantly flustered as PERSIS gives her a look*) I mean—that's what Mister Gilmore always says—so—it must be.

(*There is the sound of KEY IN LOCK, and then TO-
      BIAS GILMORE—a handsome man in his late 40s
      —enters.*)

TOBIAS. Good evening, Bianca. (*Takes key from lock, and as he pockets it, PERSIS stands up and he sees her for the first time.*) Persis! What are *you* doing here?!

BIANCA. (*sensing something juicy, hazards:*) Shouldn't she be—?!

TOBIAS. What? Oh! (*quickly fakes aplomb*) Of course she should. Just — wasn't expecting her. Business acquaintance. Unusual to see her outside office hours. (*sees BIANCA is still dubious*) Um . . . Is — er — Mrs. Gilmore in?

BIANCA. No, sir, she went out to — um — take a stroll.

TOBIAS. (*visibly relaxing*) Oh, good!

BIANCA. Why?

TOBIAS. (*tense again*) She — um — needs the exercise!

PERSIS. (*senses his panic, helps him along*) Can't get enough exercise. Speeds up the skin, firms the blood — or is it the other way round?

TOBIAS. (*anxious to be rid of her*) Bianca — don't you have something to do in the kitchen?

BIANCA. Such as?

TOBIAS. Fixing dinner!

BIANCA. It's all fixed.

TOBIAS. Cleaning the pots, then.

BIANCA. All cleaned and put away.

TOBIAS. (*thinks hard for a second; then:*) Scrubbing the floor!

BIANCA. All scrubbed.

TOBIAS. The counters.

BIANCA. Them, too.

TOBIAS. (*triumphantly*) The ceiling!

BIANCA. (*blinks, scowls*) Damn. (*exits to kitchen*)

PERSIS. Tobias — you have a maid who answers the door, mixes drinks, makes dinner, does the dishes, and scrubs floors, counters and ceilings?! A *maid's* not supposed to do *all* those things!

TOBIAS. Ssh! *Bianca* doesn't know that!

PERSIS. But —

TOBIAS. (*grabs her by elbow, steers her downstage of sofa, glancing back nervously kitchenward, and lower-*

ing his voice a bit) Never mind my maid! What are you *doing* here?!

PERSIS. Why, I—I wanted to see the decor of the place. After all, if I'm to do the upholstery in the seaplane, I want to choose something suitable to your wife's tastes!

TOBIAS. Will you please keep your voice down?! Bianca has hearing like a beagle!

PERSIS. But why *shouldn't* she hear?

TOBIAS. Because the seaplane is a surprise, for my wife's birthday tomorrow! If Bianca hears, and mentions it to her—

PERSIS. Oh, so *that's* what all the secrecy is about! You should have *told* me it was a surprise. No wonder you were so nervous about whether your wife was here!

TOBIAS. (*impatiently*) I didn't tell you it was a surprise because I never expected you to even *meet* my wife! But it *is*, and you *mustn't*! (*starts moving her doorward*) Now, you've seen the decor, so if you'll kindly get out of here—

PERSIS. But I haven't seen the bedroom!

TOBIAS. (*stops towing her, stares blankly*) So?

PERSIS. (*disengages her elbow from his grip*) A woman's *most* personal taste goes into the decor of her bedroom. That will give me the clue I'm seeking.

TOBIAS. Oh, very well, very well! It's right over here! (*points bedroomward, follows as she heads that way*) But be quick about it! Marsha may be home at any moment!

(*They exit to bedroom; an instant later, we hear KEY IN LOCK, and MARSHA enters quickly from hall, steps to desk, reaching for book—sees it's not there—stops, puzzled—jams fists against hips, looks around uncertainly—and then BIANCA enters from kitchen, sponge in hand.*)

BIANCA. Oh. It *is* you, mum. I *thought* I heard the door.

MARSHA. (*looks toward BIANCA while pointing at desktop*) The slasher seems to be creeping *again!* I could have *sworn* I left it right here!

BIANCA. (*bustles down to her*) Oh, you did, mum. I just stashed it in the drawer so Mister Gilmore wouldn't see it. (*produces book*)

MARSHA. Oh, what a quick thinker you are! (*takes book, starts to remove coat, finds book encumbers this plan, hands it back to BIANCA, and gets out of her coat, all during:*) I'd hate to see him get upset. Not that I think he'd ever do me any physical *harm* over it, you understand, but there's no point in risking a rift in domestic harmony, is there! (*has coat off, now, will hang it in cabinet, during:*)

BIANCA. Excuse me, mum, but—I thought you were going to the library?

MARSHA. So did I, until I remembered that it's after six o'clock and the library will be closed for the day. That is, closed for the night. It's open during the day. But not this late. (*has closed cabinet by now, returns to BIANCA*)

BIANCA. So it's another ten cents down the drain! (*hands book to MARSHA*)

MARSHA. (*heading with book toward chair*) How true, how true! But *The Creeping Slasher* is worth it! (*starts getting settled comfortably in chair*) It's all about this perfect ninny of a woman who hasn't the faintest idea that her husband is trying to do her in for her money, so he can run off with another woman he loves.

Why she can't *see* her peril is beyond me—but, of course, it wouldn't be much fun to read if she phoned the police and simply had him carted off to jail in Chapter One! (*is all cozy in the chair, now, well back between the wings, feet tucked up under her, opening book*)

BIANCA. (*has moved down to spot beside chair*) Excuse me, mum, but—aren't you taking a big risk?

MARSHA. Hmm? What *are* you babbling about, Bianca?

BIANCA. Well—reading the book right here in the living room—if Mister Gilmore should return—

MARSHA. (*looks up*) Return? You mean he's come home and gone out again?

BIANCA. Apparently, mum. Probably just walking that lady to her car.

MARSHA. (*closes book*) Lady? What lady?

BIANCA. A business acquaintance, mum. Name of Persis Devore. Really a smasher, in a kind of continental way—blonde hair, black trench-coat, dark glasses with jewels on them—like one of those spies in a thriller.

MARSHA. (*puzzled*) *I* know of no such business acquaintance . . . (*then abruptly dismisses puzzlement*) Of course, Tobias is a very busy broker. There must be hundreds of his clients of whom I've never heard. (*starts to re-open book, BIANCA starts kitchenward, and then MARSHA frowns and stops her with:*) A "smasher," you said—?

BIANCA. Very *much* so, mum . . . *oh,* but not compared to *you,* of course!

MARSHA. (*visibly relieved*) Well, *that's* a mercy! Well, back to the slasher! (*opens book again*)

BIANCA. (*flexing arms, exits with sponge kitchenward on:*) And *I'll* just get back on that *ceiling!*

MARSHA. (*almost absorbed in book, frowns, murmurs out front:*) On the ceiling—?

(*Looks upstage, but BIANCA is gone; shrugs, curls up into a cozy ball, and starts reading; a moment later, TOBIAS and PERSIS enter from bedroom, and will pause in area between wingback chair and archway; MARSHA's reaction, of course, to hearing TOBIAS's voice will be instant panic about holding that mystery novel: She will close it, hug it to her chest, and cuddle up even smaller to avoid being seen, and—thanks to the flaring wings of the chair—she achieves her purpose; she does this during:*)

TOBIAS. (*speaking as they enter*) Well, I hope you're satisfied, Persis!

PERSIS. Eminently! That bedroom is absolutely beautiful! (*MARSHA widens her eyes in curious uncertainty.*)

TOBIAS. Save your praises for later! If Marsha had come in there and caught us—!

PERSIS. You worry too much, Tobias. I'm sure she'll never suspect a thing!

TOBIAS. I certainly hope you're right! I mean, the whole *point* of our plan is to take her completely by surprise! (*MARSHA's curiosity starts to evolve into apprehension.*)

PERSIS. I'm *sure* we can pull it off without a hitch! After all, she has no reason to distrust you, tomorrow, when you suggest a drive down to the bay.

TOBIAS. I can hardly wait to see her face when we get there! Especially when I break that champagne bottle across her nose and the two of us stand and watch as she slides slowly into the water! (*MARSHA's eyes are wide with incipient terror, now.*)

PERSIS. (*sighs*) Seems such a waste of good champagne!

TOBIAS. But in such a good cause! (*starts escorting PERSIS toward door*) Besides, there'll be plenty of champagne to drink afterward at the party! (*MARSHA's mouth mimes an echo of "Party?!" and her attitude mingles annoyance with her basic fear.*)

PERSIS. (*as TOBIAS opens door for her*) I hope you'll let me propose a toast! Your wife has such marvelous taste — in bedroom decor *and* in husbands! (*pecks him on the cheek, which MARSHA squirms about enough to see and react to*)

TOBIAS. (*chuckles*) After my little surprise down by the bay, I fear Marsha may only be here in *spirit!* Be kind of a shame, really — you and I here, drinking champagne, while she's — (*points heavenward*) — up there floating through the heavens!

PERSIS. I really should insist you bring her back here, afterward. (*MARSHA reacts to this apparent ghoulish suggestion.*)

TOBIAS. Well — I'll try — but I suspect it won't be easy. After I surprise her down by the bay, I may well have to *drag* her away from the spot!

PERSIS. (*laughs lightly*) Well, *che sera sera!* (*Exits; he closes door, starts removing topcoat.*)

TOBIAS. *Bianca — ?!* (*will start hanging coat in cabinet*)

BIANCA. (*appears from kitchen, sponge in hand*) Oh, Mister Gilmore — I didn't hear you come back!

TOBIAS. Back? Back from where? I haven't been out.

BIANCA. (*glances chairward, sees MARSHA peeking around left wing of chair — though TOBIAS, busy with coat, does not — quickly returns her gaze to him*) Well, a moment ago, when I came in here and didn't see you or that Miss Devore —

TOBIAS. (*shuts cabinet, moves to her, fast*) Ssh! We were in the bedroom, planning a surprise for Mrs. Gilmore.

BIANCA. (*uncertainly*) What *kind* of surprise?

TOBIAS. (*wags a finger at her*) Never you mind! Oh, and — by the way — you are *not* to mention Miss Devore's visit to my wife, under any circumstances!

BIANCA. (*after an uncertain glance toward MAR-SHA, which TOBIAS does not notice*) Why — um — no, sir, I won't, if you don't want me to. . . ?

TOBIAS. (*rubs palms*) Good! Good! I knew I could count on your discretion!

BIANCA. Oh, always, sir!

TOBIAS. Good, good! (*takes step barward, stops*) Bianca, where is my martini?

BIANCA. (*moves instantly toward emptied glass on coffeetable where PERSIS left it*) Oh, that Devore lady drank it! Let me make you another. The stuff in the shaker is all diluted by now.

TOBIAS. (*as BIANCA starts barward with empty glass*) Well, wait. Matter of fact, I'd like to shower before dinner. Just have it waiting when I come out, eh? (*will exit toward bedroom during:*)

BIANCA. Very well, sir.

MARSHA. (*the moment he is gone, jumps from chair, rushes to bar*) Bianca! What am I going to do?!

BIANCA. (*behind bar, now, pouring remainder of martinis into oversized glass*) About what, mum?

MARSHA. My husband — Tobias — and that dreadful Devore woman — are planning to *murder* me!

BIANCA. Oh, come now, mum — you've been reading

too many mysteries. (*sets down pitcher, reaches thirstily for glass*)

MARSHA. (*distractedly takes glass herself, leaving BIANCA to shrug and sigh emptyhanded, moves deskward*) But I *heard* them! They're going to lure me down to the bay, bop me with a bottle, and dump me in the drink—and *then* they're coming back *here* to *celebrate!* (*drops book on desk, drains half the glass*)

BIANCA. Oh, surely you've made some sort of mistake, mum?

MARSHA. It's exactly like in *The Creeping Slasher!* (*taps book for emphasis*) With one fortunate difference—*I* caught *on* to their sordid scheme! (*drains half of remainder of drink*)

BIANCA. Well, mum—if you *are* right—why not just stay away from the bay?

MARSHA. (*impatiently*) That would only *delay* their plan. They'd find another way, another time, and the next time I might not find out about it till it was too late! (*drains rest of drink, makes a face, holds up glass*) What *is* this stuff, anyway?!

BIANCA. Martinis, mum.

MARSHA. Oh, well, that explains it. I *hate* martinis! (*moves toward bar with empty glass*)

BIANCA. Can I make you something different, mum?

MARSHA. (*setting glass on bar*) No, I don't think so. I'm much too distracted to enjoy anything right now. What I really need is a plan of action. (*sits glumly on left bar stool, one elbow on bar, facing hearthward as she muses aloud*) Bianca—

BIANCA. (*busily making fresh batch of martinis*) Mum?

MARSHA. What would *you* do in my position? I mean, if Tobias were going to murder *you* and run off with another woman?

BIANCA. I'd report him to the Domestics Union. They're very strict about things like that.

MARSHA. I mean if you were his wife.

BIANCA. Oh. (*thinks a moment before continuing*) Well, I suppose I'd call the police. They seem to be *terribly* set against people getting bumped off.

MARSHA. (*brightens*) The police! Of course! (*hops down from bar stool, heads for phone*) Why didn't *I* think of that! You *are* a treasure, Bianca. (*picks up phone, dials one digit, waits*) . . . Damn.

BIANCA. Mum?

MARSHA. I've got one of those recordings telling me not to bother the operator unless it's absolutely necessary. As if she had anything *else* to do but answer the phone! I'll never understand why they — (*abruptly reacts as operator comes on line*) Hello, operator? . . . Yes, this *is* an emergency . . . Of *course* I'm sure! . . . I will *not* cross-my-heart-and-hope-to-die! . . . I want to talk to a policeman . . . No, I *don't* know which one! Any one will do . . . Because I'm about to be murdered! . . . By my husband . . . How do *I* know why?! . . . Well, I suppose he's grown tried of me . . . Operator, really, there just isn't *time* for us to see a marriage counselor! Could I *please* speak with the police?! . . . I don't *want* the number, I want the *police!* . . . But operator —! (*grits her teeth, and deliberately lies*) Yes, I am writing it down for future reference! . . . Thank you! . . . (*waits, visibly irate, tapping one foot impatiently, then brightens and speaks eagerly*) Hello, police? . . . My husband is going to murder me, can you come right over? . . . My name? — Oh, dear, do you really have to have that? . . . Well, you know, with the scandal and all, I'd really rather not . . . But can't I just give you our address and apartment number? I'm the only wife *here* who's about to be murdered . . . Oh, all right, if you

must, you must! My name is Marsha Gilmore, and my
husband's name is Tobias . . . "Tobias" . . . T-o-b-i-a-s
. . . What? . . . Well, no, he isn't murdering me right
now . . . Tomorrow, down by the bay . . . Because I
heard him *say* so . . . Well—no—I was the only
witness—except for the woman he's in cahoots
with—but I doubt if she'd testify to it . . . But isn't there
anything you can do? . . . Now, look, you can hardly
stake out the entire bay! . . . No, I don't know *where* on
the bay he plans to do it! . . . "*Ask* him"?! Are you
nuts?! . . . But officer—! . . . Look, all I know is, he and
this woman talked about luring me down to the bay,
bopping me with a bottle, and watching me sink into the
water, and then dragging my body back here for the
party! . . . No, I have *not* been drinking! (*BIANCA
hears this, and loudly clears her throat; MARSHA
looks her way, and BIANCA taps cocktail shaker while
giving a shame-on-you shake of her head; MARSHA
guiltily returns to phone and continues:*) Well, maybe
one drink . . . Hell, if *you* were about to be murdered,
wouldn't *you* have a drink?! . . . No, this is *not* the liquor talking, this is Marsha Gilmore talking! . . .
Because I had the drink *after* I heard their plans! . . .
(*listens a moment, then holds receiver about a foot
from her face and shouts at it*) No, I will *not* cross-my-
heart-and-hope-to-die! (*slams receiver down into
cradle, folds her arms*) So much for the *police!* (*turns
her head BIANCA's way*) Any *more* bright ideas?!

BIANCA. (*who has finished the new batch and just
tasted a freshly-poured drink*) How about a martini?

MARSHA. Oh, all right, why not! (*starts for bar*)

BIANCA. (*pouring one for MARSHA*) I thought you
didn't like them?

MARSHA. I used to think a lot of things. I thought

Tobias loved me, I thought a telephone operator was there to help callers, and I thought the police would come if you called them. (*picks up drink*) Lately, I hardly know *what* to think! (*drains drink, makes face, sets glass on bar*) But I was right about martinis!

BIANCA. You know what you need, mum?

MARSHA. What?

BIANCA. You need an ally.

MARSHA. Ally? You mean like England or France?

BIANCA. Of course not, mum. I mean some person you can trust, someone to help you save yourself from doom when even the police fail you. It's done in all the best mystery stories.

MARSHA. Yes, but usually by a man who loves the heroine, so they can get together after the husband is caught redhanded and sent to the chair. I don't know anyone like that.

BIANCA. What about Mister Baxter, across the hall?

MARSHA. Virgil? *He's* not in love with me . . . *is* he?

BIANCA. Well—maybe not yet—that usually happens halfway through the book.

MARSHA. No. No, it still wouldn't work. I mean, even if Virgil helped, and fell in love with me while helping, what *good* would it do him? *I'm* not in love with *Virgil!*

BIANCA. You could *tell* him you were.

MARSHA. But—do you think that's quite fair to the man?

BIANCA. Anything's better than being bopped with a bottle and dropped in the drink.

MARSHA. But it seems such an unkind thing to do.

BIANCA. And getting murdered doesn't?

MARSHA. Well . . . if you put it that way . . . (*shrugs*) Virgil it is! (*starts for phone*) Don't know his number by any chance, do you?

BIANCA. As a matter of fact, I do. It's the same as our own, except the last two digits are reversed. We get ever so many calls for him when people dial wrong.

MARSHA. Do you suppose *he* gets calls that were intended for *us?*

BIANCA. I don't see why not. Fair is fair.

MARSHA. (*at phone, busily dials five digits, hesitates, then carefully dials last two, waits a bit, and then:*) Hello, Virgil? . . . Marsha Gilmore . . . Fine, just fine . . . Well, actually, not *that* fine, at least not emotionally . . . No, I'm not ill. The fact of the matter is, something dreadful has happened, and you are the only person in the world who can help me, and so I was wondering if—(*At this moment, TOBIAS, now in slippers, slacks, smoking jacket and ascot, enters from bedroom and heads right for waiting martini on bar; MARSHA panics at once, and says into phone:*) Never mind! (*hangs up at once, forces smile, starts barward*) Darling! Did you have a nice shower?

TOBIAS. (*turns, drink now in hand*) Well—no nicer than normal—but pleasant enough, I suppose. Who was that on the phone, dear?

MARSHA. No one!

TOBIAS. But—?

MARSHA. That is—no one we *know.* Wrong number. Total stranger. Mistake.

TOBIAS. Then why did you tell him "Never mind!"? Never mind what?

BIANCA. (*quickly*) Never mind the inconvenience he caused her!

MARSHA. Right! (*flashes grateful smile at BIANCA*)

TOBIAS. Marsha . . . is there anything wrong—?

MARSHA. (*forces a light laugh*) What an odd thing to ask, darling! Of course not!

TOBIAS. But you seem so—sort of—*tense* or something . . . (*As she and BIANCA try to think of something to say, a light frown of suspicion crosses his brow.*) Marsha—you haven't been reading those blood-and-thunder stories again, I hope?! (*BOTH WOMEN instantly look toward where book lies in plain view on desk, then instantly look back and try to look casual.*)

BOTH WOMEN. *Nonsense!*

TOBIAS. (*after a slight double-take of puzzlement at BIANCA*) You know how nervous those things make you, darling. Trash, nothing but trash. Rots the mind, you know!

MARSHA. (*backing away, maneuvering to keep herself between him and book, trying to get to it moving backward*) Yes. Yes I do know. That's why I never read them any more. That's why I'm not nervous any more. Calm. Serene. In total control. (*will feel for book, pick up memo-pad by mistake, hold it behind her back, and just as she completes last phrase, DOOR CHIMES sound right behind her and she screams in surprise and fright:*) Aaaaaah!

TOBIAS. Darling, it's only the doorbell.

MARSHA. (*will back-sidle away from door, moving bedroomward with pad behind her, keeping it out of view of TOBIAS, who is now down near upstage end of armchair*) Doorbell? What doorbell? I didn't hear any doorbell! (*DOOR CHIMES sound again and she screams again.*) Aaaaaah!

TOBIAS. (*concerned*) Marsha—?!

MARSHA. (*nearing exit to bedroom*) I didn't scream. It's therapy. Primal-scream therapy. Dreadfully good for relieving tension, relaxing nerves!

TOBIAS. *Not* for anybody within *earshot!* (*HEAVY KNOCKING starts at door.*) Bianca, will you please answer the bell?!

BIANCA. You mean the knock.

TOBIAS. (*KNOCKING is still continuing.*) Don't be so technical! *Somebody* is at that *door!*

MARSHA. Tell them I'm busy! (*finally, with a side-leap from view, completes her exit to the bedroom*)

TOBIAS. (*starts doorward*) I'm *coming*, I'm *coming!* You don't have to break the *door* down!

BIANCA. (*rushes from behind bar, beats him to door, during:*) *I'll* get it! *I'll* get it!

(*Yanks open door and VIRGIL BAXTER, a tall man with a mournful face, just entering middle age, steps in.*)

VIRGIL. I heard a woman scream!

BIANCA. (*shrugs*) *Who didn't!?* (*He is forced to backstep into hall as she shuts door.*)

TOBIAS. Bianca! Is that any way to treat a neighbor?!

BIANCA. You mean he wanted *more?* (*DOOR CHIMES and KNOCKING resume.*)

TOBIAS. Does *that* answer your question?

MARSHA. (*rushes in from bedroom minus pad*) Isn't anybody going to get the door?! (*gallops past both TOBIAS and BIANCA, opens door*) Virgil!

VIRGIL. (*steps in quickly*) Marsha! Thank heaven you're all right! After that phone call, when I heard you scream—!

TOBIAS. (*moves toward him, and BIANCA moves back so that she is out of TOBIAS's line-of-sight and can signal VIRGIL when shortly indicated*) What phone call?

VIRGIL. Why— (*sees BIANCA making frantic signals to him—pointing at TOBIAS's back, shaking her head, miming talking on phone, another headshake, hands clasped in prayerful attitude toward him, etc.; he blinks at this, then speaks with caution*) Uh . . . phone call . . . well . . . um . . . you see . . .

MARSHA. (*leaping valiantly into the breach*) *Yesterday!* When you phoned *yesterday,* we got cut *off!* Naturally, it worried you a bit, and that's why you came over to investigate! (*is nodding head vigorously at VIRGIL throughout, to indicate that this is his new story-line*)

VIRGIL. (*gets the message, turns to TOBIAS*) Right!

TOBIAS. You waited a *whole day* to investigate?

VIRGIL. Well . . . uh . . .

BIANCA. Better late than never! (*When OTHERS all look at her:*) I'd better get back on that ceiling! (*exits kitchenward*)

MARSHA. Do you know that's the *second* time she's said that! I wonder what—

TOBIAS. (*quickly*) Bianca is just conscientious, that's all. Not many maids would take it as part of their duties to clean a kitchen ceiling!

MARSHA. *Clean* it? But *she* said get *on* it!

VIRGIL. Marsha, that's an idiom for work. You have a job to do, you say you'd better get *on* it. You have a ceiling to clean, you say—

MARSHA. All right, all right, I get it. And I must say I'm relieved. But why she'd start doing such a thing so near dinner time—

TOBIAS. It's sheer conscientiousness, I tell you! It's not as though she'd been *ordered* to do it just to get her out of the *room,* or anything! (*guiltily turns away, takes hasty sip of martini*)

MARSHA. (*now narrow-eyed and totally suspicious, speaks normally*) No. No, of *course* not, darling . . .

VIRGIL. Well, I guess I'll be leaving, now—

MARSHA. (*instantly clutches his arm*) No! (*As a curious TOBIAS turns her way, she calms a bit.*) That is—can't you stay for dinner, Virgil? It's so long since we had a chance to chat!

TOBIAS. I thought you spoke on the phone only yesterday?

VIRGIL. (*sees MARSHA is foundering, so gallantly improvises*) But so much has happened since then! (*But, even as MARSHA flashes him a grateful smile:*)

TOBIAS. Such as?

MARSHA. (*sees VIRGIL is foundering, returns his favor*) That's what we're going to chat about at dinner!

VIRGIL. (*happy to be off hook, turns to TOBIAS*) Right!

TOBIAS. (*shrugs*) Oh, very well, very well! (*drains drink, sets glass on bar*) I'd better get Bianca off that ceiling! (*exits kitchenward*)

MARSHA. (*Instantly pulls VIRGIL nearer, says into his ear in an urgent* sotto voce:) No matter what happens—act natural! (*Even as VIRGIL is blinking in confusion at this, and opening his mouth to ask for more details, TOBIAS, re-enters, and MARSHA steps away from VIRGIL.*) Darling! Back so soon?

TOBIAS. (*catching her move slightly, and a bit curious*) The kitchen's *only* eight feet down the *hall*, my dear . . .

MARSHA. But you made it there and back so fast!

TOBIAS. Darling, it's not as if I had to get through a road block! (*moves to bar, starts pouring a fresh martini, his back turned to the duo*)

VIRGIL. (*sotto voce*) Marsha, what is going *on* here?

MARSHA. (*sotto voce*) I can't explain while Tobias is here!

VIRGIL. (*sotto voce*) But whyever *not?*

BIANCA. (*enters through archway, her feet moving in a fast "playing-choo-choo" shuffle, her right palm vertically against the right side of her face as if to "hide her from TOBIAS" as she scurries swiftly down between MARSHA [nearer TOBIAS] and VIRGIL [nearer door], speaking* sotto voce *toward VIRGIL as she comes abreast of him —*) Mrs. Gilmore is madly in love with you! (*— and without pause in her foot-movement, circles below VIRGIL and up between him and door and exits again toward kitchen, only shifting right palm down and left palm up between left side of face and TOBIAS as her move becomes upstageward just before her exit*)

TOBIAS. (*despite her* sotto voce, *has heard BIANCA, and turns about just in time to catch final glimpse of her before her exit*) *What's* that she said?

BIANCA. (*immediately leans around edge of archway, speaks directly to TOBIAS*) Mrs. Gilmore is in love with you! (*and even as she pops from view again:*)

MARSHA. (*leaps to TOBIAS, flings arms about him*) And I *am*, darling, I *am!*

TOBIAS. But why should Bianca *mention* it?

VIRGIL. (*who was startled — and not displeased — when BIANCA spoke to him of MARSHA's love, recovers aplomb and speaks swiftly to TOBIAS*) Well, it's hardly a *secret,* Tobias!

(*DOOR CHIMES sound; MARSHA looks surprised, VIRGIL looks curious, and TOBIAS looks panicky — all turning these looks doorward; and then:*)

TOBIAS. Marsha, why don't you take Virgil into the

dining room and show him where he'll be seated at dinner?!

MARSHA. But we're not dining till eight o'clock!

TOBIAS. Better late than never! . . . Or something.

MARSHA. Oh, very well, very well! (*links arms with
VIRGIL*) Shall we?

(*They start for dining room via archway, TOBIAS starts
for door; but the moment he has moved to a point
where he can no longer see them, MARSHA re-
verses field, grabs VIRGIL's hand, and drags him
behind bar; he opens his mouth as if to protest, but
she—always keeping an eye on TOBIAS—puts one
hand over his mouth and the other hand atop his
head, and swiftly ducks down behind bar, pulling
him down out of view with her; this is the work of a
few seconds, and then TOBIAS has door open, and
PERSIS hurries into room.*)

TOBIAS. Persis! Are you insane, coming back here?!
My wife's right in the next room!

PERSIS. Don't worry, I've figured out a cover story.
Just tell her I'm an interior decorator, come to redo the
apartment.

TOBIAS. Persis, you *are* an interior decorator!

PERSIS. That's what's so *perfect* about it! I can show
her credentials and everything! She'll never guess the
real reason I'm here!

TOBIAS. (*reluctantly shutting hall door*) And what *is*
the real reason, come to think of it?! (*will lead her down
to sofa, where they will both sit, and as they sit, MAR-
SHA and VIRGIL will raise their heads up from behind
bar, watching them*) We'd better have our stories

straight—if she suspects for a moment what we have in store for her tomorrow—!

PERSIS. She won't if we're careful. I want to knock her dead tomorrow just as much as you do!

(*NOTE: Without specifying reactions, MARSHA and VIRGIL, during the course of the TOBIAS/PERSIS colloquy, will react with appropriate horror, outrage, chagrin, bewilderment, etc., to whatever sounds sinister or criminally insane in the colloquy.*)

TOBIAS. *Ssh!* If she hears you, it would ruin everything!

PERSIS. You're right! Let's get matters settled before she returns. Here's what I came back to show you . . . (*opens purse [MARSHA and VIRGIL, of course, can see nothing but the backs of TOBIAS's and PERSIS's heads over the sofaback] and takes out a bunch of colorful swatches of various fabrics, and shows him one*) How would this look stitched to the back of her seat?

TOBIAS. Would it hold together if she squirmed a lot?

PERSIS. Hmmm. Perhaps not. Tell you what—I can attach it with a lot of upholstery nails!

TOBIAS. Ah, yes! Sounds perfect. She'd never work it loose, no matter how much she thrashed about.

PERSIS. (*shows him another swatch*) And this I thought would be dramatic cemented over her head.

TOBIAS. Cemented?

PERSIS. Well, ordinary glue wouldn't hold it in place. The bay's very damp.

TOBIAS. Oh, do anything you want. The point is, once Marcha's *in* it, I don't want to hear her complaining.

PERSIS. That reminds me—(*shows yet another swatch*) How do you like this material for the straps? Go on, give it a tug.

TOBIAS. (*doing so*) Well, *that* should certainly hold her securely!

PERSIS. I should hope so! Once she's bobbing in the bay, we don't want her popping out of the thing without warning.

TOBIAS. That's for sure! Here, now, put those things away before she comes back and sees them!

PERSIS. (*replacing swatches in her purse*) By the way, you'd better figure out some excuse to lure her down there tomorrow.

TOBIAS. I already have. Crab!

PERSIS. (*reacts*) I was *only* trying to help!

TOBIAS. (*impatiently*) Persis, I'm not calling you names, I'm referring to the sea creature. Marsha adores crab. I'll simply tell her I've discovered a new bayside restaurant that specializes in it, and pretend I'm taking her to lunch there for her birthday, do you see?

PERSIS. It sounds like a foolproof scheme! You drive her to the pier—

TOBIAS. We stroll casually down to the end of it—

PERSIS. And as she glances idly down toward the water—

TOBIAS. I take out the champagne bottle, and—

PERSIS. Crash!

TOBIAS. Splash!

PERSIS. And home for the bash! (*BOTH laugh, while MARSHA and VIRGIL react with revulsion to this apparently heartless merriment.*)

BIANCA. (*appears in archway*) Excuse me, Mister Gilmore, but—will Miss Devore be staying for dinner?

TOBIAS. (*to PERSIS*) Have you *had* dinner—?

PERSIS. Well, as a matter of fact—

TOBIAS. Good, then it's all settled. (*to BIANCA*) Miss Devore *will* be staying, Bianca.

BIANCA. Very good, sir. (*exits to kitchen*)

TOBIAS. (*stands*) Shall we join the others in the dining room?

PERSIS. (*stands on:*) All right, let's.

(*MARSHA and VIRGIL instantly—while the others' backs are to them—rush to archway, do a perfect in-unison about-face, and each raises right foot and holds it in mid-air until TOBIAS and PERSIS, moving around left end of sofa, see them, and then MARSHA and VIRGIL bring right foot down as if they'd been seen in mid-step and enter room again, smiling brightly.*)

MARSHA. Well, we're back!

TOBIAS. (*to PERSIS*) I'd like you to meet my wife Marsha, and our neighbor Virgil Baxter.

VIRGIL. (*with a gallant bow*) Happy to meet you, Miss Devore . . . (*MARSHA surreptitiously elbows him.*) . . . or whoever you are!

MARSHA. (*trying to hide his goof, makes one of her own*) Oh, don't be so formal. Call her Persis! (*realizes*) Or something.

PERSIS. (*bewildered*) Have we met before?

VIRGIL. Uh—no, but—uh—

MARSHA. But *everybody* knows the famous interior decorator!

VIRGIL. Yes! Hear your name all the time, everywhere! You must be a marvel.

TOBIAS. But how did you recognize her face?

VIRGIL. (*not quite* sotto voce *to MARSHA*) *Your* turn.

MARSHA. Saw it in the paper!

TOBIAS. Really? *I* never saw it in the paper.

PERSIS. Neither did *I*.

VIRGIL. (*quickly*) Well, you've both been so busy!

MARSHA. (*to TOBIAS*) Advising clients—

VIRGIL. (*to PERSIS*) Decorating interiors—

TOBIAS. Well, that's true enough, I daresay.

PERSIS. Oh, I'd love to see my picture—do you still have the paper?

VIRGIL. (*to MARSHA*) Do we?

MARSHA. (*to VIRGIL*) Nope.

VIRGIL. (*to PERSIS*) Nope.

TOBIAS. What a shame! (*moves toward bar*) Shall we all have a drink before dinner?

PERSIS. (*moving after him*) That sounds like a lovely idea. (*TOBIAS will go behind bar, and she will sit on right bar stool, angled toward archway.*)

MARSHA. What would you like, Virgil?

VIRGIL. Something *strong!*

MARSHA. (*as tense as he is*) I *know* what you *mean!*

PERSIS. (*as TOBIAS fixes drinks*) Mister Baxter, what is *your* line of work?

VIRGIL. I'm a pharmacist—and please, call me Virgil.

PERSIS. I wouldn't think pharmacists would be much interested in interior decorating.

VIRGIL. Uh—not professionally, of course—but—it's just—your photo was so striking. In the paper. When I saw it there. (*He has now moved to sit on left bar stool, angled to face her, TOBIAS mixing drinks between them behind bar, MARSHA moving to left end of bar.*)

PERSIS. I'd certainly like to see a copy—when exactly was it?

MARSHA/VIRGIL. Friday!/Saturday!

TOBIAS. (*looks up from his mixing*) *Both* days?

MARSHA. It was a two-part story!

PERSIS. Oh, how delightful! In which paper?!

MARSHA/VIRGIL. The Times!/The News!

PERSIS. *Both* papers?!

VIRGIL. Well, it wasn't an *exclusive* interview.

PERSIS. Interview? *I* didn't give any interviews last week.

MARSHA. Are you sure?

TOBIAS. (*now putting drinks onto bar top*) Of *course* she's sure!

VIRGIL. Say, maybe they interviewed you earlier—

MARSHA. And ran the story later! (*She and VIRGIL grab up drinks and take healthy gulps.*)

PERSIS. (*picking up her own drink*) Still and all—thank you, Tobias—it all sounds rather odd.

VIRGIL. Well, a *lot* of the news is weird lately.

MARSHA. (*before TOBIAS or PERSIS can query further*) Listen, darling, why don't you take Persis to the dining room and show her where she's to sit?!

TOBIAS. Can't that wait till dinner?

MARSHA. You made *me* do it with *Virgil*—!

TOBIAS. (*caught*) Uh—so I did! Well—Persis—if you'd like—?

PERSIS. (*caught in same trap*) I—I suppose we'd better. I mean, if *they* had to do it—? (*sets drink on bar, gets down from stool*)

TOBIAS. (*moves from behind bar to archway*) Come along, my dear, it's not far.

PERSIS. (*moving to join him*) Be back in a moment!

MARSHA. (*as PERSIS and TOBIAS exit*) There's no rush! (*The instant they are gone, rushes to VIRGIL at bar.*) *Now* do you understand why I called you? They're planning to *murder* me!

VIRGIL. You should call the police, Marsha!

MARSHA. I tried that. They wouldn't come.

VIRGIL. Whyever not?

MARSHA. Who knows?! Maybe this isn't a high-crime-rate area!

VIRGIL. But you've *got* to do *something!*

MARSHA. Such as?! I can't think of a *thing! That's* why I called *you!*

VIRGIL. You could tell them you know!

MARSHA. They'd just kill me sooner!

VIRGIL. You could move out of the apartment!

MARSHA. What excuse could I make?

VIRGIL. Say you're visiting an aunt in San Francisco!

MARSHA. Isn't that rather far away?

VIRGIL. You don't *really* go there—you come over and stay at *my* place!

MARSHA. (*recoils*) How dare you!

VIRGIL. I thought you were in love with me?!

MARSHA. (*caught*) Oh! I am! Terribly! But—what would people think?!

VIRGIL. Who's going to know?!

MARSHA. Well—that's true enough—still—it only *delays* matters. We have to find out some way to *stop* them, finally and forever!

VIRGIL. (*shrugs*) The only way to do *that* would be to murder them *first!*

MARSHA. (*elated*) Virgil! That's *it!* How shall we do it?

VIRGIL. *We?*

MARSHA. You'd let me face them alone?

VIRGIL. Well—if you put it that way—

MARSHA. Good! Now, let me see . . . there are two of them—and two of us—

VIRGIL. I don't relish the idea of a struggle—no telling which pair is the better fighter—we've got to be clever about it!

MARSHA. And fast! I've only got till tomorrow!

VIRGIL. Do you have a gun?

MARSHA. No. Do you?

VIRGIL. No. I hate guns.

MARSHA. Me, too. And even if I didn't — I'm not sure I'd have the nerve to just haul off and shoot somebody.

VIRGIL. Even if you had, things could get sticky afterward when the police came around.

MARSHA. But I could *tell* them it was to prevent my *murder!*

VIRGIL. But could you prove it?

MARSHA. I *heard* them — *you* heard them, too — wouldn't that be enough?

VIRGIL. I'm inclined to doubt it — police seldom get called to find a dead husband and take the word of a wife and her lover about why he died.

MARSHA. But you're not my lover!

VIRGIL. Try telling that to the police!

MARSHA. Oh, dear. Isn't there any way to murder them first that will leave no traces?

VIRGIL. No traces?

MARSHA. *You* know — something that would look like a natural death.

VIRGIL. You mean *two* natural deaths — *that's* suspicious enough for *any* policeman!

MARSHA. Nonsense! You can't accuse a woman and her lover of causing two *natural* deaths!

VIRGIL. Mmm — no, I suppose not. But how in the world could we cause them?

MARSHA. *You're* a pharmacist! Don't *you* know any clever poisons that look like natural death?

VIRGIL. Oh, sure, lots of them. It's one of the first things they teach you at pharmaceutical college.

MARSHA. It *is?* Good heavens, Virgil, *why?!*

VIRGIL. Well, we *have* to know what compounds are *deadly,* so we don't mix them together *accidentally,* after we find work.

MARSHA. Oh, yes, that makes sense. Well, listen, why

don't you go over to your apartment and mix up a few?
VIRGIL. *I* don't have any chemicals in my *home!*
MARSHA. Nonsense! Why, only a few months ago, I was reading in an Agetha Christie mystery that there are just oodles of things almost anyone has in their own pantry that can be combined into ever so many deadly and untraceable poisons!
VIRGIL. Yes, but the key phrase is "*almost* anyone"! Being a pharmacist, I make sure I *never* have those things on hand. I'd hate to poison myself by mistake!
MARSHA. Well, look, perhaps *we* have some in *our* kitchen—!
VIRGIL. Do you know, you probably have! The average home usually does.
MARSHA. (*vaguely insulted*) Virgil, this is *hardly* an average home! Why, Tobias is worth millions!
VIRGIL. The average *millionaire's* home usually does, too.
MARSHA. Really? Who would have thought it!
VIRGIL. (*shrugs*) You must realize, Marsha, the average millionaire doesn't have the brains of a pharmacist. (*Then BOTH look archwayward as BIANCA— wheeling a large serving-cart filled with lidded dishes—crosses from kitchen toward dining room; as she vanishes:*)
MARSHA. Virgil—now's your chance!
VIRGIL. (*clasps her in his arms instantly*) Oh, Marsha!
MARSHA. (*squirming free*) To inspect my pantry!
VIRGIL. Your pantry?
MARSHA. For would-be poisons!
VIRGIL. Oh! Oh, yes, of course. How foolish of me. I'll be right back.

(*Hastily exits toward kitchen; PHONE RINGS; MAR- SHA nearly jumps out of her skin, then recognizes*) *source of sound, hurries to desk, sees book is still there, reacts, hastily puts it into desk drawer as PHONE RINGS AGAIN, slams drawer and grabs up phone.)*

MARSHA. (*on phone*) Hello? . . . Who? . . . (*Behind her, TOBIAS and PERSIS enter from dinning room.*) *What* seaplane? (*THEY react; TOBIAS rushes toward MARSHA.*) The bay? . . . Tomorrow? . . .

TOBIAS. (*grabbing phone*) Here, that's for me! (*on phone*) Hello, this is Tobias Gilmore! . . . Plane? Don't be ridiculous! Why would I order a plane? . . . I did not! . . . I tell you, I didn't! (*smiles nervous reassurance at his lie toward MARSHA, who looks bewildered but not suspicious; then, hearing something on the phone, he shouts into mouthpiece:*) No, I will *not* cross my heart and hope to die! (*hangs up phone*) Of all the nerve! That's the last time I do business with *that* outfit!

MARSHA. You've done business with them before?

TOBIAS. (*panicky*) Of course not!

PERSIS. (*trying to help*) Their planes are so tacky!

(*Behind them all, VIRGIL re-enters from kitchen, his pockets bulging with apparently many pantry items, though all we can see is the neck of a Tabasco bottle protruding from his breast pocket; he starts careful sidle doorward, as if he could sneak out without any of them noticing him.*)

MARSHA. (*to PERSIS, puzzled*) Whose planes? I didn't even say who was on the phone!

PERSIS. (*stymied a second, blurts:*) That's true — but — isn't it *obvious* their planes must be tacky? Or else why would Tobias refuse to do business with them?!

(*BIANCA — minus serving-cart — crosses from dining*

room toward kitchen, unobserved by anyone onstage.)

TOBIAS. Exactly!

MARSHA. But why would they think that he'd ordered a plane?

TOBIAS. Promotion! You *know* how telephone salesman are! Call up a home, promise six free conga lessons if you'll only try out their product, and then have you paying off on an item you never wanted for life!

MARSHA. But he said *nothing* about conga lessons!

TOBIAS. Naturally! You—uh—you already *do* the conga!

PERSIS. (*forgetting her own role in the scheme of things*) But how would the *plane salesman* know that?

TOBIAS. (*gives her a furious glare; she remembers her role and winces unhappily as he says through clenched teeth:*) Whose *side* are you on, anyway?! (*then remembers MARSHA*) That is—the Yankees are playing the Angels tomorrow! *Whose* side are *you* on?

MARSHA. *I* thought baseball season just *ended*—?

(*VIRGIL by now has front door open and is just edging out when TOBIAS spots him.*)

TOBIAS. Baxter! You're not leaving?!

MARSHA. (*reacts to VIRGIL's presence, hastily pushes Tabasco bottle further down out of sight in his pocket*) He suddenly remembered he should change for dinner!

VIRGIL. Right! I'll be back in twenty minutes!

TOBIAS. Marsha—how could *you* know what he suddenly remembered?

MARSHA. (*defensively*) Well, *you* didn't know *baseball* season was over! Shouldn't *I* have the same privilege?

VIRGIL. Of course you should! Excuse me! (*exits fast, shutting door after him*)

TOBIAS. Marsha—what do airplane manufacturers have to do with baseball season?

MARSHA. (*thinks frantically; then, triumphantly:*) High flies!

(*TOBIAS and PERSIS react in bewilderment; then, just before they can question her logic further, BIANCA enters from kitchen, stands center archway, announces:*)

BIANCA. Last call for dinner!

PERSIS. But Mister Baxter just left!

BIANCA. (*shrugs*) *First* call for dinner, then!

MARSHA. (*anxious to be away from their questions*) I'll go bring him back! (*opens front door, but before she can exit:*)

TOBIAS. Marsha! He might not be dressed!

MARSHA. I'll tell him to shut his eyes! (*again starts to exit, but:*)

TOBIAS. He *said* he'd return in twenty minutes. Surely we can delay *that* long.

BIANCA. If you like cold soup. (*exits to kitchen*)

PERSIS. Perhaps we *should* go in to dinner, Tobias.

TOBIAS. Well—if you really think. . . ?

MARSHA. I'll just go hurry Virgil up a bit!

TOBIAS. Marsha Gilmore, come in here and shut that door! You can't intrude on the man while he's dressing!

MARSHA. (*defeated, shuts door, then brightens*) I can telephone him! (*grabs up phone, starts dialing*)

TOBIAS. You know his number without looking it up?

MARSHA. *Bianca* told me how to do it.

PERSIS. How to do *what*?

MARSHA. (*since it's obvious to her*) To dial the wrong number! (*then, on phone:*) Hello, Virgil? It's Marsha! The soup is getting cold! . . . Huh? . . . No, of *course* I'm not talking in code! Why *would* I? . . . Oh! Oh, yes, I see. But no, it's not code, it's a simple fact — the soup is getting cold, so if you want it hot, you'd best hurry back! . . . Right . . . See you shortly. (*hangs up*)

TOBIAS. Marsha — why should Virgil imagine you were talking in code?

MARSHA. Uh — why — well, "the soup is getting cold" just sounds like one of those spy-novel phrases — "The eye of the sphinx is behind the emerald mirror" — that sort of thing.

TOBIAS. My dear, there's a world of difference between emerald mirrors and cold soup!

MARSHA. Well — Virgil doesn't get out very much. (*before things can get stickier, shifts gears:*) By the way, darling — don't *you* plan to dress for dinner? You can *hardly* sit down to table in your *slippers!*

TOBIAS. (*looks down at himself, reacts*) Oh! I *am* sorry, Persis! Whatever will you think of me! (*hurries bedroomward*) I'll just be a moment!

PERSIS. But honestly, Tobias, I don't mind if you — (*But he is gone; she gives it up and turns to MARSHA.*) I *do* hope my staying for dinner isn't causing too much trouble?

MARSHA. Not if you don't take second helpings.

PERSIS. (*startled but polite*) Oh, I — seldom do. By the way — may I use your bathroom? I'd like to freshen up before we dine.

MARSHA. Oh, certainly. The guest bathroom is just down the hall, the opposite direction from our bedroom. (*as PERSIS starts to exit*) Oh, but how silly of me. You don't know where our bedroom is, do you!

PERSIS. (*stops, turns, smiles nervously*) Why—no, come to think of it. I mean, how *would* I know? (*gives unconvincing laugh*)

MARSHA. (*laughing politely, but just a shade cattily*) How indeed! (*points in proper direction*) The guest bathroom is that way.

PERSIS. (*nods, starts to exit, then—sensing an indefinable something in the other's attitude—turns back for:*) You know, my dear—Tobias loves you very much. You're all he talks about, every time I see him. I've never *seen* a man so completely infatuated with his own wife . . .

MARSHA. (*a bit shaken by this unexpected turn of conversation*) Why—uh—how nice of you to tell me, Miss Devore.

PERSIS. "Persis," please. (*smiles, then turns and exits*)

MARSHA. (*now very confused, muses aloud:*) Oh, dear. I hope I'm not making a mistake. Perhaps—yes— I'd better call Virgil and cancel our plan—(*is dialing furiously*)—at least until I'm a bit more certain . . . (*waits, then gets her party, speaks on phone*) Virgil! . . . It's Marsha. About that poison—I was wondering— . . . No, I haven't lost my nerve—well, not exactly—but it seems like such a *drastic* step, if you know what I mean . . . Well, yes, I *know* it's odorless, tasteless, and undetectable in a post mortem, but—(*thinks hard, then says, inspired:*) Is it at all *painful?* . . . (*pauses, listening to reply; her expression goes piteously sad as she quietly echoes what she hears:*) "Mortal agony"? . . . Oh, Virgil, I—There's something very important I must tell you—I've come to the decision . . . Well, you see, even if the poison is odorless, tasteless and undetectable, if it's going to cause Tobias mortal agony—(*Looks up as PERSIS re-enters; PERSIS has taken off her coat and glasses, and done something to soften the original severity of her hairdo, and she is now a sexy knockout in a terrific dress and breathtaking facial beauty; MARSHA stares at her as she stands just inside the room looking her way, then MARSHA once more speaks into the phone, completing her dangling phrase:*) Three out of four ain't bad! (*hangs up phone in quiet triumph, smiling grimly, and then folds her arms and looks toward PERSIS, who is staring at her in unsuspecting amiability, as—*)

THE CURTAIN FALLS

End of Act One

ACT TWO

Immediately following. MARSHA and PERSIS are just where we last saw them, as we continue:

PERSIS. (*extends her coat slightly*) Is there some place I might hang this?

MARSHA. Well, there's always the Museum of Modern Art. (*as PERSIS reacts with uncertainty:*) But I suppose you meant something more prosaic, didn't you! (*starts toward bedroom, calling kitchenward as she passes upstage of PERSIS:*) Bianca! Will you tend to Miss Devore's coat, please? (*exits bedroomward, just as TOBIAS enters, now in his formal dinner clothing, and she addresses him as she passes, continuing even when she is off:*) Or would *you* be a darling to her, Tobias? (*We hear her laugh mockingly at her own joke, which neither TOBIAS nor PERSIS gets; both look bewildered.*)

TOBIAS. What in the world did she mean by that?

PERSIS. She—uh—thought you might hang up my coat for me. I think.

TOBIAS. Oh, of course! How thoughtless of me.

BIANCA. (*enters from kitchen as he takes the coat*) Oh, here, sir, let *me* do that. (*Takes coat from him, and before PERSIS quite knows what's happening, BIANCA has helped her* into *the coat, turned, and exits toward kitchen again, on:*) Nice of you to stop by!

TOBIAS. That fool girl! Here, let me help you— (*removes the coat again, will hang it in wardrobe, during:*) Persis, would you mind very much acting as "lookout" for me. I wouldn't want Marsha to return while I'm on the phone!

PERSIS. But—you're *not* on the phone—?

TOBIAS. I'm *going* to be in a *moment*, Persis! Just stand guard over there and make sure she doesn't return until I've finished my call!

PERSIS. (*moving obediently but uncertainly toward archway right*) How do I stop her? Drag her screaming back to the bedroom, or just wrestle her to the floor?

TOBIAS. (*has wardrobe shut now, and is moving for phone*) Hopefully, I'll be finished before you have to make that decision! (*grabs phone up, starts dialing*)

PERSIS. But who are you calling so *urgently*, Tobias?

TOBIAS. That *airplane* manufacturer, of course! After the conversation I had with him a few moments ago, it wouldn't surprise me if he *canceled* the delivery—and *then* what would I do for Marsha's birthday?! (*Is just finishing dialing when there is a KNOCK at the door; he hangs up in annoyance.*) Damn. Probably that idiot from across the hall! (*Opens door, then reacts in pleased surprise as LYNETTE THOREN, an elegantly coiffed and garbed woman of late middle age, enters from hall.*) Why—Lynette! What a pleasant surprise!

LYNETTE. Now, Toby, you *know* I always drop by on Marsha's *birthday!* (*extends rectangular package*) Even shelled out for a present. (*notices PERSIS as TOBIAS is closing door*) I don't believe we've met—?

TOBIAS. Oh, I'm sorry—Persis Devore—Lynette Thoren.

PERSIS. How do you *do?*

LYNETTE. How do *you* do?

TOBIAS. (*will take LYNETTE's coat—she'll place package on desk while he does so—and hang it in wardrobe over next few speeches*) Persis is the lady I told you about—the one who's helping me with Marsha's birthday surprise.

LYNETTE. Oh, of course! I knew the name sounded

familiar! (*will briefly clasp PERSIS's hand*) But aren't you taking a chance, my dear? Won't Marsha be curious about who you are and why you're here? And come to think of it, why *are* you here? Shouldn't you be off in that seaplane with upholstery tacks and glue?

PERSIS. Well, I *was* going there as soon as I left here — but —

TOBIAS. (*joining them*) Matters got a bit out of hand. Had to cook up a quick story when Marsha met Persis unexpectedly, and now I'm afraid Persis has to stay for dinner, whether she likes it or not.

BIANCA. (*off*) Was that a crack?!

TOBIAS. (*calls kitchenward*) I mean whether she likes staying — not whether she likes dinner!

LYNETTE. Oh, is *Bianca* still here?

TOBIAS. I don't have enough nerve to fire her.

LYNETTE. Don't be silly, Toby. I merely meant that this is normally her night off. (*will move to desk and retrieve package, during:*)

TOBIAS. Oh, it is. She's leaving as soon as she serves dinner.

BIANCA. (*off*) And it better be soon! (*appears in archway*) I suppose *you'll* be dining with us, *too*, Mrs. Thoren?

LYNETTE. If it's not too much trouble. . . ?

BIANCA. (*hopefully*) Do you *mean* that?

TOBIAS. Of *course* she doesn't! Now go set another place at once.

BIANCA. The soup's gonna be like *ice!* (*exits toward dining room*)

LYNETTE. (*moving toward archway, package in hand*) Perhaps she can help me with this . . . (*calls*) Bianca — ? I wonder if you'd do me a small favor — ? (*exits toward dining room*)

PERSIS. Tobias, if Lynette always comes here on Marsha's birthday, why is she a day early?

TOBIAS. She's very vague about calendars. What's a day here or there, one way or the other—that's her motto. Though you'd think she, of all people, would remember the exact date.

PERSIS. (*curious*) "Of all people"?

TOBIAS. Oh, damn! *Knew* I'd forgotten something! Lynette is Marsha's *mother!* I forgot you didn't know.

PERSIS. Her forgetfulness must be contagious.

TOBIAS. Now-now, be fair. I'm not all *that* forgetful, Persis.

PERSIS. Then why aren't you phoning that airplane person?

TOBIAS. Ye gods, it went right out of my head! (*rushes to phone, will dial, during:*) I don't know what it is about tonight—everything seems sort of frantic and topsy-turvy—can't quite put my finger on exactly what I mean—there's a sort of confusing—um—*undercurrent* to matters.

PERSIS. Yes. Yes, I know exactly what you mean—and *I* can't put *my* finger on it, either. A kind of ominous crackling in the atmosphere . . . especially when Marsha is in the room.

(*Behind them, unnoticed, MARSHA—now dolled up in an evening outfit guaranteed to make PERSIS's look green with envy—appears in archway right, and reacts to all she will now overhear.*)

TOBIAS. You don't think she—*suspects?* If she found out what we were up to—!

PERSIS. It *would* certainly ruin everything we've planned!

TOBIAS. (*phone to ear, still awaiting his party*) It may

be ruined already. If you can't get over there to do *your* part before tomorrow morning, the whole thing's a bust. I want Marsha to float away from the pier in *style!* (*MARSHA reacts, of course, in something closer to total bewilderment than terror, while he continues:*) Damn! The line's busy. I'll have to try again later. (*hangs up phone, turns, sees MARSHA*) Marsha! (*PERSIS, naturally, whirls to face MARSHA in shock.*)

PERSIS. How *long* have you been *standing* there?!

MARSHA. (*can't admit the truth, but must answer the question as normally as possible*) Why — I just got here. Is there anything wrong?

TOBIAS. Of course not!

MARSHA. Then why do you two look so startled?

PERSIS. Your . . . your dress!

TOBIAS. It's startlingly beautiful!

PERSIS. And you changed into it so startingly fast!

TOBIAS. Yes! That's it! Startling dress, startling speed!

MARSHA. Perhaps I'd better change. Excitement is bad for your ulcer.

TOBIAS. (*just on the brink of annoyance*) Marsha, it's not *that* startling!

MARSHA. (*raring for a fight*) Well, just how startling *is* it?! (*The DOORBELL rings; she reacts with apprehension.*) Oh!

PERSIS. *Now* who's looking startled?!

MARSHA. (*quickly*) I'm *not!*

TOBIAS. You most certainly are! What is there in the ringing of our doorbell to put you in such a state?

MARSHA. Doorbell? Don't be silly. It wasn't the doorbell. I hardly heard it. It was . . . uh . . . the mirror! (*points while babbling:*) My reflection. Saw myself in this startling dress. Got startled.

TOBIAS. *That* startled? (*DOORBELL rings again;*

MARSHA reacts again.) Aha! The very same look, the moment the bell rang again!

MARSHA. Nonsense! I—just looked in the *mirror* again!

TOBIAS. (*definitely testy*) Well, *stop* it!

MARSHA. Gladly! (*takes them each by an arm, moves them slightly upstage*) Now, why don't you two go in to dinner while I let Virgil in?

PERSIS. Shouldn't we wait and all go in together?

MARSHA. Last one there gets the coldest soup! (*moves them upstage again*)

TOBIAS. Well, there's something to that, of course— (*takes PERSIS by the arm*) Shall we, then?

PERSIS. Oh, very well.

MARSHA. And I'll just get the door and be right with you—(*when they pause:*)—as soon as you've gone!

TOBIAS. (*shakes his head, bemused*) We'd better humor her, Persis, before *all* the soup cools off! (*DOORBELL rings again, followed by KNOCKING.*)

MARSHA. (*gaily waving them goodbye*) See you both *later!*

TOBIAS. (*now upstage of archway, facing dining-room direction*) *Much* later?

MARSHA. Oh, sooner than that.

TOBIAS. Very well, my dear.

PERSIS. But *do* hurry.

(*They exit, and MARSHA leaps to door and yanks it open to admit VIRGIL, now in immaculate evening clothes; he is carrying a rather strange sort of flask: It is both round and flat, of white ceramic structure with dark blue patterning about the edges, and with a semi-flattened bottom on the side opposite the short neck: MARSHA's upcoming observation describes it even better:*)

MARSHA. (*pulling him in and closing door*) Virgil, thank heaven you're here! Did you . . . *do* it?

VIRGIL. I had to rush a bit, but—yes—I did it. It's all in here. (*extends flask*)

MARSHA. (*looks at it but does not touch it*) What in the world is *that*?

VIRGIL. (*impatient*) What does it *look* like?!

MARSHA. A ceramic whoopee-cushion!

VIRGIL. (*will move to coffeetable and set flask on it*) This happens to be an *imported* bottle—or flagon, or whatever you call it—from Switzerland. They make a liqueur there out of gentian root—you know, those six-foot-tall yellow flowers that clutter up the Alps—

MARSHA. I thought gentian was a *blue* flower? And rather tiny?

VIRGIL. That's the American type. They're more spectacular in the Alps. Lovely craftsmanship on the flagon, don't you think? Of course, gentian root is rather bitter, and the liqueur tastes positively foul.

MARSHA. Then why have you brought it?

(*Behind, them, unnoticed, BIANCA emerges from dining room carrying identical flask, except that it has a large red bow tied about its neck, looks for a spot on the bottle-shelf behind bar to put it, finds no room, and so puts it out of sight beneath bar, all during:*)

VIRGIL. I *didn't!*

MARSHA. Well, *somebody* did!

VIRGIL. I mean brought the *liqueur!* I got it as a gift last Christmas, took one sip, and poured the rest down the sink. But the bottle was to pretty to throw away.

MARSHA. But why bring an empty bottle? . . . Oh! *You* mean—

VIRGIL. Exactly. Wasn't easy. Took me ten minutes to find a funnel!

(*BIANCA exits to kitchen and LYNETTE passes her just coming out of dining room, sees MARSHA and VIRGIL, and starts down toward them where they stand, their backs to her, between coffeetable and sofa.*)

MARSHA. Shall we bring it into the dining room, or what?

VIRGIL. I rather thought *after* dinner, out here, would be more appropriate.

MARSHA. Appropriate? *Is* there an appropriate place for murdering one's husband? (*LYNETTE reacts, a hand going to her mouth to stifle what would have been an audible gasp.*)

VIRGIL. Well, if you put it like that, I suppose one place is just as good as another. I'm rather new at this, you know.

MARSHA. Well, it's *hardly* habitual with *me!* You're sure the poison you put in the bottle is totally tasteless?

VIRGIL. Well, they *say* it is—but then, how could anyone really *know?* (*LYNETTE has looked around them and recognized—she thinks—her gift-bottle; she begins to inch backward, step-by-step, her face a study in horror, during:*)

MARSHA. I don't follow that.

VIRGIL. Well, I mean that in order to know it's tasteless, one has to taste it, and once you *taste* it, you've *had* it!

MARSHA. Oh, yes, I see what you mean. A poisoned person is hardly likely to spend his last moments alive describing flavors.

VIRGIL. However, I *am* sure it's odorless and undetectable in a post-mortem.

MARSHA. So once they drink it, it hardly matters whether they enjoyed it or not, does it! (*BOTH laugh at this, and start around left end of sofa; LYNETTE, not quite backed up to archway, does the same thing they did earlier—raises right foot, holds it in position until the moment they see her, and then brings it down as if just entering room.*) Mother!

LYNETTE. (*forcing herself to be congenial*) Marsha, my darling, how lovely you look! And who is this strange man?

MARSHA. (*as she and VIRGIL reach, and flank, her mother*) *What* makes you say he's *strange?*

LYNETTE. Well, I've never *met* him before . . .

MARSHA. Oh, *that* kind of "strange"! (*gives a relieved chuckle*) This is Virgil Baxter, my friend and neighbor. *Our* friend and neighbor! Mine and Tobias's. Both. (*as LYNETTE and VIRGIL nod politely to one another:*) Virgil, this is my mother, Mrs. Thoren.

LYNETTE. But you must call me "Lynette"!

MARSHA. Virgil is a druggist.

VIRGIL. Pharmacist.

MARSHA. What's the difference? You deal in drugs, so "druggist" would seem to be *just* as appropriate.

LYNETTE. *More* appropriate. I mean, he doesn't deal in "pharms"!

MARSHA. (*giddily*) Or his name would be "Old Mac-Donald"!

VIRGIL. I beg your pardon?

MARSHA. Oh, never mind, darling—friend—Virgil—sir! (*He has winced at each correction, so she quickly grabs him by the arm and tows him diningroomward.*) Well, whoever you are, let's get to that soup, shall we?!

(*to LYNETTE, as they exit*) Nice seeing you, Mother.
A pity you can't stay for dinner!

(*The instant they are gone, LYNETTE rushes to bottle,
grabs it up, and rushes out right toward distant
bathroom; a moment later, from that direction, we
hear GURGLING, and in another moment or so,
the unmistakeable sound of TOILET FLUSHING;
LYNETTE hastens back onstage, still carrying bottle, looks about, spots gin bottle on bar, grabs it,
and exits again toward bathroom, carrying both
bottles; a moment later, MARSHA reappears from
diningroom, on:*)

MARSHA. Or *are* you staying for dinner? . . . Mother?
. . . (*steps into room, looks around in puzzlement for
her mother, then reacts at sight of empty coffeetable*)
Oh! Now where in the world — ?! (*looks here and there,
briefly, spots identical bottle behind bar, takes it out
and hastens to coffeetable with it, on:*) I wonder how it
got back *there?* (*as she sets it down, notices red ribbon-
bow on it*) And how did *that* get there?! (*frowns, takes
bow off bottle, steps up to bar, and tosses bow behind
it, into trash receptacle, we suppose, then dusts off her
hands and exits to diningroom again; then LYNETTE
enters with both bottles — the gin bottle considerably
depleted — places gin bottle back on bar, and is just
starting for coffeetable when BIANCA appears in
upstage archway*)
BIANCA. Last call for dinner, Mrs. Thoren!
(*LYNETTE, startled, turns to face her, and thus does
not have time to notice duplicate bottle on coffeetable.*)
Oh, what's happened to the pretty bow on your birthday
present?

LYNETTE. I—I don't know—I guess Marsha must have removed it.

BIANCA. What an odd thing to do.

LYNETTE. Yes. Yes, wasn't it! (*sets bottle on bar*) Well, I guess I'd best be getting in to dinner, now! (*starts toward diningroom, but pauses for:*) Bianca, excuse me, but—I thought this was your evening off?

BIANCA. Oh, it *is*, mum. As soon as I've served dinner, I'm free as a bird. My boyfriend will be coming by for me any time, now.

LYNETTE. Oh, how nice! Well, have a pleasant evening! (*exits toward diningroom*)

BIANCA. Thank you, mum! (*takes a step kitchenward, then looks at bottle on bar, goes and picks it up and takes it to coffeetable, then sees duplicate bottle and reacts in puzzlement*) I could've sworn she only brought one! We certainly didn't have one, though . . . (*curious, picks up liqueur bottle already on table [look, for sanity's sake, let's get simpler names for the duplicates: The bottle LYNETTE just filled with gin will be known as GB, and the bottle that LYNETTE originally brought, with the liqueur still in it, will be known as OB]: anyhow, BIANCA picks up OB, uncaps — or uncorks, as the case may be — it, and takes a taste; she makes a face of appalled displeasure and sets it down again, wiping the back of her hand across her mouth*) What an *awful* thing to do to your own daughter! . . . Unless, maybe this one is spoiled—? (*experimentally uncaps GB, takes a taste, brightens*) Ah, much better! Almost tastes like straight gin! (*sets GB back on coffeetable, will exit to kitchen with OB, on:*) I'll just put *this* one into the garbage, where it belongs! (*As soon as she exits, DOORBELL rings; after a pause, DOORBELL rings again; then we hear:*)

TOBIAS. (*off*) Isn't anybody getting the door?!

BIANCA. (*re-enters from kitchen with small tray containing about eight small liqueur glasses, will place it on coffeetable beside GB, during:*) I've only got two hands!

TOBIAS. (*off*) Never mind about your hands—use your feet!

BIANCA. (*en route to door, pauses*) To open the door?

TOBIAS. (*off*) To *get* to it!

BIANCA. (*mutters under her breath, then opens door; BEN QUADE, a 25ish, nice-looking uniformed policeman steps in*) Oh, honey, it's you! I'm not even ready yet—dinner got started a little late, and— Oh! You're not ready yet, either!

BEN. Had a small emergency, Bee. Just got back from the hospital. In fact, I'm still driving the police ambulance!

BIANCA. We're going on our date in an ambulance?!

BEN. Far as my place, anyhow. I figured it'd save time if I came by for you on the way back to sign out, then we could drop off the ambulance after *I* change, and be that much ahead of the game.

BIANCA. Oh, all right. Why don't you wait here, I'll finish serving dinner, then get out of this uniform and be right with you!

BEN. You could just take off the cap and apron—the dress looks fine.

BIANCA. (*makes a face*) Have to brush my teeth, too! I just had a sip of *that* stuff—(*indicates GB as she moves kitchenward*)—and it tastes perfectly *awful!* Or the *other* one did, anyhow.

BEN. Other *what?* (*But she is gone; he looks around, feeling awkward, shifts from foot to foot; then TOBIAS enters.*)

TOBIAS. Bianca, who was at the—? (*sees BEN, reacts*

with mild surprise) Oh! Officer! Is—is there anything wrong?

BEN. Oh, I'm not here *officially*, Mister Gilmore. I'm Ben Quade, Bianca's date. But she said dinner got started late, so I'm waiting here for her to finish.

TOBIAS. Yes-yes, by all means, Officer Quade. Won't you sit down?

BEN. Thank you. (*pulls out desk chair, faces it right, sits*)

TOBIAS. Excuse me, but—do you always go out on dates in uniform?

BEN. (*chuckles*) No, not at all, sir. But I got off work late, myself. Had to take an injured pedestrian to the hospital. Matter of fact, I'll be taking Bianca in a police ambulance when we leave here, till I can get my own car at the station.

TOBIAS. Well, make yourself comfortable, and I'll—(*catches sight of GB and glasses*) What in the world is *that?*

BIANCA. Search me. Whatever it is, Bianca says it tastes *awful!* Or shouldn't I be telling you that?

TOBIAS. Probably not, but *I* won't tell her you snitched if *you* don't! (*BOTH laugh, and then TOBIAS snaps his fingers.*) The airplane! Now's my chance, while Marsha's in the other room! (*starts for phone*)

BEN. I beg your pardon?

TOBIAS. Oh, sorry. Birthday surprise for my wife. Have to get matters settled while she's out of earshot . . . (*has phone in hand, then frowns*) Damn! I forgot the number! What's become of my memo-pad?! (*starts looking in desk drawers, finds* Creeping Slasher, *picks it up, frowns, looks diningroomward, growls softly, then puts book back in drawer, on:*) No *wonder* she's been acting so jumpy tonight!

BEN. Jumpy? Who?

TOBIAS. My wife! The stuff she reads would turn *anyone's* nerves to jelly! If I've told her once, I've told her a hundred times—! (*stops as a curious MARSHA enters from diningroom; she starts toward TOBIAS pleasantly enough, on:*)

MARSHA. Tobias, what is *keeping* you? Our guests are—(*sees BEN—who stands politely*) Oh! Oh, dear! Uh—why, officer—what in the world—?

TOBIAS. Never mind him! He's just here to get Bianca!

MARSHA. (*at sea*) Bianca? But—I don't understand—?

TOBIAS. By the way, where did that bottle come from, anyhow? (*MARSHA looks at GB and reacts.*) Bianca had some and says it tastes awful!

MARSHA. (*horrified*) Bianca drank some of *that*?!

TOBIAS. Well, you know how she is—can't resist sampling things.

MARSHA. Oh, but Tobias—!

BIANCA. (*enters from kitchen in pretty dress, carrying purse, ready for her date, on:*) Okay, let's get that ambulance warmed up! (*sees the GILMORES*) Oh! I didn't know you were here—

MARSHA. Ambulance?! Bianca—you drank some of that stuff—and now this policeman is taking you away in an ambulance?!

BEN. Only as far as the police station.

MARSHA. Oh, no!

TOBIAS. Never mind about that, Marsha. There's something more important to discuss. You see, I've found out what you've been up to! (*slaps desk drawer for emphasis, which of course she doesn't connect with the book*)

MARSHA. Oh, dear! Well—I guess I may as well make a clean breast of it!

BIANCA. Clean breast of what? What's been going on?

MARSHA. Oh, Bianca! Dear Bianca! (*embraces her fondly*) It's all my fault. My fault entirely. If it weren't for me, you wouldn't be going off in that ambulance!

BEN. (*abruptly alert*) *You're* the hit-and-run driver?!

MARSHA. *What* hit-and-run driver?!

BEN. Who ran over that pedestrian!

MARSHA. *What* pedestrian?

BEN. The one I just took to the hospital!

MARSHA. (*totally confused and bewildered*) *WHAT—?!*

BIANCA. Ben, stop cross-examining her! Mrs. Gilmore hasn't been out of the apartment all day!

TOBIAS. I thought you told me she'd gone for a *stroll?*

BIANCA. Well, *you* told *me* she needed the *exercise!*

MARSHA. (*hurt*) Oh, Toby, how *could* you?!

BIANCA. Ben, come on, we'd better go.

BEN. Wait a minute, Bee! If she's got something to do with that hit-run case—

BIANCA. (*dragging him out front door*) She doesn't! Trust me!

VIRGIL. (*entering from dining room*) Is something wrong—? That soup is getting colder by the minute—(*stops, in panic-reaction to sight of BEN*) Ongh! (*starts walking backward to dining room like a film running in reverse*) Ongh-ongh-ongh—! (*says enough* onghs *to get offstage*)

BEN. What's *his* problem?!

BIANCA. I'll explain it all on the way to the ambulance! (*yanks him out front door*)

MARSHA. (*calls after them [unseen] in corridor*) You'd best hurry—she may not have much time! (*closes door*)

TOBIAS. Marsha, what are you talking about?!

MARSHA. (*amazed*) You don't *know?!*

TOBIAS. Of couse not!

MARSHA. But—Toby—you said—I'm sure you said—you knew what I'd been up to!

TOBIAS. (*slaps hand on desk again*) And I do! . . . But what's that got to do with Bianca?

LYNETTE. (*hurries in from dining room*) What in the *world* is wrong with that Mister Baxter? He just came back to the table pale as death, commandeered the wine carafe, and keeps drinking and sobbing!

MARSHA. Oh, dear, I'd better go have a talk with him!

TOBIAS. Not so fast! *I* want an explanation for your conduct, first!

LYNETTE. Oh, no! Then—you've found *out?!*

MARSHA. Mother! Do you mean—*you've* found out, *too?!*

LYNETTE. I'm sorry, dear. Yes. I overheard you and Virgil talking.

TOBIAS. What's *Virgil* got to do with it?

MARSHA. (*amazed again*) You don't *know?!*

TOBIAS. Of course not!

LYNETTE. Then don't *tell* him, darling! Now that you know *I* know, of course you're not going *through* with it, and what he doesn't know won't hurt him!

MARSHA. *That* makes sense.

TOBIAS. The *hell* it does! I *do* know what you've been doing, and I must say, I'm *very* disillusioned!

MARSHA. Only *disillusioned?*

TOBIAS. (*wistfully*) I thought I knew you. Thought I could trust you. Thought I knew everything there was to know about your moods, your temperaments. But this—! (*points toward desk drawer*) I couldn't believe my eyes. It was—like finding a *mouse*trap at *Disney*land!

LYNETTE. (*as she and MARSHA look where he points in bewilderment*) *What* was?

PERSIS. (*enters from dining room*) What is all the

shouting out here? And what in the *world* is the matter with Virgil?

LYNETTE. Well, you see—(*As she turns toward PER-SIS, she spots GB.*) How did *that* get there?!

PERSIS. (*looks toward coffeetable*) What?

LYNETTE. My present!

MARSHA. (*looks, reacts*) But—that's *Virgil's* present!

PERSIS. *What* is?

MARSHA. Virgil got it as a gift, couldn't take the taste, so he—

LYNETTE. Now, just a moment, Marsha. That is *my* present to *you!* I brought it for your *birthday!*

MARSHA. (*a hand going to her throat*) What? Oh, how could you! My own mother!

LYNETTE. Marsha, watch what you say—Tobias knows nothing about it!

TOBIAS. About *what?*

LYNETTE. (*to MARSHA*) *There,* you *see?!*

MARSHA. (*as a woozy, bleary-eyed VIRGIL plods defeatedly into room, arms extended before him stiffly, wrists together like a man expecting to be handcuffed*) But Tobias said he *knew* what I was up to!

VIRGIL. Then it's over! All over! All right, officer, I'm ready to go quietly! The things a man does for love! (*Looks around uncertainly—he is more than a bit tipsy.*) Officer—? Where did he go?

MARSHA. He took Bianca away in an ambulance!

LYNETTE. Ambulance?!

MARSHA. (*flails finger at GB*) She *drank* some of that! You *know* what happened next!

PERSIS. The *hell* I do!

VIRGIL. Oh, no! This is monstrous, dreadful! (*will head for sofa, sit and sob, on:*) The poor sweet innocent child!

LYNETTE. Hush, not another word! She'll surely be all

right when he gets her to the hospital!

TOBIAS. But he's not *taking* her to the hospital! He's taking her up to his apartment!

MARSHA. Whatever *for?*

TOBIAS. So he can get out of his uniform!

MARSHA. (*quickly clapping her hands over LYN-ETTE's ears*) Toby! Not in front of mother!

VIRGIL. Then it's too late! It's all over! We're doomed! Doomed! I'm ruined! And why, *why?!*

TOBIAS. That's what *I'd* like to find out!

MARSHA. Toby, make up your *mind!* You say you know *everything,* and you keep trying to find everything *out!*

VIRGIL. (*sits up straight, a ghastly look on his face*) Oh, dear!

PERSIS. What is it?

VIRGIL. I think I'm going to be sick! (*stands, looking frantically right and left*) I never *could* handle cold soup. . . !

MARSHA. (*part dragging him, part pointing the way*) Quick! The bathroom! Down the hall to your right! (*She stops at archway; he continues off.*)

TOBIAS. Now, Marsha—while there's relative peace and quiet—would you *please* clear up what's been going on here tonight?

MARSHA. Uh—well—

LYNETTE. Marsha, be careful—!

MARSHA. Say! *I* have an idea! Why don't *you* tell me what you *think* is going on, and then I'll tell you if you're right or wrong?

PERSIS. Wouldn't it be simpler if *you* explained?

LYNETTE. (*airily, as if events were perfectly natural*) But what is there *to* explain? Tobias and Marsha were having some people in for dinner, and one of the guests got sick. Hardly a cause for cross-examination.

TOBIAS. Well, when you put it like that—(*then remembers*) No, wait! What was all that stuff about Marsha being to blame for Bianca having to go off in that ambulance?!

MARSHA. Uh—why—all I meant was that if I paid the child better wages, she could have gone off in a Mercedes!

TOBIAS. But you were practically *weeping* about it!

MARSHA. That was for *your* sake!

TOBIAS. *My* sake?!

MARSHA. Of course, darling! I mean, think of the drain on your finances if you had to *pay* her that much!

TOBIAS. Oh. Never thought of that part.

PERSIS. But why did *Virgil* get so upset when he walked in here?

MARSHA. Hates to see a woman cry!

LYNETTE. (*proud of MARSHA's ingenuity*) Oh, you *are* clever!

TOBIAS. Clever?

LYNETTE. I mean, *truthful!*

PERSIS. That's not the same thing.

MARSHA. That's what's so *clever* about it!

TOBIAS. Wait a minute—I'm getting all confused!

MARSHA. (*inspired*) Then what *you* need is a *drink!* (*Rushes to GB, will pour two servings, as she says to PERSIS:*) And you'll join him, of course?

PERSIS. I will?

MARSHA. Well, it wouldn't be polite for him to drink and not offer some to a guest, would it?

LYNETTE. (*who knows, of course, that the gimmicked bottle has been flushed*) Uh, Marsha, there's something I should tell you—

MARSHA. (*busy handing drinks to TOBIAS and PERSIS*) *After* they drink, Mother, *after!*

TOBIAS. But damn it, I don't *feel* like a drink!

MARSHA. Not even to wish me a happy birthday?

TOBIAS. Oh. Well. If you put it *that* way—(*He and PERSIS almost drink; then:*) Oh, but *Lynette* doesn't have a drink!

MARSHA. Mother doesn't drink!

TOBIAS. She drinks like a fish!

MARSHA. But she's given it up!

PERSIS. She drank her wine at dinner—?!

MARSHA. *Since* then! Drank her wine, had remorse, quit.

PERSIS. Just like that?

MARSHA. Why not? You have to swear off *some*time!

TOBIAS. Oh, all right, all right! (*raises his glass*) Happy birthday, darling! (*sees PERSIS has not raised hers*) Aren't you going to join me?

PERSIS. I hate to be the only other person drinking.

LYNETTE. (*trying to speed matters up*) Oh, for heaven's sake, I'll join you! (*starts for bottle*)

MARSHA. *No!* (*starts pulling her away*) Fight it! Fight the terrible urge! Never give in! Never!

LYNETTE. (*pulls free*) Nonsense! Why shouldn't I have a drink if I feel like one?

MARSHA. Why? *Why?* But—Mother—you said you *overheard*—you said you knew *everything*—doesn't *that* give you a clue?!

LYNETTE. Yes, but there's *one* thing you don't know—!

TOBIAS. There's at least *ten* things *I* don't know!

MARSHA. Oh, hush up and drink your toast!

TOBIAS. Oh, very well! . . . Persis?

PERSIS. (*raises her glass*) May as well get it over with!

BOTH. (*raise glasses toward MARSHA, just as a now-sober-if-shaky VIRGIL enters from bathroom*) Happy birthday!

VIRGIL. (*reacts like a madman, waving his arms and*

shrieking as he rushes toward them) No! Don't! You can't! You mustn't!

BOTH. (*slightly terrified by this apparition*) Why *not?!*

VIRGIL. (*stops, thinking desperately*) Because . . . because . . . (*Inspiration strikes.*) Her birthday's not till *tomorrow!*

LYNETTE. Oh, where's the harm in anticipating?!

TOBIAS/PERSIS. Right! (*Both drink entire contents of glasses.*)

VIRGIL. *Aaaaaghhhh!* (*falls in dead faint onto floor*)

PERSIS. (*rushes to look down upon him, OTHERS following*) Whatever is *ailing* that man?

LYNETTE. The life of a pharmacist is very hard.

TOBIAS. (*points at fallen body*) *That* hard?

PERSIS. Well, perhaps he's not very *good* at it.

MARSHA. (*who has been smiling in triumph since they drank*) He's better then you know! (*will take each of their glasses from them, during:*) Better than you know! He knows things—oh, so many things—that one would never suspect to look at him! (*starts for kitchen, taking tray, GB and cordial glasses*)

PERSIS. Well, he *certainly* knows how to louse up a dinner party!

TOBIAS. Dinner! We've completely forgotten dinner! (*starts for dining room*) No wonder I feel so hungry! Come along, Persis, or *everything* will be cold!

MARSHA. Perhaps even you and Tobias! (*gives wild laugh of devilish glee, exits to kitchen*)

PERSIS. Now, what did she mean by *that?*

TOBIAS. (*pausing short of exit*) I'm tired of trying to figure out her conduct tonight. Let's just go and eat!

LYNETTE. You're just going to leave Virgil *lying* there?

TOBIAS. It's as good a place as any! (*exits*)

PERSIS. (*starts after him just as MARSHA returns minus glasses*) Perhaps I'd *better* eat—that drink had the *oddest* taste. . . ! Almost like . . . *gin* . . .

MARSHA. (*smiling in almost sinister fashion*) Yes, I suppose it did. After all, even plain *water* isn't *entirely* tasteless. It's all a matter of degree.

PERSIS. (*very uneasy near her, if unsure why, starts backing away toward dining room*) Uh, yes. Yes, to be sure. . . !

MARSHA. (*ominously*) I've never been surer!

PERSIS. Uh . . . of course you haven't . . . uh . . . none of us has. . . ! (*turns and dashes off to dining room*)

MARSHA. (*claps her hands and dances about*) Revenge! Revenge! Revenge!

LYNETTE. Marsha, darling, you simply *must* calm down!

MARSHA. Calm down? Now? At my moment of total triumph?

LYNETTE. Darling, there's something I should tell you about that bottle—

MARSHA. Mother, don't you understand? I've *done* it! (*points to VIRGIL*) *We've* done it! Odorless, tasteless, undetectable—and very soon, mortal agony!

LYNETTE. Oh, but darling—

VIRGIL. (*starts to stir*) Mmmmph . . . oooh . . . what—where—my head hurts—why am I on the floor?

MARSHA. (*helping him to his feet*) Be calm, Virgil, be calm! It's all over! We've won!

LYNETTE. Marsha—

VIRGIL. Won? You mean—? Your husband and that woman—? They're—? (*He stops, too horrified to finish.*)

MARSHA. Well, not *yet*, of course, but I'm sure it's

only a matter of minutes till they curl up and fall over and writhe about on the floor. That last part is my favorite.

LYNETTE. Marsha—

MARSHA. (*finally paying attention*) *Yes,* Mother, what *is* it?

LYNETTE. There's something I must tell you, tell both of you—but—before I do, there's something *you* must tell *me . . . Why,* darling, *why?*

VIRGIL. Why what?

LYNETTE. (*impatiently*) *You're* not darling!

VIRGIL. Sorry.

MARSHA. But Mother—why what?

LYNETTE. Why did you want to murder your husband? And that Devore woman?

MARSHA. Believe me, Mother, if you knew what *I* know about them, you'd murder them, too!

LYNETTE. (*very surprised and curious*) Know about them? You don't mean—that he and she are—were—?

MARSHA. Oh, Mother, if you only knew what they had planned for tomorrow morning!

LYNETTE. Tomorrow morning?

VIRGIL. Down by the bay.

LYNETTE. (*as it becomes—she thinks—clear*) Oh, *that!*

MARSHA. Mother! You *know* what they were planning to do?!

LYNETTE. Why—of course I knew! Tobias told me all about it last week!

MARSHA. (*aghast*) And you didn't tell *me?!*

LYNETTE. How could I? He said it was a surprise!

MARSHA. (*backing from her*) Mother! How could you! Your own daughter! And not a word of warning!

LYNETTE. But if I had warned you, it would have spoiled everything! And after all, you certainly had it coming to you!

VIRGIL. (*totally shocked and scandalized*) *What kind of a mother* are *you?!*

MARSHA. Coming to me? Coming to me? But I've always been so nice to him, so caring, so devoted—!

LYNETTE. Of course you have! That's why he decided to *do* it!

VIRGIL. What! Take Marsha down to the bay, pretending he'd found a new crab restaurant, take her to the end of the pier, raise the champagne bottle, and—?!

LYNETTE. Why *not?!* I thought it was very clever of him to think of it!

MARSHA. *Mother!*

LYNETTE. Oh, darling, look at it from Tobias' point of view: Year after year, giving you such silly little presents on your birthday—meaningless things—a pair of earrings here—a bottle of perfume there—he just couldn't stand it any longer, and decided he had to do something that would knock you dead! And about *time*, if you ask *me!*

(*MARSHA can stand no more; staring at her mother in horrified disbelief, she clutches her temples and starts screaming, over and over, wordlessly, louder and louder; TOBIAS and PERSIS, of course, come rushing into the room in reaction to the sound, see her, and—with MARSHA constantly screaming— we have the following dialogue/action:*)

TOBIAS. (*rushing for MARSHA*) Good heavens!

PERSIS. (*standing dumbfounded*) What's happened?

TOBIAS. (*wrestling with MARSHA, who is trying to*

fend him off—while continuing repeated screams, of course) She's gone berserk! *Help* me with her!

VIRGIL. (*grabs PERSIS as she starts to move*) No you don't! Keep away from her, do you hear?! (*wrestles her to floor*)

PERSIS. No! Stop! Have *you* gone berserk, *too?*

VIRGIL. Don't play innocent! I'm *on* to you!

PERSIS. Well, get *off* of me! (*starts screaming of her own*)

TOBIAS. Lynette! Don't just stand there, *do* something!

LYNETTE. Such as?

VIRGIL. Keep fighting, Marsha! It won't be long now! Five minutes at the most!

MARSHA. (*between screams*) *What* won't be long now?

VIRGIL. The poison!

PERSIS. (*between screams*) *What* poison?

VIRGIL. In that *drink* you just had!

LYNETTE. Now, listen—please listen—everybody listen—!

(*At this moment, front door bursts open, and BEN— BIANCA just behind him—leaps into room, his gun steadied before him in two hands, legs spread apart, knees slightly bent in classic cop-on-the-job stance, his leap landing him simultaneous with his cry:*)

BEN. *FREEZE!* (*ALL FREEZE, looking at him in silent shock.*)

BIANCA. (*pointing to both interlocked couples*) There! What did I tell you!

TOBIAS. What *did* she tell you?

BIANCA. Everything! I *knew* what you were planning for tomorrow morning, and I told it all to Ben as soon as we got out of here!

PERSIS. So is that any reason to pull a *gun* on us?

BEN. *Quiet,* while I tell you your rights! "You have the right to remain silent—"

TOBIAS. (*releasing MARSHA*) Now just a moment—!

BEN. Hold it right there! One more move and I start shooting!

PERSIS. (*squirming free of VIRGIL and getting to her feet, which he does, too, while she speaks*) But you're trying to shoot the wrong people! *These* two tried to *poison* us!

MARSHA. That's utter nonsense!

VIRGIL. Of course it is!

LYNETTE. Please, if everybody will just *listen* to me—!

BEN. (*gun-gesturing TOBIAS and PERSIS*) Come on, you two, raise those hands, and be quick about it!

TOBIAS. (*as he and PERSIS raise their hands*) But officer, you've got to listen to me! We have less than five minutes before the poison takes effect!

BEN. Don't hand me that!

TOBIAS. (*starts gesture toward coffeetable*) It's true! Just take that bottle and have it analyzed—(*stops at sight of empty coffeetable*)

BEN. What bottle?

TOBIAS. (*lamely*) Well, it was there a minute ago—!

BEN. Okay, that's enough! Come along, you two, you're going for a ride!

BIANCA. *Now?* But what about our *date?*

BEN. *Really,* Bee! This is *important!* (*has turned slightly to her while speaking, and TOBIAS and PERSIS start to lower their hands, and he catches, and reacts, to movement by again gun-threatening them on:*) No you don't!

BOTH. (*hands going high again*) We *didn't!*

BIANCA. (*angry with BEN*) Well, I guess I know how *I* rate with you! (*starts stomping off kitchenward*) If I'd known you were going to be *this* devoted to duty, I never would have told you at *all!*

BEN. Bee—! (*But she exits to kitchen without replying; furious, he starts gesturing TOBIAS and PERSIS into hall.*) Oh, boy, *now* you two are *really* gonna get it!

TOBIAS. (*moving toward hall, hands high*) That's not fair!

PERSIS. You can't take your love-problems out on suspects!

BEN. Why *not?*

TOBIAS. He's got a point, Persis.

PERSIS. He *has?*

TOBIAS. Well, he's got a gun, and the person with the gun always has a point—whether he has or not! (*TOBIAS and PERSIS exit, BEN following close after them, on:*)

BEN. Mrs. Gilmore, I'll take these two downtown and book 'em, but we'll need a statement from you . . .

MARSHA. Oh, of course. Any time at all, Officer. (*BEN exits, MARSHA closes door after him.*)

VIRGIL. I feel so unclean! They'll be dead before he even pulls away from the curb!

LYNETTE. *Enough!* If you two will stop gloating and agonizing for a moment, I have something very important to tell you!

MARSHA. Oh, all right, Mother—what?

LYNETTE. *Nobody* has been *poisoned!*

VIRGIL. But they *drank* from the bottle—they *must* be poisoned!

LYNETTE. Well, they *would* have been, but luckily, I overheard the two of you plotting, and I took the bottle and emptied it down the commode in the hall bathroom!

MARSHA. That's impossible! I'm *sure* there was something in their glasses—?!

LYNETTE. That was *gin!* I wanted *something* in the bottle so I could see just how *far* you two would really *go!*

VIRGIL. Let me get this straight—you *stole* some poison that didn't *belong* to you and you *flushed* it?!

LYNETTE. Well, you had no right to put poison into my birthday present!

MARSHA. Mother, what are you talking about?! That was *Virgil's* present!

LYNETTE. Nonsense! I brought that bottle here tonight, as a birthday present to you! If you don't believe me, ask *Bianca!* (*At this moment, BIANCA enters, carrying OB.*)

BIANCA. Say, do you suppose *this* is the bottle Mister Gilmore was talking about just before he left? I found it in the garbage.

MARSHA. You couldn't have! I stashed it in the kitchen cabinet with the cordial glasses! (*to VIRGIL*) I was going to wash it out later, with the glasses, to conceal the evidence.

BIANCA. But I distinctly remember throwing it into the garbage!

VIRGIL. Well, of course, *that* gets rid of the evidence rather well, too.

LYNETTE. You two are idiots! (*will go to BIANCA, take bottle, and fill small glass from it at bar, during:*) Here, give me that! This will show you, once and for all, that I know what I'm talking about! I *dumped* your precious poison, put *gin* in its place, and *that's* what Tobias and the Devore woman drank! (*raises glass*) Now, just take a taste of this, if you don't believe me!

MARSHA. No way!

VIRGIL. Not on your life!

BIANCA. They have a point, Mrs. Thoren. . . !

LYNETTE. Oh, don't be ridiculous, Bianca! This is gin! I know it's gin because I put it there! Look, I'll prove it! (*takes large swallow from glass, reacts to the taste of the gentian—remember, this is the OB she has*) Oh! . . . *Oh!* . . . OH! (*drops glass onto bar, clutches her throat*)

MARSHA. *Mother!* What have you *done?!*

BIANCA. Maybe she got the wrong bottle!

MARSHA. What?!

VIRGIL. You mean there *were* two bottles?!

BIANCA. Of course! But—which one had the poison in it?

LYNETTE. I think I *know!* (*rushes madly toward front door*) Wait! Officer—wait! Hold that ambulance! (*exits to hall, fast, slamming door behind her*)

MARSHA. (*accusingly, to VIRGIL*) *Now* see what you've done!

VIRGIL. But how did *I* know there were two bottles?!

BIANCA. You could have *asked* me!

VIRGIL. *Wait* a minute! Bianca! *You* drank some of that stuff yourself!

BIANCA. (*horrified*) That's right! I did!

MARSHA. But—from which bottle?

BIANCA. (*growing terrified*) I don't *know!* I don't *know!*

VIRGIL. Well, how do you *feel?*

BIANCA. Panic-stricken! (*rushes for front door*) Ben! Ben, don't go! Wait for me, please! (*exits, slamming door behind her*)

VIRGIL. (*numbly, turns to MARSHA*) Well . . . what do we do *now?*

MARSHA. (*thinks hard a moment, then offers brightly:*) How about some *dinner?!* (*And, as she smiles cheerily, and he stares at her in slack-jawed unbelief—*)

THE CURTAIN FALLS

End of Act Two

ACT THREE

Immediately following. MARSHA and VIRGIL just where we left them.

VIRGIL. Marsha, how can you even think of sitting down to dine, with all those lives on our conscience?

MARSHA. Virgil, be sensible! Tobias and Persis were trying to *murder* me, and my mother was *in* on it! She *said* she knew all about their plans for tomorrow, *didn't* she?

VIRGIL. I'll grant you, they probably had it coming to them—but what about Bianca? She was entirely innocent!

MARSHA. Well, you can't blame us for Bianca being poisoned—after all, she shouldn't be drinking our liquor in the first place. I'll miss her, of course, but at least poisoning her was an accident, so we can't really feel guilty about it, now can we!

VIRGIL. Speak for yourself. I feel perfectly rotten!

MARSHA. (*slumps*) Well, if you must know—so do I! (*starts to cry*)

VIRGIL. (*goes to her, holds her*) Why Marsha—you do have a conscience, after all!

MARSHA. Of course I do! Why, if I hadn't been so afraid—if it hadn't been for that Devore woman—I'd never have gone through with it!

VIRGIL. I don't follow that.

MARSHA. Oh, Virgil, if you knew how much I adored—do adore—always will adore—my darling husband! If he'd been planning to murder me all on his own—well, I just might have let him succeed. The notion that he hated me so much would make my life no longer worth the living anyhow!

VIRGIL. But knowing he had another woman waiting—! Ah, yes, I see!

MARSHA. It wasn't his planning to murder me that hurt so much—it was his planning to murder me so he could go to her!

VIRGIL. Say, now, wait a moment—if you adored—do adore—and always will adore—Tobias so very much—how can you be insanely in love with *me?*

MARSHA. Oh, dear. Virgil—I have a confession to make—

VIRGIL. (*releases her, takes a backstep*) Oh, Marsha! I can see it in your eyes! You never *did* love me! You just needed an *ally!* You—you *used* me!

MARSHA. Yes, but, what are helpful neighbors *for?!*

VIRGIL. Oh, what a fool I was! When I think of it—throwing away all my scruples, all my values—all for the love of a woman who never loved me in the first place! Who probably despises me, in her heart of hearts!

MARSHA. Well, now, don't be too hard on yourself, Virgil. You *are* rather *nice,* in a kind of mousy way. And I certainly appreciate all the help you've given me, and I may even come to love you a little after we're married—

VIRGIL. Married?! What are you talking about?

MARSHA. Virgil, we *have* to get married! Every book I've ever read where the wife and lover bump off the husband, they get married so they can keep an eye on one another, since each one knows all about the other one's capital crime!

VIRGIL. Marsha! This is not a mystery novel! This is real life! Do you know the difference?!

MARSHA. Oh, Virgil, you're such an innocent! There *is* no difference! Husbands and wives are murdering

each other right and left, all over the place. You find a
case in almost every morning paper!

VIRGIL. Because they were all *caught! That's* what you
read about — all those love-blinded *idiots* who have been
arrested for *murder!*

MARSHA. Well, if we *are* arrested, at least we know we
had it coming to us. But I doubt that we will be. We've
been far too clever. Of course, there's always *one* problem in such cases . . . (*is staring at him shrewdly*)

VIRGIL. Problem? What problem?

MARSHA. (*eyes locked on him*) *One* of the killers is
always the *nervous* sort — the kind who fidgets and wor-
ries and fusses and panics until his very face is like a
neon sign displaying his guilt . . .

VIRGIL. (*her implication sinks in*) Uh. Well — I — I cer-
tainly *hope* you don't mean *me?!* (*with lame bravado*)
Why, I *never* panic — steady as a rock — nerves of steel —
(*PHONE RINGS and he screams in terror.*)

MARSHA. You were saying — ? (*He bites his lip in
shame, and she answers phone.*) Hello? . . . Who? . . .
He *what?* . . . Oh. Yes. I see . . . No, I'm sure that was
some sort of mistake . . . Yes, by all means, go right
ahead as scheduled . . . All right . . . Goodbye. (*hangs
up*) Now, if that isn't the oddest thing!

VIRGIL. What? What thing? What's odd?

MARSHA. That man on the phone. He said Tobias has
purchased a seaplane, due to be down at the bay tonight
so Tobias will be able to get to it there tomorrow morning. Now, why do you suppose he'd do a thing like that?

VIRGIL. Perhaps for his getaway, in case he flubbed
your murder somehow.

MARSHA. But *Tobias* can't fly a plane!

VIRGIL. Maybe he knows somebody who *can. Does*
he?

MARSHA. Only *me*. But I could hardly do that once he'd murdered me.

VIRGIL. But if he *flubbed* the murder, you'd still be *alive!*

MARSHA. Yes, but hardly in the mood to offer him my assistance!

VIRGIL. That's true enough — oh, but, by the way, why did you tell the airplane man to go *ahead* with the plan?

MARSHA. Well, if things don't work out for *us*, then *we* could use it for a getaway!

VIRGIL. With the Law in hot pursuit? Marsha, the *police* have planes, and their planes have *machine*-guns!

MARSHA. But they wouldn't be *chasing* us in planes if we started our getaway in my *car* — and by the time we got to the bay and took off, they'd waste all *sorts* of time getting their *own* planes into the air, and we'd be long gone off into the blue!

VIRGIL. (*with weary patience*) Marsha — look — use your head — just *where* on the bay is this plane going to be?

MARSHA. *I* don't know.

VIRGIL. What *make* is it?

MARSHA. *I* don't know.

VIRGIL. Where would you get the *ignition* key for it?

MARSHA. *I* don't know.

VIRGIL. What is its *flight* range?

MARSHA. Really, Virgil, do you expect me to be well informed on every last petty detail?!

VIRGIL. *Petty?!* You don't know where the plane *is*, what it *looks* like, how you're going to *start* it, or how far it will *take* us, and *this* is how you've planned our *getaway?!*

MARSHA. I suppose my plan *does* need a little work . . .

VIRGIL. (*aghast*) A little *work?!* It's in a major *recession!*

MARSHA. Well, if you're going to be critical, you can just eat dinner by yourself! (*starts bedroomward*)

VIRGIL. (*Her vector hasn't registered.*) Dinner?! Who can think of food at a time like this?! We've got to come up with a plan, a solid alibi, a—(*It registers.*) Marsha, where are you going?

MARSHA. (*pauses short of exit*) To have a nap, of course. It's been an absolutely *exhausting* evening! (*exits*)

VIRGIL. *But—?!* (*No use; she's gone; distracted, he totters to bar, almost pours himself a drink from OB, reacts, sets it down in distaste, grabs the gin bottle and drinks from it without a glass, then moves down to sofa and sits, staring out front with glazed eyes, now and then taking a sip from the bottle, mumbling half-aloud:*) A nap . . . at a time like this . . . after lying to a policeman . . . four attempted murders . . . no plan of escape . . . our entire future in jeopardy . . . sucking me into her sordid scheme. . . !

(*As he mumbles, hall door slowly opens, and there enter —one by one, on tiptoe, very stealthily— TOBIAS, PERSIS, LYNETTE, BEN and BIANCA [who quietly closes door after her] until they have him semi-surrounded, TOBIAS standing at right end of sofa, BIANCA at left end, remaining trio along the back of sofa, all looking grimly down at him; as he reaches final phrase of the mumble, he senses other presences, abruptly looks left and right and behind him in a fast series of spastic head-and-body moves, and then—in one motion—drops the bottle and clutches his heart and opens his mouth to scream in*) *terror, and BEN neatly gets his hand over VIRGIL's mouth in time to prevent a sound; then:)*

BEN. (*quietly*) Not a sound! Nod your head if you promise not to scream. (*VIRGIL nods, eyes wide with fear.*) Okay, then. But one peep, and you'll regret it! (*releases VIRGIL, who gasps some air in a couple of contorted gulps; then:*) Where is Mrs. Gilmore?

VIRGIL. (*a bit too loudly*) She—(*OTHERS all make threatening moves inward toward him, and he frantically lowers his voice and manages:*) She—went into the bedroom—to take a nap.

TOBIAS. (*disgustedly*) Wouldn't you just know! After all she's done tonight!

(*NOTE: To save time and space describing players' inflections, suffice it to say that ALL—including VIRGIL—will play remainder of this sequence* sotto voce; *they need not actually lower their voices (since spectators in the back rows of the audience have a right to hear the dialogue), but by modifying their voices give the impression—an accurate one—that they do not want MARSHA to hear what they're saying.*)

VIRGIL. I don't understand. I thought you all were—?

PERSIS. (*accusingly*) Dead?

VIRGIL. No, of course not! There wasn't any poison in that bottle! In *either* bottle! But I thought you'd all be off in the ambulance by now!

LYNETTE. No poison? What are you saying?

VIRGIL. Wait a minute. First things first! (*Curiosity is now overmastering fear in his delivery.*) Why are you all back here so *quickly?* You couldn't *possibly* have had time to get to a hospital and find out you *weren't* going to die!

BEN. That's simple enough. By the time we got down to the street, Mister Gilmore was able to explain what he and Miss Devore had *really* planned for Marsha tomorrow morning, and it certainly made sense—

LYNETTE. And when *I* got down there, I'd finally realized that it was only that foul-tasting liqueur that had panicked me—*obviously* I hadn't been poisoned if the poison were totally *tasteless*—

BIANCA. And when Mrs. Thoren *assured* me that the doctored bottle had been flushed, I knew *I* wasn't poisoned—

PERSIS. Which brings us back to *you,* Virgil! What do you *mean* you didn't try to poison us?!

VIRGIL. You sound disappointed!

BEN. Now *listen,* creep! I'm giving you a lot more leeway than you deserve! We want some answers, and the *right* answers, fast! I *still* feel I ought to be arresting everybody in sight!

BIANCA. (*pats his arm soothingly*) Now, Ben, we've been all *over* that! You can't arrest Mister Gilmore and Miss Devore because they *weren't* planning to murder his wife—and you can't arrest *her* because the attempted poisoning was only *self-defense* on her part!

BEN. Damn it all, *something* illegal's been going on here, if I could only figure out *what!*

TOBIAS. Keep your voice down! We don't want Marsha to hear us!

BEN. Okay, okay! But what's all this about no poison in that bottle?

TOBIAS. (*to VIRGIL*) And why did you get panicky and faint when we drank some if you knew it wouldn't *kill* us?!

VIRGIL. *Because* I knew it wouldn't kill you! Once you drank the stuff and *didn't* keel over, Marsha would know I'd been lying to her about it, and then the whole ghastly truth would come out!

PERSIS. *What* ghastly truth?

VIRGIL. (*miserably, hanging his head*) I'm not a pharmacist. Never have been. Don't know the least little thing about it, either!

BIANCA. Then why did you tell Mrs. Devore you *were?* And let *Marsha* believe it?

VIRGIL. She was *so* anxious for me to help her—it was the only thing I could think of that might sound like I was in a position to do her some good. I couldn't tell her what I *really* was!

LYNETTE. And just what *are* you?

VIRGIL. (*almost inaudible in his shame*) A kindergarten teacher!

OTHERS. *What?!* (*Then ALL start shushing each other immediately; when quiet has been restored:*)

BEN. I think you'd better explain yourself, Baxter!

TOBIAS. Yes! How did you let yourself get dragged *into* this mess?

VIRGIL. (*shrugs unhappily*) It was an adventure. I've never had an adventure before. Kindergarten teachers seldom do. (*gives a wistful sigh; then:*) I had to be convincing—Marsha gave me the idea for my plan when she quoted some Agatha Christie book that said everyone's pantry was full of potential combinations that could be poisonous—so I filched a bunch of stuff to convince her I knew what I was doing, took it next door, left it all on my kitchen table, and just filled up the liqueur bottle with plain water.

BIANCA. Just *water?*

VIRGIL. (*shrugs*) Well—the poison was supposed to

be tasteless and ordorless — I thought water would come up to those specifications nicely.

TOBIAS. I can see now that all my warnings to Marsha weren't foolhardy. All her mystery-reading *has* softened her brain! That she could for one moment *imagine* that I — a loving husband of many years — would even *think* of doing her in — !

VIRGIL. Now, *wait* a moment! Marsha and I *eavesdropped* on your conversation with Persis! You two even had *me* convinced Marsha was right!

PERSIS. What do you mean?

VIRGIL. You said you were going to take her down to the bay, break a champagne bottle across her nose, watch her go off into the water — and then come back here for a *party!*

TOBIAS. Oh, but Virgil —

VIRGIL. (*to PERSIS*) And *you* were talking about straps to hold her, and something you were going to cement over her head, and —

PERSIS. Oh, dear. Tobias — we were. We really were!

BEN. Going to *murder* her?

PERSIS. *Saying* those things!

BIANCA. They sure *sound* like murder!

LYNETTE. No-no! Virgil and Marsha had the wrong *nose!*

BIANCA. I don't follow that.

TOBIAS. We were going to break the champagne bottle over the nose of Marsha's *birthday* present — a new *seaplane!*

VIRGIL. Seaplane! Then that explains the phone call!

BEN. What phone call?

VIRGIL. While you were out. A man called, said the seaplane was going to the bay tonight, and Marsha okayed it.

PERSIS. Oh, damn! Then she knows about the surprise!

VIRGIL. Well, hardly! She thought you wanted the plane for your getaway!

TOBIAS. Getaway from *what?* We haven't committed a *crime!*

VIRGIL. *Marsha* didn't know that!

LYNETTE. It seems to me the main point is — what are we going to do *now?*

TOBIAS. We are going to teach Marsha a lesson she'll never forget! If she wasn't addicted to reading that mind-rotting junk like *The Creeping Slasher,* none of this would have happened!

PERSIS. Uh, Tobias —

VIRGIL. Say, you know, you may be right! She *said* the book was about a woman whose husband was trying to bump her off!

TOBIAS. It's a shame none of *us* has read it. We could use its plot to really give her a scare!

PERSIS. Tobias —

TOBIAS. It's a pity none of us has the requisite rotted mind! But only an idiot would read that sort of trash.

PERSIS. Tobias!

TOBIAS. Hmm? What?

PERSIS. *I've* read it!

BIANCA. Oh! Why, of *course* you have! It was the very first thing you said when you walked *in* here this evening!

TOBIAS. Oh, my. Persis — how can I ever apologize!

BIANCA. You might not *have* to — maybe her mind *is* rotted.

TOBIAS. Bianca!

LYNETTE. Ssh! Keep your voice down!

PERSIS. Look, the point is, I *have* read it, and I think I

know how we can use it to teach Marsha that lesson. It's about time she learned the difference between fact and fiction!

TOBIAS. Amen to that!

BEN. So what's your plan?

PERSIS. (*gestures them to huddle in closer to her, and VIRGIL leaves sofa to join the huddle as well*) Well, in the book, the woman's begun to suspect her husband—

VIRGIL. Just like Marsha.

PERSIS. She's tried calling the police, but they think she's a wacko, and won't come—

VIRGIL. Just like Marsha.

PERSIS. Now, this woman is having a torrid love affair with another man—(*OTHERS all turn their gazes expectantly upon VIRGIL.*)

VIRGIL. I didn't say a word. (*ALL re-focus on PERSIS again.*)

PERSIS. —so the husband forces the lover to telephone her, so that when she comes to the phone, the husband can come creeping out of the kitchen behind her, with the huge butcher knife he's used for all his other killings—

TOBIAS. That's perfect! Let's *do* it!

VIRGIL. But what if she struggles?

PERSIS. She can't. The husband's girl friend ties her up!

BIANCA. Gee, this is exciting! What happens next?

PERSIS. (*caught up in BIANCA's dementia*) Well, a long time ago, when the heroine was a little girl, her grandfather told her that if she was ever in trouble, she should—

TOBIAS. Persis, *please!* We have *enough* information!

LYNETTE. But what did the grandfather *tell* her?

TOBIAS. Enough!

LYNETTE. Sorry.

BIANCA. Okay, now, let's do it!

VIRGIL. How? Marsha doesn't have a lover.

TOBIAS. *You* be her lover.

VIRGIL. Why *me?*

BIANCA. You were *almost* her lover *already!*

VIRGIL. But I can't!

TOBIAS. Why not?

VIRGIL. Well, for instance, what would I say to her on the phone?

LYNETTE. Anything that pops into your head!

VIRGIL. Such as? All I can think of is "Nice weather we're having!"

PERSIS. The book! Where's the book?! He can read the conversation right out of that!

TOBIAS. Of course! (*leaps to drawer, gets book, hands it to VIRGIL*) Here, just read what it says in here, and do it!

VIRGIL. Well—I guess that should be simple enough . . .

PERSIS. All right, then, is everything set to go?

BEN. Now, wait a minute—I'm not sure this kind of this is legal.

BIANCA. Ben.

BEN. Yes, honey?

BIANCA. Do you ever hope to date me again?

BEN. Of course!

BIANCA. Then it's legal.

BEN. . . . All right.

TOBIAS. Good! Now, Virgil, you go back to your apartment, wait about a minute, then telephone here. That'll bring Marsha out of the bedroom. I'll get the butcher knife from the kitchen, and wait just around the corner of the archway—

LYNETTE. Wait a minute! Where do the *rest* of us go?

TOBIAS. Why—uh—out in the hall, I suppose . . .

BIANCA. Not on your life! I don't want to miss this!

PERSIS. Neither do I!

TOBIAS. But you can't stay in *here!*

BEN. We can hide! I feel as if I should be on the premises, anyhow—just in case you get caught up in your role as the slasher and—

TOBIAS. Now, really!

PERSIS. Oh, be a sport, Tobias!

TOBIAS. Okay-okay. Everybody hide! Virgil, get over to your apartment! I'll go get that butcher knife! (*VIRGIL hastens out front door, BEN gets into coat cabinet with BIANCA, LYNETTE grabs gin bottle, goes behind bar, leaves bottle on bar, and ducks down out of sight, and PERSIS exits with TOBIAS toward the kitchen; about two seconds pass; then:*)

BEN. (*from cabinet*) Aw, but honey!

BIANCA. Later, Ben, later!

BEN. Aw, c'mon!

LYNETTE. (*rushes from behind bar to cabinet, yanks it open, and we see BIANCA struggling in BEN's arms*) Now, cut that out! The phone's going to ring any second, and—(*PHONE RINGS.*) Yipe! (*BEN and BIANCA disengage and shut cabinet doors as LYNETTE gallops back to duck behind bar; PHONE RINGS AGAIN; a half-second, and we hear:*)

MARSHA. (*off*) Virgil? . . . Virgil, is that the phone? . . . (*She enters from bedroom, sleepily, in nightgown, robe and slippers, looks vaguely around room.*) Virgil—? (*PHONE RINGS AGAIN; she heads for it, on:*) Where in the world has *he* gone? (*gets phone, on:*) Probably out buying a false beard! (*then, on phone:*) Hello. . . ? (*She comes fully awake.*) Virgil? . . . Virgil,

where *are* you? . . . My grandfather? *What* grandfather? . . . Yes, of *course* I have a grandfather — *two* of
them, as a matter of fact! What I was wondering is why
you — ? *What?* . . . Virgil, you're not making sense!
You're talking just like the heroine's boy friend in *The
Creeping Slasher!* . . . (*Behind her, TOBIAS — with
butcher knife and feigning a fiendish glee — and
PERSIS — carrying a large coil of rope — come tiptoeing
out of kitchen and toward her.*) Yes, Virgil, of *course* I
remember what Grandfather said to do in a time of peril
. . . Not *my* grandfather, the one in the silly book! . . .
Virgil, why are you *saying* all those things? You're scar-
ing me! It's just like the part in the book where the
heroine doesn't know that just behind her . . . (*Her
voice stops, she becomes uneasy.*) . . . that — just behind
her . . . with a huge gleaming butcher knife in his hand
. . . her — her husband . . . is . . . is . . . (*turns head, sees
TOBIAS, screams and drops phone*) No! No, don't!
This isn't *happening!* It *can't* be happening! (*Despite
her denials, she is already backing from him as she
speaks, in an arc that will take her backward to spot between center of sofa and coffeetable, while PERSIS
moves in mirror-image arc that will bring her down just
behind MARSHA with rope.*) Toby! That knife! What
does it mean?!

TOBIAS. (*gives sinister chuckle, then says:*) Three
guesses!

MARSHA. (*screams as PERSIS grabs her and starts ty-
ing her up*) No! Stop! Let me go!

TOBIAS. (*sets knife on coffeetable, helps PERSIS
truss her up*) Make those knots good and tight! We
don't want her wriggling while we kill her!

MARSHA. (*During her speech, they will finish binding*

her, and deposit her lying on sofa, her head right on sofa-arm.) Toby! That's *just* what the husband said in the *book!*

PERSIS. Save your breath for shrieking!

MARSHA. And *that's* just what his *girl friend* said!

TOBIAS. You're doomed, Marsha, doomed! Now that I have you bound and helpless, you'll be no match for the razor-sharp blade of my knife! (*picks knife up, leans over her, smiling evilly*)

PERSIS. How many victims does this make, Slasher?

TOBIAS. She will be my seventh!

MARSHA. Seventh?! Toby, what does this mean?!

TOBIAS. That I am going to stab you seven times, of course!

PERSIS. He stabbed the first victim once—

TOBIAS. The second victim twice—

PERSIS. The third victim thrice—

TOBIAS. And so on and so on.

MARSHA. Aw, shucks!

PERSIS/TOBIAS. "Shucks!"?

MARSHA. I've always wondered what came after "thrice"! *You* know—Is it "frice" or "fice" or—?

TOBIAS. Cut that out! This is serious!

MARSHA. Sorry.

PERSIS. We're wasting time! Start that stabbing!

TOBIAS. Very well! (*Raises knife; as he does so, BEN and BIANCA peek out of cabinet, and LYNETTE peers up from behind bar, ALL enrapt by the downstage tableau.*)

MARSHA. Oh, but Toby—*seven times?!*

TOBIAS. Of course! It's a behavior pattern for the police to detect. Of course, they won't figure it out till about the tenth victim or so.

PERSIS. One murder, one stab—two murders, two stabs—and the police still haven't decided if there's a connection between them all!

MARSHA. (*sighs*) Why are the police always so infernally stupid?! (*BEN, resenting this, almost steps out of cabinet and speaks, but BIANCA gets a hand over his mouth and restrains him with an insistent headshake.*)

TOBIAS. Enough chitchat! Prepare to die! (*raises knife again*)

PERSIS. Oh, by the way, Slasher—

TOBIAS. Yes?

PERSIS. When you *do* stab her seven times—

TOBIAS. Yes?

PERSIS. Try to make it look like an accident!

TOBIAS. (*drops out of "Slasher" character*) An *accident?!* Persis, that's *silly!*

MARSHA. But Toby—*all* of Anton Dupré's books are silly!

TOBIAS. They *are?*

PERSIS. Of *course* they are! Why do you think I *read* them?

TOBIAS. But—?

MARSHA. Toby, use your brain! Would anyone writing a *serious* mystery novel ever call it anything like *The Creeping Slasher?*

PERSIS. And would anyone ever *end* a serious novel like the finale of *The Creeping Slasher*, where the heroine decides to—

MARSHA. Don't tell me! Don't tell me! I haven't finished it yet!

TOBIAS. (*getting back into character with an effort*) And you're not *going* to, either, when *I* get through with you!

MARSHA. Wait! Don't kill me yet! Let me do the one thing my grandfather always told me to do in times of peril!

TOBIAS. (*out of character*) *Which* grandfather?

PERSIS. In the *book,* in the *book!*

TOBIAS. Oh, *that* guy! (*back into character, menacing with knife*) And just what *did* your grandfather tell you to do in times of peril?

MARSHA. (*in an automatic singsong:*) "Now I lay me down to sleep—" (*TOBIAS guffaws, turns away.*) Toby, you're not supposed to laugh!

TOBIAS. (*turing back, almost helpless with laughter*) But that's utterly ridiculous!

PERSIS. I *told* you those books were silly!

TOBIAS. (*forcing himself back into character*) Well, silly or not, you're going to die! Do you hear? Die!

PERSIS. Seven times!

TOBIAS. (*out of character*) Now, cut that out!

MARSHA. Oh, Toby—if I *must* die—would you honor one final request?

TOBIAS. *What* request?

MARSHA. Would you take *The Creeping Slasher* back to the library?

TOBIAS. *What?!*

MARSHA. It's *already* two days *overdue!*

TOBIAS. All right, all right! As soon as I finish killing you, I'll take it back.

MARSHA. Actually, I was hoping you'd take it back *first,* and *then* come back and kill me.

TOBIAS. But you might escape while I was out!

MARSHA. Yes, that was the general idea!

TOBIAS. Enough! (*raises knife*) Your time has come!

PERSIS. No-no! *That's* not what the Slasher says!

TOBIAS. Damn it all! All right, what *does* he say?

PERSIS. "Soon your radiant beauty will be lying here in seven pieces!"

TOBIAS. You're kidding!

PERSIS. I told you the books were silly.

TOBIAS. But that's such lousy arithmetic! If I slash seven times, that leaves *eight* pieces!

PERSIS. It *does?*

TOBIAS. Picture Marsha as a loaf of bread—if I slash it *once,* it's in *two* pieces—if I slash a *second* time on one of the two pieces, it's in *three* pieces—if I slash it a *third* time—

PERSIS. Wait, not so fast!

TOBIAS. What's the matter?

PERSIS. I'm still trying to picture Marsha as a loaf of bread.

TOBIAS. Persis—!

MARSHA. She *told* you the books were silly!

PERSIS. Look, this is taking *forever!* Will you just *make* your final threat and get *to* it!

TOBIAS. Oh, all *right*, damn it! (*into character, hovering over MARSHA with knife*) Soon your radiant beauty will be lying here in seven pieces! (*Then ALL look doorward as door flies open with a crash, and VIRGIL leaps into room, a large pistol in both hands, just as BEN did earlier.*)

VIRGIL. Take your clothes off!

TOBIAS. *What?*

VIRGIL. I mean—Get goosebumps!

TOBIAS. *What?*

VIRGIL. Wait a minute, I'll get this right . . . Oh, of course—(*has dropped stance, gets into it again for:*) *FREEZE!*

MARSHA. (*who cannot see him or eavesdroppers over back of sofa*) Virgil, is that *you?*

VIRGIL. (*springs to position where she can see him, into that stance again, meancing* her *with gun*) I said, *freeze!*

PERSIS. Not *her,* you idiot! Me and the Slasher!

VIRGIL. Sorry, I'm new at this.

TOBIAS. Virgil, what the hell is going *on* with you?!

VIRGIL. You *told* me to read the book, and whatever it said, *do* it! I'm *doing* it!

MARSHA. Well, stop it! Stop it this instant!

ALL OTHERS. *What?!*

MARSHA. I don't want you to spoil the ending!

TOBIAS. Marsha, what are you *talking* about?!

MARSHA. Well, I only read up to the part where the Slasher has the heroine on the sofa. If Virgil does the next part, he'll spoil it!

TOBIAS. Damn it, do you seriously expect me to let you live to read it?!

MARSHA. You have no choice. Virgil's here now, and he's going to shoot you dead, I have no doubt, and then I can get back to my book.

TOBIAS. Marsha—!

PERSIS. (*bends to undo MARSHA's ropes*) She's right, Tobias. We mustn't spoil the ending for her.

TOBIAS. But damn it all—! (*By now, of course, it's too late to maintain the charade: OTHERS have come out of hiding and down to the sofa, and the atmosphere is becoming genial.*) Oh, what's the use! (*starts helping untie MARSHA*)

VIRGIL. I *wish* someone would give me a *cue!* Do I *shoot* him or *not?*

PERSIS. Well, actually—

MARSHA. Don't tell me, don't tell me! I want to find out for myself!

VIRGIL. Damn it, so do I! (*starts out still-open front door*) Excuse me, I have to get that book! (*exits*)

PERSIS. (*calls after him*) By the way, Virgil, that was nice work picking up your *last* cue!

VIRGIL. (*off*) *I* thought so!

TOBIAS. (*MARSHA is now sitting up, freed of rope.*) Persis, do you mean that you *knew* he'd pop in on cue?

PERSIS. Of course! Why do you think I made you say the Slasher's line *exactly* as *written?*

MARSHA. Virgil would *never* pick up on a *paraphrase!*

LYNETTE. Well, he *might* have, darling . . .

MARSHA. A kindergarten teacher?! Don't be silly, Mother.

TOBIAS. Hold it! You *knew* he wasn't a pharmacist?

MARSHA. Of *course* I did! Toby, dearest, do you think I'd let a *real* pharmacist go off to mix up a batch of poison? You might have been killed!

BEN. Then you *knew* it wasn't real poison?

MARSHA. Why would I want to poison *Toby?* I'm in *love* with him!

BIANCA. Excuse me, mum, but—how did you know Mister Baxter *wasn't* a pharmacist?

MARSHA. I've seen him leaving for work in the morning.

OTHERS. *And—?*

MARSHA. I *ask* you—would a real pharmacist have a *Sesame Street* lunchbox?

TOBIAS. But—wait—none of this is making sense—I thought you thought Persis and I were plotting against your life, and—and—?!

MARSHA. Oh, I *did,* darling, at first! I mean—the *things* you two were *saying—!* But the moment Persis came back into this room after she took off her topcoat and glasses and fluffed up her hair, and I got a good look at her, I know it couldn't be true.

OTHERS. *Why?!*

MARSHA. (*takes TOBIAS' arm, fondly*) Darling, that woman just is *not* your *type!*

TOBIAS. Oh? And just what sort of woman *is* my type?

MARSHA. (*prettily*) *My* type, of course! (*He stares at her, then melts.*)

TOBIAS. (*to OTHERS*) She's got me *there!* (*He and MARSHA embrace and kiss.*)

LYNETTE. Ah! I just *love* happy endings!

VIRGIL. (*rushing in with book*) Does it *have* a happy ending?

PERSIS. As a matter of fact—

MARSHA. (*breaking from kiss*) Don't tell me, don't tell me!

TOBIAS. Marsha, I'm shocked! Do you mean to say that after all that's gone on here this evening, you *still* intend to read *that book?*

MARSHA. Don't *you?*

TOBIAS. (*tries to remain stern, but can't*) Damn it, of *course* I do!

LYNETTE. Virgil, bring it along into the dining room! You can read it aloud to us while we eat! (*will exit to dining room, during:*)

BIANCA. That reminds me, I'm starved! Come on, Ben, let's go out for pizza!

TOBIAS. Oh, hell, there's enough to go around. Why don't you two join *us* for dinner?

BEN. Well—if you think it'd be okay—?

BIANCA. We'll get to hear how the book comes out—!

BEN. Hey, that's right! Come on, Bee! (*He and*

BIANCA exit to dining room.)

VIRGIL. *(moving after them)* I don't know about this—if I have to read aloud during the dinner, I won't get a chance to *eat!*

MARSHA. But cold soup makes you nauseous anyhow.

VIRGIL. *That's* true enough, I guess ...

MARSHA. By the way, Virgil, where *did* you get that *gun* you rushed in here with? You told *me* you didn't *own* one!

VIRGIL. I don't. I confiscated that from one of my pupils.

TOBIAS. Your *kindergartners* carry *pistols?!*

VIRGIL. It hasn't been easy. *(exits)*

PERSIS. *(starts after him)* I'll eat fast, then get down to do the interior to that plane!

TOBIAS. Oh, Persis, by the way—considering the events of this evening, and what you've been through—I want you to know that I intend to *double* your *fee!*

PERSIS. *(pauses in archway)* Tobias—considering the events of this evening—I intend to *triple* it! *(exits)*

TOBIAS. *(sighs, links arms with MARSHA)* Shall we, dearest—?

MARSHA. Yes, I'm simply famished—? *(They start up around left end of sofa, then both stop as PHONE STARTS BEEPING, in the way telephones do when they're left off the hook as long as this one has been; TOBIAS picks it up from floor.)*

TOBIAS. Forgot all *about* this thing! *(Hangs it up; starts back toward MARSHA; PHONE RINGS; he answers it.)* Hello? ... Yes, this is he ... *Police?* ... She said what? ... No, officer, I assure you, I love my wife very much and have absolutely *no* intention of murdering her, tonight or any night ... *(listens a moment, then growls into phone:)* No, I will *not* cross my heart and hope to die! *(slams down phone, takes MARSHA's arm)* Happy birthday, darling!

MARSHA. *(as they start off toward dining room)* And many happy *returns?*

TOBIAS. You've *got* to be kidding! *(And as they exit, arm-in-arm—)*

THE CURTAIN FALLS

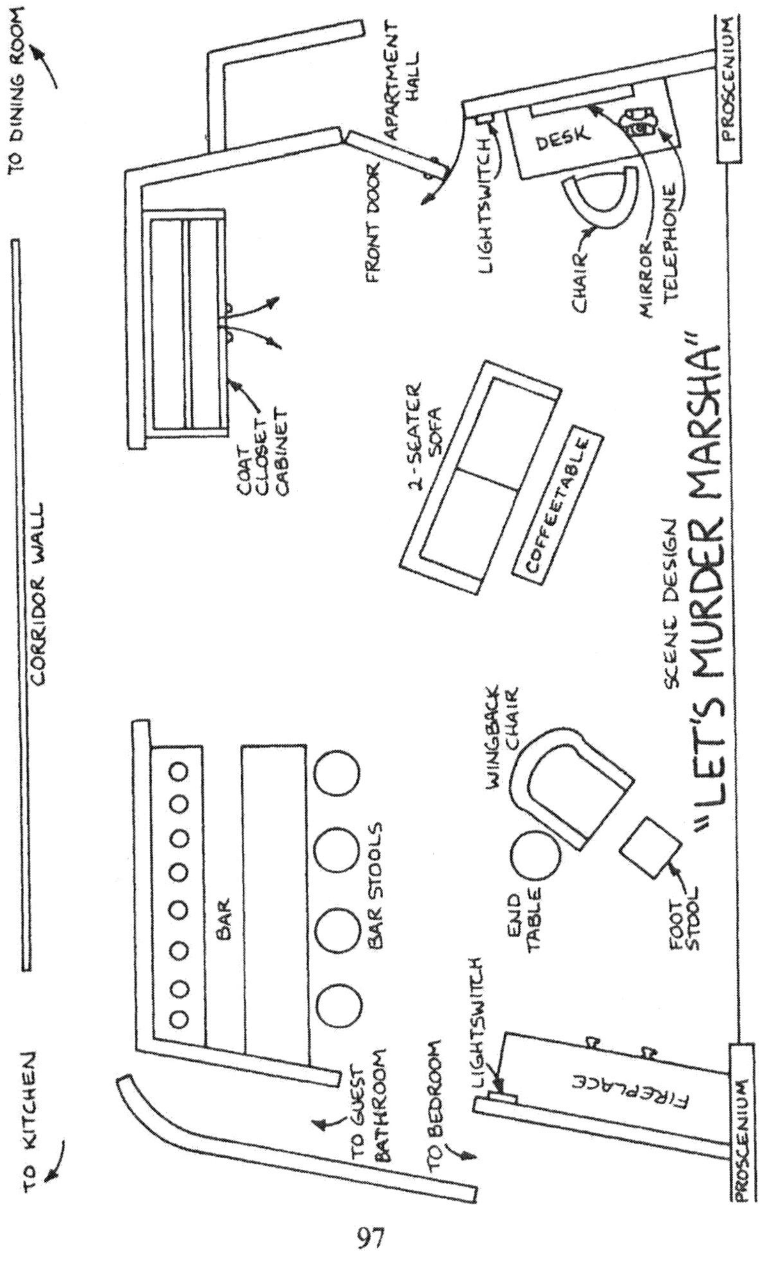

SCENE DESIGN

"LET'S MURDER MARSHA"

TO KITCHEN

TO DINING ROOM

CORRIDOR WALL

TO GUEST BATHROOM

TO BEDROOM

BAR

BAR STOOLS

LIGHTSWITCH

FIREPLACE

PROSCENIUM

END TABLE

WINGBACK CHAIR

FOOT STOOL

COFFEETABLE

2-SEATER SOFA

COAT CLOSET CABINET

FRONT DOOR

APARTMENT HALL

LIGHTSWITCH

DESK

CHAIR

MIRROR

TELEPHONE

PROSCENIUM

97

MUSIC USE NOTE

Licensees are solely responsible for obtaining formal written permission from copyright owners to use copyrighted music in the performance of this play and are strongly cautioned to do so. If no such permission is obtained by the licensee, then the licensee must use only original music that the licensee owns and controls. Licensees are solely responsible and liable for all music clearances and shall indemnify the copyright owners of the play(s) and their licensing agent, Samuel French, against any costs, expenses, losses and liabilities arising from the use of music by licensees. Please contact the appropriate music licensing authority in your territory for the rights to any incidental music.

IMPORTANT BILLING AND CREDIT REQUIREMENTS

If you have obtained performance rights to this title, please refer to your licensing agreement for important billing and credit requirements.

Walking the Disused Railways
of Sussex

David Bathurst

Photographs by David Bathurst

S.B. Publications

By the same author:

The Selsey Tram
Six of the Best!
The Jennings Companion
Around Chichester In Old Photographs
Financial Penalties - Enforcement in Magistrates' Courts
Here's A Pretty Mess!
Magisterial Lore
The Beaten Track
Poetic Justice
Walking the Coastline of Sussex
Best Sussex Walks
Let's Take It From The Top

Contributions to:
Introduction to *While I Remember* - autobiography of Anthony Buckeridge
The Encyclopaedia of Boys' School Stories

Map reproduced by permission of Ordnance Survey on behalf of The Controller of Her Majesty's Stationery Office, © Crown Copyright 10042719

To Jeff, Jenny, Rosie and Heather

First published in 2004 by S.B. Publications
14 Bishopstone Road, Seaford, East Sussex.
Tel: 01323 893498   Email: sbpublications@tiscali.co.uk

ISBN 1 85770 292 1
Reprinted 2006

Typeset by EH Graphics, East Sussex (01273) 515527

CONTENTS

Front Cover:	West Grinstead station on the Shoreham to Christ's Hospital line.
Title Page:	On the Rye to Camber Sands line.
Back Cover:	On the Chichester to Midhurst line.

ACKNOWLEDGMENTS

The author wishes to acknowledge the assistance and support of Jeff Vinter of the Railway Ramblers who provided so much useful information; the staff of SB Publications for their efficiency and encouragement; and his wife Susan for her constant loving support.

ABOUT THE AUTHOR

David Bathurst was born in Guildford in 1959 and has enjoyed writing and walking all his adult life. He has written twelve books and walked most of the designated National Trails of England and Wales as well as the two principal long-distance routes in Scotland and Wainwright's Coast To Coast Walk. His book The Beaten Track, a guide to walking these routes, was published in 2001. The following year his guide to walking the coastline of Sussex was published by SB Publications. David also enjoys amateur acting and singing, but his chief claim to fame was reciting the four Gospels from memory in July 1998. He works as a legal adviser to magistrates sitting at Chichester and Worthing. He is married with one daughter and lives in Barnham, between Chichester and Arundel, in West Sussex.

INTRODUCTION

Disused railway walking has deservedly become extremely popular in the last twenty years. Not only does it provide stimulating exercise and a chance to enjoy delightful countryside, but it places us in touch with a very important part of our past and gives a fascinating insight into an era in which the railway, rather than the car, was the principal means of transport between both rural and urban centres.

Sussex once boasted a formidable collection of railway lines. Whilst the main towns and cities of Sussex are still well served by train, a great many of the lines that opened during the railway boom of the late nineteenth century have now closed down, several of these closures having taken place in the Beeching era of the 1960's. Now, forty years later, although some of these old lines have been hopelessly overgrown and some have been obliterated by modern development, many stretches of old line are still very easy to trace, and an increasing number have been converted into cycle paths and pedestrian walkways, passing through beautiful countryside and providing an invaluable leisure facility. Moreover, there is still plenty of evidence of the old lines even where the former trackbed itself is impossible to follow, in the form of old bridges, tunnels, station platforms and even station buildings.

The purpose of this book is to provide a definitive and exhaustive guide to the walker wishing to follow the disused railway lines of Sussex, with information as to the length of each walk, details of availability of public transport and refreshments, and a potted history of each line. It should be stressed that the book does not cover old urban tramways, what might be called "pleasure" trains through e.g. public parks, museum/zoo grounds or along seaside esplanades, or the narrow-gauge industrial/non-passenger railways. It does however cover every single railway line that was on the passenger railway network in Sussex, including lines that crossed the border into the neighbouring counties of Surrey, Hampshire or Kent.

My aim is to offer a continuous walk based around each line. In many cases it is impossible to follow or even gain access to the trackbed itself, so nearby roads and footpaths are used instead. The directions make it clear when the walking along the old line involves following paths and tracks that at the time of writing are not designated rights of way. If you are in any doubt as to whether to follow these sections, it may be prudent for you to consult the landowner and seek permission in advance. You should make it a rule, as this book does, NEVER to disobey a sign telling unauthorised persons to keep out, and NEVER to try to surmount obstacles deliberately erected to prevent trespass on to land through which there is no public right of way. It does the reputation of walkers in general, and railway ramblers in particular, no good whatsoever if one of their number is caught causing damage or disturbance to land to which they have no right of access. Many landowners are in fact extremely accommodating and quite happy to allow access but you should not take this for granted. Discreet advance enquiry, initially perhaps at the nearest public library, should yield information as to the ownership of a particular stretch of land. It is worth equipping yourself with the relevant 1:25000 OS map in case you need to find a way round a section which has become unexpectedly unavailable to walkers and where no detour is suggested in this book. Please note that land usage changes all the time, and one can never rule out the possibility of sections of old line, or access tracks, that were available at the time of writing becoming inaccessible in future years. Conversely, hitherto inaccessible sections may become available for walking in due course.

Although no hillclimbing is involved, the terrain can often be difficult. Expect the ground to be muddy and slippery in winter, and at any time of year you should expect to have to negotiate a fair amount of overhanging branches and undergrowth - although where this does become intolerable, a parallel route will usually have been suggested! Do not forget wet weather gear when rain is forecast and drink plenty of water when the weather is likely to be hot. Do not wait till you are thirsty before you do. Refreshment opportunities are infrequent on many of the walks, so do stock up with food and drink before you set out. Public transport opportunities en route may also be scarce so it may be prudent to take a mobile phone and the numbers of local taxi firms!

I would like to express my thanks to Jeff Vinter, chairman of the Railway Ramblers, for his assistance and support in preparation of this book; my wife Susan for her patience and indulgence as I took time out to put the book together; and my long-suffering two-year-old daughter Jennifer, who accompanied me on most if not all of my exploration with hardly a complaint!

Happy walking.

David Bathurst
Barnham, West Sussex
Christmas 2003

SECTION 1 - **CHICHESTER TO SELSEY**
(The Selsey Tramway)

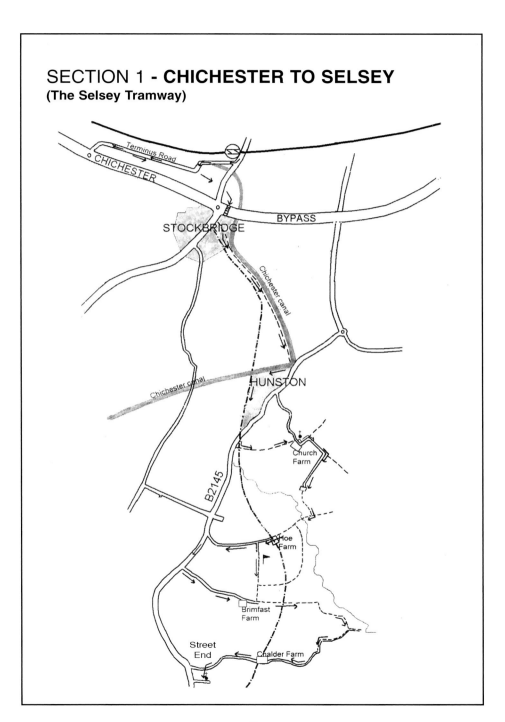

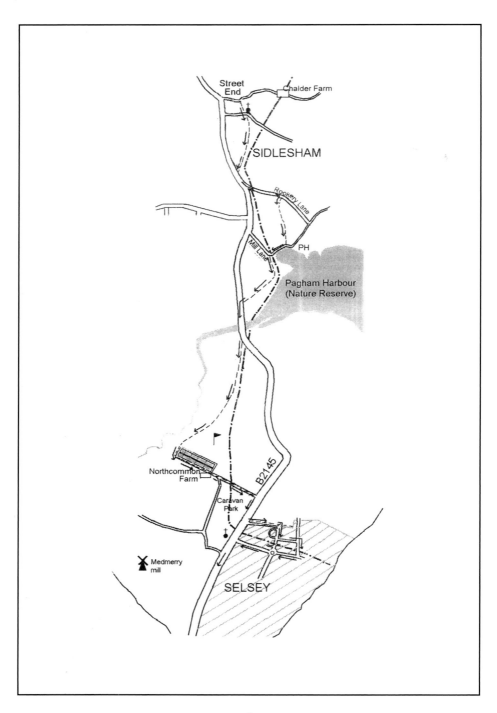

SECTION 1 - **CHICHESTER TO SELSEY** (The Selsey Tramway)

Length:	8 miles.
Start:	Chichester railway station.
Finish:	Selsey town centre.
Public Transport:	Chichester is well served by train from London Victoria, Brighton and Portsmouth, also by bus from Brighton and Portsmouth. There are regular bus services daily, including Sundays, from Selsey back to Chichester.
Conditions:	There are a number of small sections of the old line that are still walkable, and sufficient public footpaths linking them up to ensure road walking is kept to a minimum. The walking is across the flat Manhood Peninsula, with lovely views back to the Downs and across Pagham Harbour. It can be extremely muddy after wet weather.
Refreshments:	Shops, pubs and cafes in Chichester; shops and pub in Hunston; pubs and (off route) shop in Sidlesham; shops, pubs and cafes in Selsey. RECOMMENDED PUBS: CHICHESTER - THE FOUNTAIN(South Street) - popular pub, excellent food; SIDLESHAM - THE CRAB & LOBSTER - fresh seafood, good wines and beers, glorious setting; SELSEY - LIFEBOAT(Albion Road) - wide food choice.

History

The Selsey Tramway was one of the most remarkable railway lines in England, consisting of a stretch of line just eight miles long boasting no less than eleven stations. It was constructed in response to a perceived demand for a rail link between the bustling cathedral city of Chichester and the seaside community of Selsey. The railway had arrived in Chichester in 1846, but it was not until fifty years later that a company, known as the Hundred of Manhood and Selsey Tramway Company, was formed and duly built the line from Chichester to Selsey. It was officially designated as a tramway rather than a railway to enable the company to escape the rigorous safety measures required for it to become a Light Railway. The engineer was one Holman Stephens, universally acclaimed as a champion of the small railway, and involved in the construction and management of at least 15 different railways. These lines were

*A fine section of the Chichester to Selsey line
beside Pagham Harbour.*

characterised by primitive rolling stock, dilapidated buildings and minimal facilities, but boasted a bucolic charm and individuality that other railway operations lacked. The Selsey Tramway, which opened on 27th August 1897, was typical of Stephens' work. It was constructed on a shoestring, with very basic station architecture, extraordinarily old rolling stock - one locomotive was 58 years old when it arrived on the Selsey Tramway - and no crossing gates or signalling. In later years, Stephens introduced railbuses on to the line, which although economical gave passengers a particularly uncomfortable ride. The number of stations was amazing, considering how few settlements of any size existed between the two termini. The first stop out of Chichester was at the village of Hunston, followed by the three halts of Hoe Farm, Chalder and Mill Pond, and the village stop at Sidlesham. Beyond Sidlesham was the tiny Ferry station, Golf Club Halt, and then three stations in Selsey itself, namely Selsey Bridge, Selsey Town and Selsey Beach. The stretch of line between Town and Beach did not open until nearly a year after the rest of the line, and was to close shortly before the First World War. Even the "village" stations, Hunston and Sidlesham, boasted no more than corrugated iron sheds, while Golf Links Halt offered just a solitary platform. The journey times varied; in summer 1913 one train was timetabled to complete the journey in 25 minutes whilst a 1934 timetable shows a journey time of 45 minutes. By the time war broke out in August 1914, more than 80,000 passengers were using the line each year, for both work and leisure-related activity, and this figure rose to over 100,000 during the penultimate year of the war. The railway also carried a tremendous variety of freight, ranging from milk and sugar to bricks and stone; two particularly colourful users of the line were Emidio Guarnacchio who transported ice cream to sell to holidaymakers in Selsey from his store in Chichester, and Colin Pullinger who had a flourishing mousetrap business in Selsey and used the Tramway to transport mousetraps away from the village.

The line suffered a setback in December 1910 when a heavy storm resulted in the breaching of the shingle bank separating the sea from reclaimed agricultural land at Pagham Harbour, and submerged the Tramway between Sidlesham and Ferry. Thankfully funds were available to effect the necessary repairs and the line reopened six months later. Disaster then struck in September 1923 when a northbound train was derailed just beyond Golf Links Halt, and one of the crew was killed. With many passengers already deserting the Tramway for road transport, the accident, which was at least partially attributable to neglect in the upkeep of the line, could not have come at a worse time. The 1920's and early 1930's saw a steady decline in the number of passengers and trains, and whereas a dozen trains each way had run on weekdays in 1913, that number had halved by 1933. Passenger traffic continued to decline during the early 1930's; it is recorded that the 11.40am train from Chichester to Selsey on a Saturday in August 1933 carried no passengers at all, and a typical day in 1934 might see just eighteen passengers board the train at Selsey for the journey to Chichester. Meanwhile, the railway company plunged deeper into debt, and with the Southern Railway unwilling to purchase the line, it was only a matter of time before the line closed for good. The last train on the Selsey Tramway ran on 19th January 1935. The line was gradually dismantled and the buildings were demolished; the absence of conventional signalling and other railway landmarks such as bridges meant that evidence of the line's existence was virtually obliterated. It does however live on in the memory as a line of special and unique character, and, as one commentator put it, "It created few artefacts but it left a legacy of admiration and nostalgic smiles."

Walking the Railway

Starting from the main forecourt of Chichester railway station, turn right and cross over the railway, continuing in the same direction along Stockbridge Road. Shortly, immediately opposite the Richmond Arms pub, you come to Terminus Road, a narrow residential road that is not accessible from Stockbridge Road for vehicles. The Chichester terminus of the Tramway was at the junction, and the old line followed wasteland behind the gardens of houses in Terminus Road, before swinging from west to south and proceeding across ground that is now covered firstly by the new Chichester Gate leisure complex, then the A27 Chichester bypass, and then housing. Follow the narrow Terminus Road to its end, turn right at the T-junction, then go first left into Chichester Gate. By following this road and then walking down to the Kentucky Fried Chicken restaurant behind which is the A27 Chichester bypass, you are following approximately the course of the old line. It is impossible to continue across the bypass, so walk back through the heart of the Chichester Gate leisure complex, aiming for the Chicago Rock café. Turn right to pass the café and two other premises, Wetherspoons and Cannons, and arrive back at Stockbridge Road. To pick up the course of the old line again, turn right into Stockbridge Road, follow the road to the A27 roundabout and go straight over, using the footbridge provided. Follow this road - the A286 Witterings road - briefly, then turn left along a tarmac footpath marked "Selsey Tram Way." The footpath takes you through a modern housing development, then having crossed a road brings you to the west bank of the Chichester Canal, being reasonably faithful to the course of the old line throughout. Now following the course of the old line, you enjoy a delightful canalside walk. After a few hundred yards the old line struck out slightly west of south; it is not possible to follow beside it, but you can follow the course of it from a distance as you continue along the canal bank to Hunston. Arriving at the road at the northern end of the village, turn right on to the road, then almost immediately turn right again along the left bank of the canal as it heads south-westwards. In a quarter of a mile or so you arrive at what remains of the old drawbridge used to convey the Tramway over the canal. Turn left on to a public footpath which follows the course of the old line past housing on the edge of Hunston, including a road named Tramway Close, and in due course you arrive at the B2145 Chichester-Selsey road.

So far you have been able to follow the old line for most of its course from Chichester, but for the next couple of miles you will be unable to follow any of it, the course of the old line being across private farmland and then a golf course with no means of access. Cross the B2145 and turn left to follow it briefly, as far as a public footpath sign just before a children's play area on your right. Join the footpath and follow it past the play area, going on to the little church with the unusual dedication of St Leodegar (pronounced Ledger). Turn right on to a driveway that passes the main entrance to the church and goes forward to a T-junction of paths. Turn left at this T-junction, shortly right at the next junction of paths, and shortly right again along a track that brings you to the golf course. The course of the Tramway is to your right, but quite impossible to discern. You reach a T-junction of paths; turn right to follow a metalled track that leads you past the golf clubhouse, the clubhouse complex situated on the site of Hoe Farm station on the Tramway. Just beyond the complex a signed footpath goes off to the left, leading southwards to a point just east of Brinfast Farm, the site of the Tramway following very roughly parallel with this path and just to the left (east) of it. You pass more golf holes and across a plank bridge over a narrow stream. It should however be noted that at the time of writing this path is shut; if it remains shut, to reach the south end of it you will need to go forward to the B2145, turn left to follow the road for a few hundred yards, then left again along the concrete road signposted Brinfast. You reach the junction with the closed footpath just beyond the buildings of Brinfast.

Between Brinfast and Chalder, there is again no prospect of following the Tramway, but it is possible to make the link by means of a delightful footpath through the fields just to the east. Follow the footpath heading eastwards beyond Brinfast, which swings right and then left, then sharply right again, passing a junction with a footpath going off to the left. The main path then swings right, now heading westwards, turns sharply left (southwards) and then right on to a wider track through the Chalder Farm

The former bridge on the Chichester to Selsey railway over the waters of Pagham Harbour.

complex. Beyond the complex, follow the track just north of west, and if you look carefully through the vegetation, you can see what remains of Chalder station platform on a field edge to your left, though you really would have no idea a railway line ever existed here at all! Again, however, you will be unable to follow the old line southwards from Chalder and will not see it again until around Mill Pond Cottage. Continue on past Holborow Lodge, a cat and rabbit rescue centre, to enter the village of Sidlesham. As the track widens and bends sharply to the right, cross over through the main gates leading to the parish church, and follow the church path. Instead of going up to the church door, however, bear left along a path that runs past the left hand side of the church, up and then down some stone steps and down to a metalled road. Cross straight over the road and proceed just west of south along a public footpath through a field. The old line ran roughly parallel to this path, to your left. The path brings you back to the B2145, and you turn left to walk beside this busy road as far as the turning to Rookery Lane; fortunately a pavement is provided. On this short stretch of roadside walking, look out on your left for Mill Pond Cottage, reminding you that very close by was Mill Pond Halt, one of the stations on the old line but without sidings or station buildings.

Turn left into Rookery Lane, crossing the course of the old line almost at once, and proceed along the road in a south-easterly direction. Very soon the road bends subtly to the left, heading roughly eastwards, but if you look in a south-easterly direction from the bend, across an area of uncultivated rough grass, you can see the course that the old line took. Again, however, it is out of bounds to the public. In a few hundred yards turn right on to a public footpath and follow this path; it soon bends to the left and proceeds pleasantly in the shade of trees down to Mill Lane, the course of the Tramway running virtually parallel with it to your right. At Mill Lane, you reach the edge of the quite beautiful Pagham Harbour. By detouring left here you will soon reach the inviting and popular Crab and Lobster pub, but your way is to the right along the road, shortly reaching a signed path which goes off to the left and which follows the course of the old line. Before turning left on to the path, look to the right to observe the course of the old line heading north-westwards back towards Mill Pond Halt. It is, however, inaccessible, even though the track immediately beyond the gate looks easy enough to walk.

There now follows what is unquestionably the highlight of the walk, with a quite delightful promenade along the shores of Pagham Harbour, following the course of the old line. It was this section that was submerged in 1910. Today it forms part of the Pagham Harbour Nature Reserve, and you are likely to share this part of the walk with birdwatchers as well as daytrippers. Sidlesham Station building was situated immediately beyond Mill Lane; in the early days of the running of the old line, the name was spelt Siddlesham on the signboard, reflecting its pronunciation. Following the 1910 floods the station building was lifted and replaced at right angles to the track, so that it had its back to the prevailing winds. You proceed through the nature reserve, sticking to the course of the old line; initially you head just east of south then swing just west of south. In due course you approach a rife, that is a channel of water which is effectively an inlet of Pagham Harbour, and as you do so, you can clearly see the site of the old railway bridge crossing straight ahead. There is no bridge crossing, so swing right to follow the path away from the course of the old line, parallel with the water channel and almost up to the B2145 where you reach a T-junction of paths. Turn left at the T-junction and proceed round the edge of the water, arriving at another T-junction of paths on the other side. You need to turn right here to continue towards Selsey, but if you want to walk a little more of the Selsey Tramway you can detour left here and follow a good path along the south side of the water, soon drawing level with the old bridge crossing. At this point, you can look and walk to your left, following the line back to the water, and/or look to your right into the back garden of the house "Wayside" to see how the line continued. Then retrace your steps, going forward to the B2145.

Cross the road with care, and turn left round a sharp bend. Almost immediately after rounding the bend, turn right along a signed footpath towards the buildings of Ferry Farm. This runs parallel with, and just to the right of, the course of the old line. As you reach the farm buildings, a signed footpath leads off to the right, round the side of the buildings, then swings left on to a wide track which is on the course of the old line. [At the time of writing it was possible to turn left just before the farm buildings then right on to the track, meeting the official right of way a bit further down and allowing a little more time on the course of the old line itself. This is not a designated right of way.] Sadly your walk along the old line is short-lived. Soon you arrive at the northern end of Selsey golf course, and a public footpath sign which draws you away from the old line. The old line continued along the east fringe of the golf course but strict warning signs make it clear that it cannot be followed. Instead you must proceed along a rather muddy path along the west side of the golf course, gradually getting further away from the old line! However there are compensations: there is a good view to Medmerry windmill, and looking back there are splendid views to the Downs which Tramway passengers would have enjoyed. Beyond the golf course is a caravan park, and it is here that you need to look out for a signed footpath pointing to the left. Take this footpath which heads south-eastwards, initially past rows of caravans and then the buildings of Northcommon Farm. Shortly beyond the farm a tarmac drive leads off to the left, up to the golf clubhouse. Looking just to the right of this drive you can identify the route of the old line by the course of the electricity wires along the right-hand side of the golf course. Golf Links Halt used to stand just a little beyond where the clubhouse is sited today.

You continue south-eastwards along the public footpath, effectively a driveway and the main access road to the golf club from the main road. The course of the Tramway is over a field to your right and then through a caravan park. In a few hundred yards you reach the main road and turn right, following the main road south-westwards. You follow the main road until you reach house number 30 on your right, while a signpost on the opposite side points to Warners Farm Touring Park and the White Horse Caravan Park. Just beyond number 30 on your right you can look down at an embankment at the foot of which is a small pond. This is the site of Selsey Bridge Station and the point at which the old line went under the main road. On the opposite side of the road is a signed footpath leading away to the east. Follow this path, while looking to your right at the course of the old line, set in a cutting that is now quite thick with vegetation. This is the last evidence of the old line that you will see. The path continues rather muddily round the right hand edge of a new housing development, and soon reaches the north fringe of a red-brick housing estate. Turn right to access and follow the road heading southwards through the estate, passing the crescent-shaped Denshare Road, which lies to your right, almost immediately. Just beyond Denshare Road, Mountwood Road goes off to your left; the point at which it does so is very roughly the site of Selsey Town station, and by following Mountwood Road you are virtually on the course of the old line on its final leg towards Selsey Beach. At the T-junction, however, the rest of the course of the old line becomes lost in new housing. To get back to the main road, turn right at the T-junction into Manor Lane and follow it down to the junction with Beach Road. Turn right into Beach Road, right again into Church Road, and then left at the T-junction at the western end of Church Road, passing St Peter's Church and soon reaching the centre of Selsey with its variety of amenities and buses back to Chichester.

SECTION 1 - **PULBOROUGH TO PETERSFIELD**

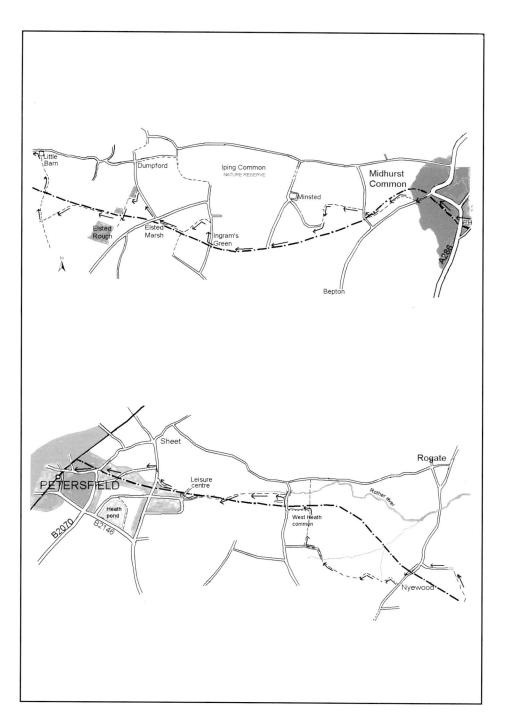

SECTION 1 - **PULBOROUGH TO PETERSFIELD**

Length:	19 miles.
Start:	Pulborough railway station.
Finish:	Petersfield railway station.
Public Transport:	Two trains an hour on weekdays (one on Sundays) to Pulborough from London Victoria via Gatwick Airport and Three Bridges, and from Portsmouth and Havant via Chichester and Arundel. Two trains an hour from Petersfield to Havant.
Conditions:	Only a fragment of the old line is now a designated right of way. However many sections are still walkable, and these sections provide some really enjoyable and rewarding walking. The old stations at Fittleworth, Petworth and Selham are beautifully maintained.
Refreshments:	Pubs, shops and cafes at Pulborough; pub and shop at Fittleworth; pubs, shops and cafes at Petworth; pub at Selham; pubs, shops and cafes at Midhurst; pub at Elsted Marsh; pubs, shops and cafes at Petersfield. RECOMMENDED PUBS: FITTLEWORTH - THE SWAN - 14th century inn, big inglenook log fire, well-kept beers; PETWORTH - BADGERS(2 mins from path) - attractively presented bar food, well-kept beer, good range of house wines; SELHAM - THREE MOLES - well-kept beers, guest beers from small breweries (no food); MIDHURST - BRICKLAYERS ARMS - good "local" atmosphere, well-kept beers; ELSTED MARSH - ELSTED INN - well-kept ales, lovely downs-view garden.

History

The Pulborough-Petersfield line, built during the railway boom in the mid-19th century, was opened in three stages. The first section to open was between Hardham, just south-west of Pulborough, and Petworth on October 15th 1859, being a branch of what became known as the Arun Valley line between Horsham and Arundel. The section between Midhurst and Petersfield was opened next, on September 1st 1864. The section that linked these two strands, from Midhurst to Petworth, was the last to open, on October 15th 1866. The London, Brighton and South Coast Railway (hereinafter referred to as LBSCR) built the sections between Hardham and Midhurst, and the section on to Petersfield was constructed by the London & South Western Railway (LSWR). Initially it was not possible to run through trains between the LBSCR-owned and the LSWR-owned sections because the connecting line across the Bepton Road bridge was capable of carrying only the weight of a single wagon. There were therefore two stations at Midhurst, one providing services eastwards via Selham, Petworth and Fittleworth to Pulborough and Horsham, and one offering services westwards via Elsted and Rogate to Petersfield. It was not until 12th July 1925, after the two companies had been incorporated into the Southern Railway, that the Bepton Road bridge was replaced, the LSWR station was closed, and through services became possible. Not all the stations opened at the same time. Selham station, a simple wooden building with one platform, opened in 1872 and Fittleworth station, another modest construction with wooden canopy, opened in 1889. Petworth station became a grander affair, to be blessed not only with a large and generously canopied station building but also a goods yard and goods shed as well as a small locomotive shed and signal box. The station was actually a mile and a half from the town of Petworth itself; the fact that buses were subsequently able to travel conveniently to Midhurst from the centre of Petworth must have been a significant disincentive to would-be passengers to travel between these town centres by train. West of Midhurst, with its two stations, there were just two intermediate stations: Elsted, over a mile north of the village of the same name, and Rogate, known also as Rogate for Harting and situated a mile and a half from both Rogate and Harting in the village of Nyewood where there was an important brickworks.

Initially the LSWR section offered five return journeys daily, but by 1913 the number had increased to eleven, reducing to ten by 1922. The LBSCR route to Petworth also provided five return journeys in its early years, increasing to eight on extension to Midhurst. When through trains became possible, a large number of journeys still started and ended at Midhurst. The 1938 timetable shows seven trains between Pulborough and Midhurst and eight between Midhurst and Petersfield, but only two through services daily (none on Sundays) between Pulborough and Petersfield with a journey time of 51 minutes, and just one (curiously, two on Sundays) between Petersfield and Pulborough. The 1942 timetable saw a significant increase in the number of through trains. A number of trains running from Pulborough to Midhurst continued on to Chichester via Cocking, Singleton and West Dean, and there was one remarkable train which for some years left Brighton at 6.25am and proceeded to London Victoria via Chichester, Midhurst, Petworth and Pulborough, giving a journey of 101 miles! Freight conveyed on the line included not only elephants (see above) but also coal, grain, sugar, milk, bricks and timber. One of the proudest moments of the life of the line was on December 6th 1899 when the Prince of Wales and his suite travelled to Petworth by Royal Special Train. The train left London Victoria at 4.28pm and arrived in Petworth at 5.57pm. The line prided itself on the personal service it offered to its patrons, and a number of former passengers recall acts of kindness, such as holding a train to allow a pram to be placed in the guard's van, and locating a precious dress cap which had been blown off a passenger's head and out into the countryside. There were also some amusing incidents, such as the occasion on which a family which had used the line to travel to Petersfield was delayed on the homeward train because the engine had gone off without the carriages.

After the 1939-45 war there was a steady decline in passenger usage, due largely to the competition from the roads, with many trains running empty. British Railways, which came into being in 1948, claimed to be losing £31,000 per year on the service. Passenger trains ceased throughout on 5th February 1955, as did goods services between Petersfield and Midhurst. Goods yards east of Midhurst closed gradually over time, with Petworth being the last to close on 20th May 1966. Ironically, in contrast to the very subdued final day of the Chichester-Midhurst passenger services, Midhurst station saw more people than possibly ever before for the last day of passenger operations on the line to Petersfield, and it was reckoned that only Bank Holidays prior to the First World War had seen such crowds.

Walking the Railway

The nearest public transport stop is Pulborough, and it is at Pulborough Station that your walk begins. Descend the station approach road to the village street and turn left, soon reaching a roundabout with the A29 signposted to the right. Turn right to follow the A29, soon crossing over the River Arun, and continue alongside it. You pass the village of Hardham and, a short way beyond the road leading off to Hardham Church on the left, turn right off the A29 along a narrow road which crosses the railway and passes a pumping station. Just beyond the railway turn left on to a signed footpath which initially follows a driveway then shortly swings left to arrive at a gate. Go through the gate and turn right; you are now on the old line only a few yards from where it branched off from the still existing Pulborough-Arundel line, and you may see trains plying this route as you begin.

At the time of writing it was possible to follow the old line for just under a mile, along what has been designated a right of way. The scenery is delightful, with woodland to your left and the picturesque Rother valley to your right. Further progress is obstructed by a secure gate, and it is necessary to follow a signed path directing you to the right (a). Unfortunately the future of the right of way along the old line is far from certain, and access may well become impossible by the time this book appears. Should that be the case, you will need to return to the A29 very shortly after joining the old line - a footpath leads off to the left over the existing railway just before the "restricted" section begins, and reunites you with the A29 - and follow this road south-westwards. Cross over the existing railway, ignore the first right turn into Old London Road but take the second right turn into Old London Road, forking left again almost

A pleasant section of the Pulborough to Petersfield line near Hardham.

immediately along Kings Lane. The lane peters out and becomes a path; keep going along the path and shortly you will arrive at the old line just beside the secure gate referred to earlier in this paragraph. You cross straight over the old line to follow the signed path leading away from the old line referred to as (a) above. The path leading away from the old line can be soggy after wet weather but in dry conditions is most pleasant; extremely well signposted throughout, it emerges from the trees, continues across fields and makes for the south bank of the Rother, having arrived at which it proceeds pleasantly north-westwards along the bank to the B2138 Bury-Fittleworth road. As you approach this road you can see the course of the old line slightly above the valley floor to the left.

Arriving at the road, turn left to follow it, shortly reaching a bridge over the old line. Looking back towards Hardham, you will note how overgrown (and waterlogged in winter) it has become, while looking westwards you will be able to admire the beautifully restored and maintained Fittleworth station which is situated immediately in front of you. It is a private residence so access is impossible. You must continue south very briefly along the B2138 and then turn right along the minor road, heading for the little village of Coates. In a few hundred yards a track leads off to the right, keeping a piggery field to the left; by following the field edge firstly along the track and then round to the left, you will find yourself going parallel with the old line which is in a cutting below you and quite accessible. However, although you can follow the cutting for a couple of hundred yards in each direction, you are unable either to get back to Fittleworth station or go forward to Coates, and you will have to return to the road. Continue along the road which goes downhill and then straight uphill. As you rise, there is an opening to the right, giving access to a field; follow the southern then the eastern edge of the field, and as you reach the north-eastern corner of the field you can easily access the old line, turning left (westwards) to follow the old line, there being no possibility of backtracking eastwards. This is very attractive walking indeed, with good views to the Rother valley to the right. You pass the fine Coates Barn house which is on your left, and arrive at a green track leading back to the Coates road; you need to follow this track to proceed with your walk, but it is possible to continue to follow the old line for a further half-mile or so past the back of the houses of Coates, before the surrounding vegetation makes further progress impossible and you are forced back whence you came. There is, however, one collapsed bridge crossing shortly after you embark on the detour which requires an awkward drop down and climb back up, and if in doubt, don't try it. None of the segments of old line between Fittleworth and Coates are designated rights of way.

Follow the green track past Coates Barn, then turn right on to the road which has now arrived at Coates. The road passes the very attractive houses of the village and then swings left. Immediately beyond this left bend, look out for a signed path going off to your right; now follow this path, getting good views to line to your right. The path heads initially just north of west then swings south-westwards, passing to the left of some buildings and reaching the northern fringe of an area of woodland. Sight of the old line is lost as you now follow the footpath, now a good track, along the northern edge of the wood. A further area of wood comes in from the right; at the junction of tracks at this point keep to the right-hand one, shortly emerging from the wood and reaching a junction of footpaths. Take the right-hand one which climbs quite steeply, keeping the wood to the right. On reaching the brow of the hill the path swings even further right and proceeds due north downhill to meet and cross the old line and then rejoin the bank of the Rother. The path then goes forward to reach a minor road which crosses the river here by what is known as Shopham Bridge. Turn left on to the road to arrive almost at once at a bridge crossing of the old line; there are good views to the course of the old line but access on to it is absolutely impossible. Beyond the bridge, continue along the road and very shortly you will see a signed path going over a stile to your right. Go over the stile and follow the path which goes uphill along the left-hand edge of the field, parallel with the road. You reach the top left-hand edge of the field; here bear right, keeping the wood to your left and the field to your right. Continue until you reach, shortly, a signed footpath going off left into the wood, then follow the path through the wood downhill to arrive at a road with the delightful Burton Mill Pond beyond. Turn right to follow the road and continue north-westwards along it for about a mile, bearing right on to a footpath opposite the left turn signposted Burton Park Farm. Follow this path through the wood to arrive at the A285 at Heath End, then turn right on to the A285 and follow it downhill, crossing a bridge over the course of the old line, and soon afterwards reaching the Badgers pub on the right hand side. Just before the pub you will see an access road which leads to the old station at Petworth; the old station building has been quite beautifully restored, and now offers bed and breakfast accommodation. Note also the collection of railway carriages adjoining the station building, and a large industrial estate behind the station, built on or around the course of the old line and rendering it impossible to backtrack eastwards along it.

Returning to the road, retrace your steps to just short of the bridge over the old line, and you will see a signed public right of way going off along a track to the right. Follow this track until you reach a house on the right hand side, no more than a few hundred yards along. Across the track from the house is a gate leading into a field; turn left through the gate and go across the field to a gate at the far end. The way across the field is not a designated right of way but there was no difficulty of access at the time of writing. Go through the gate at the far end of the field to find yourself on the course of the old line. Although your way towards Selham is to the right, you could detour left to follow the line almost back to the bridge under the A285, but the last little bit is inaccessible. Retrace your steps, therefore, and keep walking, heading north-westwards for Selham. Although not a designated right of way, there is an unobstructed walk along the old line virtually all the way to Selham, and it is disused railway walking at its very best. To begin with you are in the shade of woodland, with the Rother below you and to your right, but you then emerge from the woods to enjoy really fine open walking through the Rother valley, the course of the old line stretching invitingly ahead of you. You pass Cathanger Farm which is to your left, and enjoy views to the pretty village of Tillington that is situated your right. Sadly a collapsed bridge over the Selham-Fitzlea Farm track means you are forced off the old line and down to the track, and although it is possible to regain the old line on the other side, progress is almost immediately blocked yet again. Simply return to the track and follow it westwards, passing farm buildings, to arrive shortly at Selham. Turning left on to the little village street, you soon reach the Three Moles pub, which has an outstanding reputation for the quality of its beer; immediately beyond is the remnant of the bridge carrying the old line over the road, and if you feel sufficiently agile, it is possible to shin up the bank beside it to get a glimpse of the old line just east of the Three Moles. Further access eastwards is not feasible.

Assuming you have enjoyed a pint at the Three Moles, retrace your steps along the street and turn next left along the South Ambersham road. Soon you reach the little village church, just beside which is a signed footpath leading off to the left. Follow this path across a field, and look out to your left for the old Selham station building. It is possible to discern the course of the old line both to your left and to your right here, but to make further progress it is necessary to bear right just beyond the course of the old line along a track which, though not a designated right of way, leads to a T-

Near Fittleworth on the Pulborough to Petersfield line

junction with a track which is a right of way and which leads southwards to Smoky House. Immediately to your right is what remains of the bridge carrying this track over the old line, while just opposite is a stile taking you into what is now a polo field. All traces of the old line have been obliterated across the eastern end of the field, but incorporated into the field is an embankment which bore the old line. Although you won't be following a designated right of way, you can actually cross the stile and follow the polo field to the embankment then walk along the embankment - but it is impossible to progress further than that! You will have to retrace your steps to the Smoky House track and turn left, following the track northwards and returning to the Selham-South Ambersham road. Turn left on to this road and follow it for just under a mile to South Ambersham, then turn left at the T-junction on to the Heyshott road which climbs into woodland. You pass under the remains of a bridge which carried the old line over this road, then shortly turn right on to a wooded track, which is a signed public right of way. You very soon reach a junction of tracks; the signed right of way is straight on, but you take the track going off to the right and almost at once find yourself back on the old line. Turn left to continue along the old line towards Midhurst, although you could detour right (eastwards) to follow the old line back to the bridge over the Heyshott road. Retrace your steps to proceed towards Midhurst.

There follows a superb stretch, the course of the old line continuing along a clear unobstructed track, although this is not a designated right of way. The track passes through beautiful woodland, but there are breaks in the trees which allow views towards Cowdray Park to the north. You pass under a fine brick bridge, shortly beyond which you meet signed footpaths going off to the right and the left. To reach Midhurst you will need to turn right here, but it is in fact possible to follow the old line for a fair distance further, still in the shade of woodland, until you arrive at the buildings of

Oaklands. It is impossible to progress further on, so you need to go back to the footpath turning and bear left, following the path and shortly arriving at a T-junction of paths. Turn left at this junction on to a wider path that proceeds picturesquely through firstly open countryside, and then in the shade of woodland. At a sharp right-hand bend you will notice a signed path branching off, effectively in the same direction in which you have just been travelling; follow this path uphill then quite steeply down, taking care as you descend for it can be hideously muddy. At the foot of the hill you reach a T-junction. Turn right and proceed to a crossroads then turn left along the road, ascending and passing through the village of West Lavington. You leave the village centre behind and continue along the road in the same direction, keeping woodland to the right. As the road bends left, you will find yourself on a bridge over the course of the old line, and you can look down to see just how inaccessible it is! This is the only sighting of the old line you will get between Oaklands and Midhurst; just west of here the old line having entered thick woodland plunged into a tunnel, emerging from it on the other side of the A286 Chichester-Midhurst road. Follow the road to the pub on the right just a short distance further on, and then cut through to the A286 by means of the pub garden and car park. Turn right on to the A286 and follow this towards Midhurst. Descend with the road, which bends sharply left at the junction with Chichester Road. Just beyond the sharp bend, turn left into Bourne Way and left again into The Fairway. The junction of Bourne Way and The Fairway is the approximate site of Midhurst LBSCR station. By continuing up the Fairway you can look ahead of you to the boarded up mouth of the tunnel referred to above.

Beyond Midhurst LBSCR station, there was then an overlap between the line going on to Petersfield and the line going south to Chichester, both lines following the course now taken by Bourne Way. [Also see next chapter.]. To resume your Petersfield-bound journey you need to return via the Fairway and Bourne Way to the A286 and follow it past the fire station to a sharp right-hand bend, turning left here on to Bepton Road. The old Petersfield line ran along the embankment just to your left beyond Holmbush Way, but its course is now obscured by housing development. [The Chichester-bound line branched off hereabouts, following the approximate course now taken by Holmbush Way - see next chapter.] Having turned left into Bepton Road, turn right almost at once into Station Road, although by detouring a little down Bepton Road you can see traces of the old railway bridge. Following Station Road, you soon arrive at the old LSWR station, which has been splendidly restored. Continue past the station and on through an industrial estate, the road running parallel to and just to the right of the old line. In due course the road peters out at a sort of crude mini-roundabout, but you keep on in the same direction into a sort of "no man's land" guarded at the far end by a bank. You need to climb up over the bank - it isn't difficult - continuing in very much the same direction. Once over the bank, you find yourself in an open area with extensive woodland to your right and a lake to your left. Maintaining the same direction initially but then swinging south of west, follow a path which charts an obvious course through the middle of this open area. In a few hundred yards you will arrive at a track running at right-angles to the path, and immediately beyond the track you will see a section of old railway embankment in the shade of trees. A path runs parallel with and to the right of it; simply follow this path to arrive on Severals Road in the little village of Bepton Common.

Turn left to follow Severals Road, noting the course of the old line to your left and right, although the old line quite inaccessible just here. You follow the road very nearly to its junction with Bepton Road but just before the junction turn right along a signed path, heading initially just south of west then veering very gently north of west to cross a field, aiming for a stile. You go over the stile on to the course of the old line, crossing the line and following the path through the woods. It is actually possible to detour on to the old line here, but progress south-westwards is soon obstructed by a fence and north-eastwards by vegetation. Having crossed the line and proceeded through the woods, you arrive at a T-junction with a metalled driveway, which is a public right of way. Turn left to follow it. The right of way then swings round the front of a quite beautifully positioned house on the edge of the woods, and brings you on to the course of the old line once again; you can follow it back to the fence but must then retrace your steps. Return past the front of the house, but having done so bear left on to a signed path which swings north-westwards. You can see the outbuildings of Tyeland Farm just up ahead, with a field to your left; as you get closer to the outbuildings you will see an unobstructed track leading southward through the field to join the old line. You will also see a pathway which gives access from the public footpath to that field track, and which at the time of writing was partially but by no means totally obstructed. Neither this "link" pathway nor the field track are designated rights of way and in view of the partial obstruction it is suggested you endeavour to seek permission before using them. Once you are back on the old line, however, you can enjoy a splendid stretch of old line, nearly two miles in length, which takes you all the way to Ingrams Green Lane. Your progress south-westwards is initially rather difficult, with a lot of vegetation to negotiate, and just south of Minsted you will need to drop down the embankment to pass round a collapsed bridge, but you can pick the old line up again at once. The scenery is quite superb, with breathtaking views to the South Downs escarpment to your left. None of this stretch is along designated rights of way. At Ingrams Green Lane there is an overbridge, and further progress along the line becomes temporarily impossible. An obvious track takes you on to the lane itself, on the south side of the old line. Turn right on to the lane, cross the bridge and proceed up the lane for just under half a mile. You then arrive at a signed footpath going off to the left. Follow this path just south of west, the path proceeding picturesquely through fields and arriving at a crossing of a stream. Turn sharply left, crossing the stream, and head southwards across a field, then swing south-westwards, aiming for a collapsed bridge on the old line. As you walk you can see the course of the old line coming up from Ingrams Green Lane, although the thickness of the vegetation makes it impossible to follow the old line back to this lane. However, just to the right (west) of the collapsed bridge it is possible to join the old line and follow it all the way to the industrial estate at Lower Elsted. This is not a designated right of way but there is no difficulty of access. As you reach the estate you must leave the old line, forking to the right of the units and making your way up to Elsted Road. There is a convenient pub immediately to your right as you reach the road.

You are now once again forced away from the old line. Cross straight over Elsted Road to follow Trotton Road, passing the buildings of Greenacre Farm. Shortly beyond the farm buildings there is a signed footpath leading off to the left; follow this footpath south-westwards along the left-hand edge of woodland, to arrive at the old line. It is possible to detour left to follow it (or parallel with it) briefly back towards Elsted, but to progress north-westwards towards Petersfield, turn right. You can now proceed along the old line initially along the south fringe of Park Copse and then through open fields. It is not a designated right of way, but access is unobstructed. All too soon you reach another area of woodland, where the old line follows the top of an embankment and becomes difficult to follow; to make further progress you need to enter the field

immediately to the right of the embankment and follow the left-hand field edge parallel with the embankment, soon arriving at a track. Turning left, you immediately see the remnants of a collapsed bridge. It is possible to climb back on to the line on the other (west) side, following it for a few yards until you reach a stile to your left. Ahead of you the old line is impassable and indeed you will be unable to proceed along it until beyond Nyewood, the next village. You must therefore turn left to cross the stile and follow a public footpath which proceeds south-westwards in a straight line across fields. You go over a field and cross a footbridge over a stream into a second field, then go forward to the next field boundary and into a third field. Halfway across this third field you reach a "path crossroads" with a path heading south-north. Turn right on to this path to proceed virtually

A golden afternoon on the Pulborough to Petersfield line.

due north, crossing into another field and then, following a clearly signed route, going on into a strip of woodland. You soon cross the old line again - it is impossible to follow it more than a few yards in either direction! - and continue north-westwards past some lakes, following signs leading you to a driveway that skirts the west end of Clarefield Copse. Go uphill to reach Dumpford Lane. Turn left to follow this road for half a mile or so to the Rogate-Harting road, and here turn left to enter the little village of Nyewood.

Proceeding along the village street, you soon reach the railway bridge and, looking left, can see how the site of the old line has been redeveloped. You can detour left, downhill, to look at the old Rogate station, which has been superbly converted into offices. Return to the village street and continue in a south-westerly direction until you reach a signed footpath going off to the right opposite the phone box. Follow this path into an area of woodland. Just before emerging into a field you pass a signboard which is on your left, and opposite this signboard a narrow path goes off to your right. Follow it through the woods and under a line of pylons to arrive at the old line which, although not a designated right of way, you can follow very briefly north-westwards but more satisfyingly south-eastwards back towards Nyewood, arriving beside the warehouse/shop of John Jenkins, porcelain and crystal manufacturers, with the bridge conveying Nyewood village street just a little way in front of you. It is then necessary to retrace your steps to the signboard referred to above, and forsake the old line for a while. Emerge from the woods and continue along the footpath through a field, heading in roughly the same direction; you arrive at the edge of a strip of woodland and now bear left, along the extreme right hand edge of the field. At the end you turn sharply right, entering a larger field and following it to its end, then bear right to enter another field and follow it just west of north, aiming for a line of pylons. Passing just to the right of a pylon you find yourself on a track which swings sharply left round the buildings of Down Park Farm. Shortly a signed path goes off to the right. Take this path - part of the Sussex Border Path - and follow it across the very picturesque West Heath Common to be reunited with the old line at a collapsed bridge. You will note that it is impossible to follow it back eastwards towards Nyewood but there is no problem in turning left to join the line on the west side of the collapsed bridge, and following it. The going is rough but not especially difficult, with steep banks rising up on each side. After a few hundred yards a short and sharp but easily negotiable climb takes you on to a track; turn right to follow it downhill to the Maidenmarsh-West Harting road, the old line easily identifiable to your right. Turn right on to the road, immediately passing what is left of the railway bridge crossing over the road.

Following the road briefly, you soon meet a narrow road going off to the left, leading to Durford Mill. Go along this road and, as the road swings right, do not swing right with it but go on in the same direction along a path that now strikes out south-westwards across a large field. You can see the a portion of the old railway embankment to your left, but this fizzles out and the course of the old line is lost in flat fields.

However, you can use the location of the surviving sections of embankment to guess the route it took. You cross a stream by means of a footbridge and continue to the left-hand edge of a wood beside the banks of the River Rother. You follow the river for a short distance then just before reaching another patch of woodland - you can see another stretch of railway embankment through the trees - turn right over the Rother by means of a footbridge, crossing the border from West Sussex into Hampshire. You go on in the same direction, keeping a fence to your left, then at the corner of the fence, swing left, now heading just north of west and with the river to your left. Proceed just above the river, separated from it by a fence and an area of marsh, and arrive at a stile. Go left over the stile and descend to the river, crossing the footbridge, then beyond the bridge, continue just north of west past some bushes and up to an open grassy area. Ahead of you is now another stretch of railway embankment but as before you can only guess the course the line took to get there from the previous section of embankment in the woodland, since it is now anonymous farmland. This next section of embankment cannot be walked on; you will need to pass the eastern end of it, almost immediately arriving at the east end of Durford Road. Follow this road to a crossroads, with Penns Place going off to the right. You are now on the outskirts of Petersfield.

Turn right to follow Penns Place, almost immediately passing the collapsed bridge carrying the old line over this road; just beyond is a field, and if you wish you could detour right into it and follow the right-hand field edge parallel with the embankment back towards Durford Mill, but it is not a designated right of way and you will need to retrace your steps. The way forward is left off Penns Place on to a signed footpath which initially takes the form of a tarmac drive, with the centre of Petersfield stated to be a mile and a half away. To begin with you can easily identify the course of the old line on your left but you are forced away from it, keeping a large green area to your right and shortly entering Heathfield Road. Follow this down to a T-junction with Pulens Lane (B2199). Although you could detour left to inspect the remains of the old railway bridge over this road, just a couple of hundred yards or so along, your way is right at this road. Very soon you reach a bridge over a stream. Cross the road and then the bridge, then turn left to follow a stream-side path. Initially you pass through a modern housing estate, which has obliterated any evidence of the old line, but just after crossing Holt Down you reach another section of railway embankment and it is possible to scramble on to it and follow it to its end, although you may prefer simply to follow parallel with it to the left. At the far end of it you arrive at Marden Way; turn right on to Marden Way and follow it to a T-junction with Moggs Mead.

Two further sections of embankment remain. To get to the next, bear left into Moggs Mead, and shortly right into the cul-de-sac Lower Heyshott, following it to its end and then using an alley-way to enter Upper Heyshott. Turn right up this road which bends right and again peters out into an alley-way leading to Love Lane. Cross the road and turn left, and you will be confronted by another rather less accessible portion of

Disused railway walking at its clearest and best on the Pulborough to Petersfield line.

embankment. Follow the unnamed road parallel with and to the right of the embankment, soon reaching a T-junction with the B2070 Ramshill. Cross over and turn left, entering Station Road; in a few yards, and opposite Tilbrook House, you turn right along a footpath which runs parallel with and to the left of the third and final section of embankment. You pass under a bridge, the last piece of railway engineering on the old line that you will see on this walk, and turn immediately left, now keeping the embankment, which is inaccessible, to your left. You reach a junction with the top end of North Road, beyond which there is no further trace of the old line. However you are now very close to the surviving London-Portsmouth line and the point where the Pulborough line met it. To get to that point, turn right up the alleyway linking North Road with the existing railway, turning first left to arrive at the top end of the Sandringham Road cul-de-sac. An alleyway soon leading off this road to the right leads to a green area where you can deduce the point at which the old and existing lines met. To get to Petersfield railway station, walk down Sandringham Road and then turn right into Station Road. The town centre of Petersfield, with its excellent range of amenities, can be reached by turning left into Winton Road shortly after joining Station Road. The station is a few hundred yards further along Station Road. To return to Pulborough by train, you will need to catch a train to Havant and then another to Pulborough via Chichester and Arundel.

SECTION 1 - **CHICHESTER TO MIDHURST**

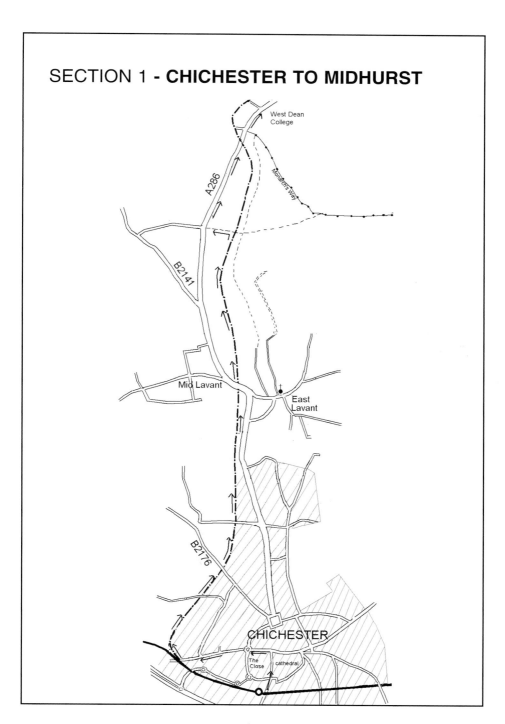

West Dean College

A286

Monarch's Way

B2141

Mid Lavant

East Lavant

B2176

CHICHESTER

The Close   cathedral

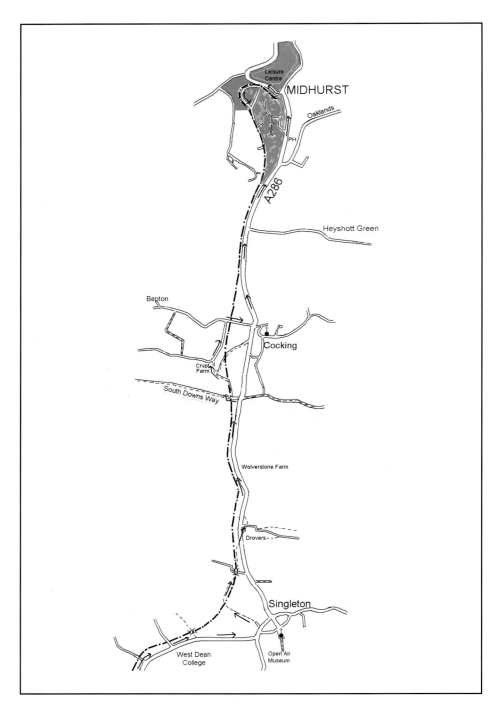

SECTION 1 - **CHICHESTER TO MIDHURST**

Length:	12 miles.
Start:	Chichester railway station.
Finish:	Midhurst town centre.
Public Transport:	Chichester is well served by train from London Victoria. Brighton and Portsmouth, also by bus from Brighton and Portsmouth. There are regular bus services daily, including Sundays, from Midhurst back to Chichester.
Conditions:	There is some excellent walking available along the course of the old route between Chichester and West Dean, through quite delightful countryside. Beyond West Dean there is virtually no access at the time of writing. However the route suggested below is very easy to follow and walk.
Refreshments:	Shops, pubs and cafes in Chichester; pub and shop in Lavant; shop, pub and café in Singleton; shop, pub and café in Cocking; pub at Cocking Causeway; shops, pubs and cafes in Midhurst. RECOMMENDED PUBS: WEST DEAN - SELSEY ARMS - well-kept beers, good value wines; SINGLETON - FOX AND HOUNDS - well-kept beers, decent wines, good food with excellent cheese platter; COCKING - BLUE BELL - "friendly village local," well-kept ales; COCKING CAUSEWAY - GREYHOUND - pretty tile-hung pub, beams, old fireplaces.

History

The idea for a line between Chichester and Midhurst emerged in the 1860's, during a time of intense railway-building activity. The prospectus stated that among the aims of the line was to allow Chichester and Midhurst to sustain their important agricultural and mercantile connection, but also at the forefront of the minds of the Chichester to Midhurst Railway Company must have been the appeal of a direct route from the busy town of Midhurst towards Goodwood and its racecourse, the historic cathedral city of Chichester, and of course the sea. Authorisation was given to the rail link in 1864 and work commenced in 1865, only for the project to be abandoned in 1865 because of lack of funds. The scheme was revived in 1876 by the LBSCR, who had initially been less than enthusiastic. The line linking Chichester and Midhurst finally opened on 11th July 1881, the West Sussex Gazette pointing out that what had been a three hour journey by train to Midhurst from Chichester, via Pulborough or Petersfield, could now be accomplished in forty minutes. The first train of the day left Midhurst at 7am, reaching Cocking at 7.10am, Singleton at 7.21am, Lavant at 7.30am and Chichester at 7.41am. No expense was spared by the LBSCR in the construction of the line, all three intermediate stations, at Lavant, Singleton and Cocking, boasting impressive mock timber-framed buildings with moulded stucco panels. Singleton station was built to cater for Goodwood race traffic, with two island platforms and extensive sidings, and indeed the summer months saw thousands of race-goers alighting at this station; at the end of the 19th century the Prince of Wales used the station when visiting West Dean Park nearby. One curious feature of Singleton station was that it boasted one of the largest gentlemen's toilet blocks ever built for a country station! Cocking station building was another impressive structure, with extravagant ornamentation and floral patterns in the plasterwork. The line involved a climb towards a gap in the South Downs and subsequent descent to Midhurst, and three tunnels were needed: West Dean (443 yards), Singleton(744 yards) and Cocking(740 yards). One former passenger recalls his anxiety as the train gathered speed downhill through Cocking tunnel, accompanied by a whistling sound that affected his ears! With the lavish station buildings and the three tunnels, it is not surprising that the cost of the line was considerably higher than average, working out at £25,000 per mile.

An 1890 timetable shows six passenger trains every weekday and Saturday in both directions, but no passenger services on Sunday, although for just a few years prior to World War I there were three Sunday journeys, and there was an extra Wednesday train for the Chichester market. After World War I the six daily trains were reduced to five. Most of the trains in fact ran to and from Pulborough, and for a time in the 1920's there was a train leaving Chichester at 8.15am on the Midhurst line that ran all the way to London Victoria. The line never attracted the number of passengers expected of it, and as early as World War I passenger traffic was declining. Buses proved more convenient, comfortable and economical, and although for a while the railway company tempted some passengers back with the introduction of a railmotor train, they still could not provide cheaper fares than the bus company. After the war, many people started coming to Goodwood races by car.

There were few especially memorable incidents in the line's history. In September 1904 near Cocking there was a derailment of a locomotive working a goods train from Midhurst to Singleton. During World War II, the Singleton and Cocking tunnels on the line were both used for the storage of wagons containing shells, landmines, torpedoes and other naval ammunition, all of which had to be shunted out as and when required - a particularly laborious task. The Germans even attempted to bomb the tunnels on one occasion but the bombs fell on West Dean tunnel where no

The southern section of the Chichester to Midhurst line provides splendid walking.

ammunition was stored! The most destructive incident in the line's history, however, was the collapse of a bridge north of Cocking on 19th November 1951, the bridge having been undermined by heavy rain. The line was thus left without a supporting bank at a time when a goods train was approaching, but mercifully the crew saw the danger in time and jumped clear.

During the 1920's and 1930's more and more traffic, both passenger and freight, was lost to the roads. Passenger services were withdrawn on 6th July 1935 and freight services ceased at Cocking and Singleton on 28th August 1953, less than two years after the bridge collapse north of Cocking. Lavant, however, was in that year to become the railhead and loading point for sugar beet from a wide area; it remained in use for freight until 3rd August 1968 and for sugar beet until January 1970. Curiously, the line from Chichester to a point just south of Lavant was reopened in 1972 for the transport of gravel from Lavant to Drayton just east of Chichester, but this usage ceased in 1991 and the track was duly pulled up in 1993. A railway preservation society was formed in the hope of reviving services as far as Singleton, but to no avail. As will be seen below, much of the southern section of the line was converted into a cycle track and pedestrian walkway.

Walking the Railway

Turn left out of the forecourt on the south side of Chichester railway station and walk northwards via Southgate and South Street to the Cross in the city centre. Turn left at the Cross into West Street which you follow past the cathedral to a roundabout, going straight over into Westgate, and following Westgate to a mini-roundabout with Sherborne Road leading off to the right. Go straight over the mini-roundabout and continue along what is a cul-de-sac for vehicles, towards a pedestrian crossing over the main Chichester-Havant railway line. If you continue to the crossing, known as the Fishbourne Crossing, and look down the railway to your right, you can see the point at which the Chichester-Midhurst railway branched off to the right, and in fact until recently there was a signal box here. Just before you reach the crossing, you will see a bus turning area on the right-hand side; from this area a concrete path leads off to the right, with a signpost proclaiming Lavant to be three and a half miles away. You follow this path to a tall metalled gate, beyond which are the grounds and buildings of Bishop Luffa School, turn left just by the gate and almost immediately find yourself on the course of the old railway. (There is no right of way along the course of the old railway back to the junction.)

The good news is that save for a very short section at Lavant, you can now follow the course of the old line all the way to Binderton. This section of the old line has been converted into a first-class footpath/cycle track known as the Centurion Way, and has become immensely and justifiably popular with walkers and cyclists. Until the first overbridge, carrying the B2178 Chichester-Funtington road, there is open countryside to the left and, beyond the Bishop Luffa school buildings, suburban housing to the right.

Beyond the B2178 overbridge, the line begins to take on a more rural feel; cuttings that are thick with vegetation line each side of the path and although there is housing occasionally visible to the right, you feel as though you are moving out of suburbia. There follow two overbridges in close succession, the second conveying the picturesquely-named Brandy Hole Lane, and if you fancy a scenic detour, there is a signpost to Brandy Hole Copse just before this bridge. Beyond the Brandy Hole Lane bridge, you pass further modern housing to the right, followed by a tall embankment, and for a while the path actually runs slightly to the left of the course of the old railway. To the left of the path, beyond a more modest cutting, is a sizeable area of rolling grassland, and you can look beyond this grassland to the attractive hills of Kingley Vale Nature Reserve. Your path now rises quite abruptly, and as you ascend to meet the top of the embankment you are reunited with the course of the old line. Note the extraordinary modern sculpture by David Kemp right beside the path close to this point; named The Chichester Road Gang, it is one of a number of pieces of sculpture work close to or on the Centurion Way. Very soon you pass under the bridge carrying the road known as Hunters Race, and beyond the bridge, although the countryside is still open to your left, the houses of Lavant are now visible to your right, and you are aware of traffic noise from the A286 Chichester-Midhurst road. The path enters a small cutting, goes under another bridge and then shortly beyond that bridge passes under the A286 bridge. Just beyond the A286 bridge is some modern housing to your left, and amongst this housing is a tall quite distinctive building that is the redevelopment of the old Lavant station building. There is no possibility of access into the building, as it is now a private dwelling.

The pedestrian/cycle track is temporarily halted here, and for the next mile there is really no evidence of the existence of a railway line at all. However you can remain reasonably close to the course of the old line throughout. When the trusty metalled path comes to an abrupt halt beyond the new development, don't be tempted to swing left to join the road, but go forward towards a long narrow strip of grass, following the same line as the old railway, and take a flight of steps down the right side of a small embankment. Turn left at the bottom to follow a good path. The scene to your right is most pleasant, with the river Lavant, active during most winters, below you to your right, and splendid rolling countryside beyond. You pass a children's play area, also to your right. The path loses its identity beyond the play area, but you continue in the same direction along the grass, the river now immediately below you to your right. Directly ahead is housing, and the course of the old line is now completely lost in this comparatively new residential development. When you reach the housing, bear to the right of No. 97 "Riverview" to briefly follow a metalled path beside the river, but you are soon forced left, away from the river, along a concrete drive to Lavant Down Road. Turn right to follow this road. The houses to your right are built along the course of the old line, and you can only imagine what a lovely view passengers would have had across the river to the beautiful countryside to the east, including the masts on the well-known hilltop beauty spot known as the Trundle. The road, having passed St Roche's Close, East View Close and St Mary's Close, bends left; just before the left bend is a small crescent which at the time of writing bore no signboard but which you need to follow, choosing between the two offshoots, and aiming for a track leading off between no. 15 and no. 17. Go forward, past a Centurion Way information board, and you will again find yourself on the course of the old line, which, as far as Binderton, has been converted into another stretch of pedestrian/cycle track.

This next section of the Centurion Way which you now follow as far as Binderton, was completed and opened in November 2002, and is if anything even more rewarding than the stretch between Chichester and Lavant with its splendid scenery. The A286 is now of course to your left and provides a constant and not too intrusive companion as you proceed onwards. You soon cross two bridges over watercourses, one being the river Lavant and the other being a tributary; when I walked this section one January day both streams were very full after weeks of heavy rain, and made an extremely picturesque sight in the cold winter sunshine. There are still delightful views to the Trundle on your right and Kingley Vale Nature Reserve on your left, and one other very attractive feature of this section is the line of trees on each side of the path for a time. Beyond the line of trees you continue through lovely open countryside and approach what is the first overbridge since just before the old Lavant station. Just before the bridge, a gate provides access to the continuation of the old line under the bridge and forward for about 200 yards to another gate. There is no access through the second gate; beyond the gate you can see that the old line has been turned into a track used by farm vehicles, and beyond that, the line is strictly private, running beside farm buildings. If you have made the detour, you have no alternative but to retrace your steps, back under the bridge. Follow the Centurion Way westwards, going downhill to cross the river Lavant then uphill to just short of the A286, arriving at the hamlet of Binderton.

The Centurion Way turns right to follow the right-hand side of the A286 heading north-eastwards towards West Dean. You are now looking down on the old line, its course evident from the lines of vegetation bordering it. Simply follow the metalled track for approximately three quarters of a mile until you reach the old bridge underneath which the old line passed. Just beyond the bridge there is a track leading off to the left; turn left on to the track and arrive very soon at a crossroads of tracks. By turning left you find yourself on the course of the old line, and although this is not a designated public right of way at the time of writing, you can follow the old line on from here for about half a mile back towards the point where you left it at Binderton. It is lovely walking, in the shade of woodland with beautiful views to West Dean Park to your left. Further access is frustrated by a fence, but you aren't far short of the farm buildings that halted your progress northwards from Lavant! Retrace your steps and having gone under the A286 road bridge, continue on over the crossroads of tracks and follow the old line (again not a designated public right of way) all the way to the

A delightful wooded interlude on the Chichester to Midhurst line near Lavant.

boarded-up mouth of the West Dean Tunnel. The surrounding countryside is quite delightful; note the attractive grouping of flint buildings to your left and a particularly fine flint and brick house to your right just beyond the bridge over the West Dean-Staple Ash Farm road. Frustratingly you must now retrace your steps to the crossroads of tracks and return to the A286, turning left to continue beside the road.

The next mile, as far as Singleton, is disappointing. Fortunately there is a pavement which you follow past the Selsey Arms pub that is on your right, while to your left is the wooded hill through which West Dean Tunnel was built. You pass signed turnings to West Dean Church and West Dean College, both to your right; immediately opposite the college turning is a signed public footpath going off to your left which takes you under a bridge beneath the old line. By following the footpath beyond the bridge uphill along a pleasant green track you can look down on the line, it having emerged from the tunnel and now proceeding along a wooded embankment. Access to the line is however impossible. Returning to the A286 and continuing towards Singleton you very soon come to a metalled road going off to the left, which also provides an opportunity to view the embankment of the old line from below. Once again you go back to the A286 and shortly a metalled drive leading off to the left takes you gently uphill to a private residence which is the site of Singleton station. Until recently this was a vineyard with visitor access, but this has now gone, and indeed, immediately north-east of the site of the station, the old line appears to have become a dumping ground. Sadly you return to the A286 and follow it to the village of Singleton, the old line barely discernible through the hedgerow.

Things now look up somewhat. As you arrive at the village, look out for the signed public footpath leading off to the left immediately in front of a prominent white-painted house, which was formerly the village stores. The path leads round the back of the cricket pavilion then bends sharply right over a stile and across a little footbridge over a stream. Once over the bridge bear right and almost at once, at the Drovers Estate signboard, turn left. You cross over a stile, and follow a signed path uphill, soon going over a bridge above the old line and able to look down on the line which lies in a deep cutting and is totally overgrown. It is in a particularly sorry state on the Chichester side of the bridge. Once over the bridge don't climb up the stone steps ahead but instead bear immediately right and continue to a stile; cross the stile and now follow the field edge, keeping the old line below you to the right. Walking on the grassy hillside can be quite tiring on the feet, but soon you pick up a track, continuing in the same direction, and the views ahead of you are beautiful. A track leading right gives you the opportunity to detour on to the line as it emerges from the cutting, but then you need to return to the track you've been following. You descend quite steeply, turn right at the bottom as directed by the signpost, and go under a bridge, the old line now above you. However, almost immediately beyond the bridge you turn left to enter a field, there being a right of way along the left-hand field edge. You climb, again quite steeply, and are soon on the same level as the old line; in fact you can gain access through a gate on to the line although progress along it is impossible in either direction. Return to the field edge and follow it to the top left corner. You are now above the old line and must temporarily bid farewell to it as it disappears into Singleton tunnel. There is a good view from here to Goodwood, and it must have been with good cheer that racegoing train travellers from Midhurst and beyond emerged from the tunnel to see the hillside on which the racecourse is situated, with Singleton station just a couple of minutes away.

Bear right to follow the edge of the wood, going downhill, then at the corner of the wood bear left along a good path, still keeping the wood to your left and the A286 to your right. The OS map shows the designated right of way swinging right to meet the A286 at Drovers, but it appears possible to continue on a grassy surface for a couple of hundred yards further, joining a track which takes you down to join the A286 by a bus stop. Turn left and proceed along the verge beside the A286 for another couple of hundred yards until a track, signposted as a public right of way, goes off to the left with a sign warning NO CARS. The track proceeds past a delightful old flint house and buildings of Littlewood Farm and enables you to view the railway embankment, the old line having emerged from Singleton tunnel and the thick woodland around it. Access to the embankment is not possible and the bridge carrying the line over the track has gone, so you must return to the A286 and content yourself with continuing along the roadside and following the embankment which runs close by. Shortly you reach the buildings of Wolverstone Farm on the right, but just before the buildings bear left off the A286 up a signed bridleway that takes you to a very splendid bridge over the old line. It is worth detouring slightly either left or right, having crossed it, so you can admire the quite magnificent brickwork. You can see that the line has now entered a deep cutting with thick woodland on its west side, but the line itself is massively overgrown. There were even some fallen trees among the vegetation at the time of writing. Return to the A286 and follow it uphill, the deep cutting through which the old line was built clearly visible to the left; as you near the crest of the hill, and the woodland relents, watch for a public bridleway sign on the left. Follow the bridleway and very soon you will find yourself looking down, to your left, at the mouth of Cocking tunnel, the last of the three tunnels on the Chichester-Midhurst line.

Return to the A286 and follow it to the crest of the hill where you will see Cocking Hill car park to your left. Walk through the car park and at the end turn left on to the South Downs Way. You follow it for just a few moments, turning right just before the farm buildings down a path indicated by a fingerpost as "Public Right Of Way." The path drops very steeply indeed then turns sharp left. At the bend, go straight on; in a few yards look round to your right, and you will see the northern mouth of Cocking tunnel. This is one of the best spots on the whole walk, offering a marvellous combination of impressive railway engineering and beautiful unspoilt natural surroundings. It is in fact possible to drop down to the old line and follow it back towards the tunnel, although this detour is not a designated right of way. At the time

A sunny summer's evening on the Chichester to Midhurst line near Binderton.

of writing the tunnel was not sealed off, but you enter it at your own risk and you are strongly advised to seek permission from the owner before doing so. Progress along the old line north of the tunnel is frustrated by trees and other vegetation, so you must return to the bend in the path and continue downhill. The path arrives at a junction with a metalled road at Crypt Farm; it is recommended that you detour to the right here, passing a lovely pond, to view the embankment of the old line either side of a very fine bridge. To continue towards Midhurst, however, turn left at Crypt Farm and proceed past the buildings. Beyond the farm take the track forking right, and proceed gently uphill to reach a T-junction with another track; turn right on to this track and follow it all the way to the Cocking-Bepton road. This is a most rewarding walk, for on your right you will see the course of the old line and at a footpath signpost with fingers pointing ahead and behind, there is a path (not a designated public right of way) leading off to your right, taking you on to the line itself. If you take the path to the line here, you will be well rewarded, for to the east and south you have spectacular views to the South Downs and surrounding countryside, and to the north you can see Cocking station building. Although you cannot follow the line to the station you can at least see the direction it took and the surrounding terrain. Return to the public footpath and proceed to the Cocking-Bepton road, the old Cocking station building situated to your right just before you reach the road; the building has ben magnificently restored and developed as a private dwelling. Turn right on to the road, pass under the railway bridge and proceed along the road into Cocking.

The three-mile walk into Midhurst beside the A286, running more or less parallel with the old line, is a real anticlimax after the fine walking around and to the north of Cocking tunnel. It is true that there is pavement beside the A286 throughout, and that the course of the old line is easily visible to your left for much of the way, as far as the Greyhound pub at any rate. If it is any consolation, the countryside bordering the old line is really no more or less scenic than that bordering the A286 hereabouts. There are just three rights of way which allow you to inspect the old line close up: a footpath going off left immediately opposite the road leading to Graffham and Heyshott just under a mile from Cocking, which takes you to the embankment; the metalled Pitsham Lane just before the Greyhound pub at Cocking Causeway half a mile further on, which takes you to a fine bridge under the old line; and, just beyond the Greyhound, a signed public footpath which brings you to what is your last view of the embankment before the outskirts of Midhurst are reached. There is no right of access on to the old line from any of these three routes, although if you are agile you may scramble up the bank from Pitsham Lane on to the course of the old railway to be met with dense undergrowth which makes even negligible progress impossible. In the absence of tunnelling or significant development on or even near the old line, it would be grand to think that the Cocking-Midhurst section of old line might become a leisure facility as much of the Chichester-Binderton section has.

Having returned to the A286 along the path beyond the Greyhound, you now face a dull trudge on to Midhurst. The old line passes through the woodland to your left and is totally inaccessible. You rise slightly, soon passing another pub (across the road), then begin a steady descent. The road bends sharply left, then almost as sharply right. Continue to follow it, then just past the fire station turn left into Holmbush Way and follow that. You pass through the industrial estate - no pavement is available - and continue straight ahead into Barlavington Way. Proceed as far as number 34 on the right-hand side, beyond which is a concrete pathway with garages down the side. By following this pathway to the bottom and then proceeding down a flight of steps you will find yourself on a back alley which provides residents' access to their back gardens and sheds. Immediately beyond the back alley and running parallel with it is the old line, and beyond the old line is woodland and attractive countryside. At this point you are in fact very close to where you last saw the line, just beyond the Greyhound pub. Access to the back alley is also available between numbers 20 and 22, heading back towards Holmbush Way. Returning to the northern end of Barlavington Way, look to your left and you will see a stream with what was evidently a bridge conveying the old line; on the Barlavington Way side of the stream you can clearly see the course of the old line heading back towards Cocking.

Returning to the A286 via Holmbush Way, you are now following the course of the old line. Note how as the road swings from north-west to north-east, so did the line; you will see in a few moments how the old line then swung south-east to arrive at

Midhurst station. Turn right back on to the main road and pass the fire station, just beyond which on your right is the stream and further evidence of a railway bridge crossing. Now head back up the A286. At a sharp left-hand bend turn right into Bourne Way, soon reaching a T-junction which marks the site of Midhurst (LBSCR) railway station. If you were to turn right at the T-junction, continuing in fact along Bourne Way, you would be walking on what was the very last section of the old line from Chichester, but it is hardly worth the effort. By turning left at the T-junction, along The Fairway, you would be following the course of the old line which headed eastwards towards Petworth (see chapter devoted to the Pulborough-Petersfield line) but there is no more walking to be done on the former Chichester-Midhurst line. Buses are available back to Chichester from bus stops situated very close by, both on Bourne Way and the A286 itself; if you want to explore the delightful town of Midhurst with its many amenities and refreshment opportunities, return to the A286 and turn right on to it, then shortly bear left down Chichester Road, going forward into South Street. Continue to a T-junction with North Street, Midhurst's main thoroughfare. The bus stand is at the north end of North Street on the right.

It would be great to think that the whole of the Chichester to Midhurst line might one day provide disused railway walking of this quality.

SECTION 2 - **ALDRINGTON TO DEVIL'S DYKE**

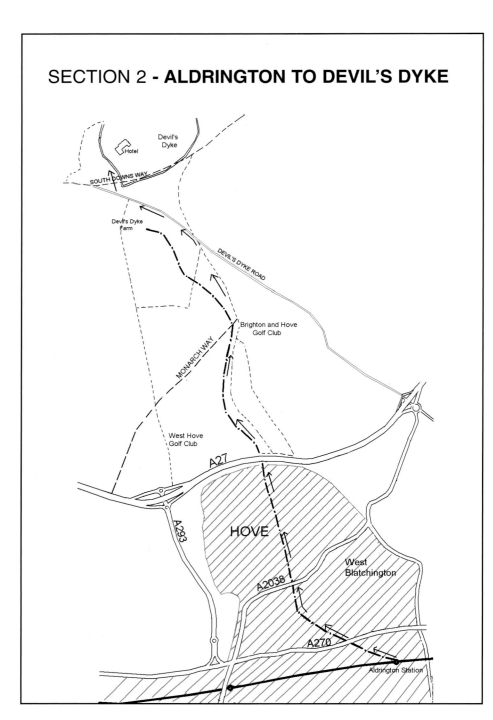

SECTION 2 - ALDRINGTON TO DEVIL'S DYKE

Distance:	3.5 miles.
Start:	Aldrington Station, Hove.
Finish:	Devil's Dyke.
Public Transport:	Aldrington is served by regular train services on the Worthing-Brighton line. There are regular buses from the Devil's Dyke restaurant/picnic area into central Brighton.
Conditions:	The first half of the walk is along roadsides and is relatively unrewarding. The second half is much better, offering good walking along the course of the old line or by the side of it, with fine surroundings and superb views.
Refreshments:	Shops on Rowan Avenue; shops and pub on Hangleton Road.; pub and restaurant at summit of Devil's Dyke. RECOMMENDED PUB: DEVIL'S DYKE HOTEL is a popular family pub in a stunning setting with a good range of snacks and more substantial fare.

History

Devil's Dyke has a timeless attraction, boasting magnificent views from the top of the South Downs escarpment to the Weald, as well as the extraordinary natural phenomenon which is the Dyke itself. It has always been popular with visitors, and towards the end of the 19th century a company called the Brighton & Dyke Railway Company was formed with a view to creating a rail link from central Brighton - by then a bustling and popular resort - to the Dyke. The go-ahead to build the line was given in 1877 but it was not until 1st September 1887 that the line opened. It followed the main Worthing line to Dyke Junction (a halt was opened here in 1905, renamed Aldrington Halt in June 1932) and branched off at this junction. Although trains initially ran non-stop from Hove to the terminus, named "The Dyke" in Bradshaw's Timetable, two intermediate stations were subsequently opened on the branch to attempt to encourage further passenger usage. Golf Club Halt, just under a mile from the terminus, was opened in 1891 to serve the nearby golf course, and Rowan Halt, half a mile beyond Dyke Junction, opened on 12th January 1934 to serve nearby housing developments. Station design was very basic, and the terminus was a bleak proposition indeed in winter, its location being exposed and isolated. There was normally just one staff member there, acting as booking clerk, shunter, porter and

An information board for users of the Dyke Railway Trail, incorporating a substantial part of the Aldrington to Devil's Dyke line.

signalman! Because the branch was starting at virtually sea level and climbing to virtually the top of the downs, an almost continuous gradient of 1 in 40 was required. The 1905 timetable showed eight daily trains travelling to The Dyke direct from Brighton with a usual journey time of 20 minutes for the uphill slog to the top, and just 1 minute chopped off for the descent back to Brighton. Six trains made the return journey on Sundays. Although the line was intended chiefly for passenger use, there was a small goods yard at the terminus which received coal and cattle food and sent out hay. The line was temporarily closed during the First World War and closed for good on 31st December 1938. Dyke Station became a farm, and there is now no trace of any station building beyond Aldrington.

Walking the Railway

From Aldrington Station take the exit on the north side and proceed down the path to the bottom of Aldrington Avenue, going straight ahead into Amherst Crescent. It is just to the left of the junction of Aldrington Avenue and Amherst Crescent that the old line left the main line. Following Amherst Crescent up to the A270 Old Shoreham Road, you are keeping the course of the old line immediately to your left and parallel with Amherst Crescent; the site of the old line is now occupied by Sussex House Industrial Estate and is inaccessible. At Old Shoreham Road turn left, then cross over and turn right into Holmes Avenue. The old line crossed Old Shoreham Road a fraction beyond the junction with Holmes Avenue and then swung from north-west to just west of north, through what is now another industrial estate and past the southern end of Maple Gardens. You will need to walk up Holmes Avenue and then turn left at the first crossroads, passing the cul-de-sacs of Acacia Avenue and Maple Gardens and going forward along Elm Drive. Once past the junction with Maple Gardens (obviously you can detour down this road and back, but there is nothing much to see!) you are again following parallel with the course of the old line, which ran along the west side (left side as you look at it) of Elm Drive. You reach a small parade of shops; don't turn right to continue along Elm Drive, but continue along what turns into Rowan Avenue, still keeping the course of the old line immediately to your left. In fact a little further up Rowan Avenue an alleyway leads you left into a park, and although you would never guess it now, by walking along the grass parallel with Rowan Avenue in either direction, you are actually on the course of the old line. Return to Rowan Avenue and continue to the junction with Hangleton Road. Turn right on to this busy road then shortly, just beside a pub, turn hard left into West Way and right into Poplar Avenue. The old line ran immediately parallel with and to the left of Poplar Avenue; looking both back towards Rowan Avenue, and back up Poplar Avenue, it seems inconceivable that there was once a railway line here! At the end of Poplar Avenue cross Hangleton Way and arrive at a signboard signifying the start of the "official" Dyke Railway Trail. Beyond the signboard, which gives a brief history of the old line, the way forward is obvious; you are now on the course of the old line, following an exceedingly good path northwards. Very soon you cross over the A27 Shoreham/Brighton bypass, then ignoring a right fork continue along the path, keeping to the course of the old line.

This is now quite delightful walking; at last you have left the sprawl of Brighton and Hove behind and are now in open country, with West Hove golf course immediately to your left. Looking back, you can enjoy superb views across the Brighton/Hove/Shoreham conurbation out to sea. It will perhaps only now strike you just how much height you have gained since Aldrington and how hard the engines would have had to work to haul the trains up to this height from virtually sea level. The path swings north-westwards from the A27 crossing, but then swings east of north, still sticking to the course of the old line. Having passed the northern end of West Hove golf course to your left, you now become aware of another golf course - Brighton & Hove - to your right, and the clubhouse comes into view. It is hereabouts that the old Golf Club Halt station was situated. At this point the path swings more decisively to the right, and a footpath sign points you upwards past the clubhouse, away from the course of the old line. If you wish to continue along the old line you need to proceed straight on along a rougher track, in a northerly direction, rather than obeying the footpath sign. Initially it all looks very promising, and you might ask yourself why walkers are signposted away from it, but your satisfaction is short-lived for almost without warning the rough track stops. If you wish to make further progress you will need to follow the right hand edge of the field, keeping the course of the old line - easily discernible in the form of an embankment - immediately to your right. There is no possibility of following the embankment itself. After progressing along the field edge for a few hundred yards, you will see the way ahead is blocked by a fence. It may be possible, just before the fence, to cross over the course of the old line using a break in the embankment, then follow the left-hand edge of the field in front of you, now keeping the course of the old line immediately to your left. At the corner of the field, swing right and ascend, still following the field edge, to Devil's Dyke Road; to gain access to the road you will need to follow the field edge south-eastwards to a gate and a gap in the hedge. [If the traverse of the field edges, either side of the old line, is rendered impossible by the presence of crops (and none of this is designated as a public right of way) you will need to backtrack all the way to the footpath sign by the Brighton & Hove golf course clubhouse. Follow the public footpath briefly then turn left along a track virtually opposite the clubhouse; this is a public right of way and leads you to Devil's Dyke Road. Turn left on to the road and you will soon pass the gate and gap in the hedge referred to above.] Now simply follow Devil's Dyke Road north-westwards. Looking to your left as you follow the road you will see the course of the old line running roughly parallel with the road and to your left; sadly although the course is very clear there is no access to it. Devil's Dyke Road can be extremely busy, especially at weekends and holiday times, and although you get a much better view of the old line by walking along the left-hand side of the road, you may find the going pleasanter and safer by crossing over and using the footpath running along the right-hand side of the road. Just before a right-hand turn leading to the clubhouse of the Dyke golf course, you will see a track leading off to the left and soon swinging sharp left again, on course for Dyke Farm. This is private property but is built on the site of the terminus of the old line. Rather than entering the farm area, stop on your way down to the farm buildings and you will clearly see, just ahead of you and to the right, the final few yards of the old line and the point at which it would have come to an end. There is no means or right of access to it, however, but just by looking at it you will see how isolated and windswept the terminus was!

Return to Devil's Dyke Road and turn left to continue along it, passing the turning to the club house mentioned above. Soon you will cross the South Downs Way and see the impressive ravine to your right, and shortly beyond that you will arrive at what is marked on maps as the Devil's Dyke Hotel, now an immensely popular pub and restaurant. You are now right on the edge of the South Downs escarpment and can enjoy fantastic views to the Weald; a topograph situated close by will help you identify the places you can see from here on a clear day. There is one further feature for the "old railway" buff to see before partaking of a well-earned drink or meal at the pub and then

steps back to Hartington Road. Pausing at the crest of the bank, looking just west of north, you can see the existing Brighton-Lewes line in the middle distance and using the section of old line you have just followed as a marker you can see roughly the course that old line would have followed to link with the still existing line.

There is no access through the tunnel. Having returned to Hartington Road turn almost immediately right into Bonchurch Road, and at the end turn right into Elm Grove, getting a good view of the small strip of existing line you have just walked. It was at this point that the line entered the tunnel. Take the second left turn into Bentham Road, then turn right at the T-junction into Queens Park Road and join it briefly before taking the first left turn into St Luke's Terrace. Follow this to the junction with Freshfield Road and turn right to follow this road. Soon you find yourself looking down on the Freshfield Industrial Estate to your left. Passing the estate, you turn left into Freshfield Way and left again into Stevenson Road to gain access to the estate itself. Beyond you can see the steep cliffs from which the old line emerged to arrive at the station on the site of which the estate now stands. To return to the station from the estate, make your way to the south end of Freshfield Road and its T-junction with Eastern Road. Turn right on to Eastern Road and follow it westwards; in due course it leads into Edward Street, which in turn drops down to the south end of Grand Parade. Cross over to the far west side of Grand Parade and go straight on into Church Street, which goes uphill, slightly north of west, to arrive at Queens Road. Turn right into Queens Road and keep going until you reach the station.

Kemp Town Station circa 1968.

SECTION 2 - **THREE BRIDGES TO GROOMBRIDGE TOWARDS ERIDGE**

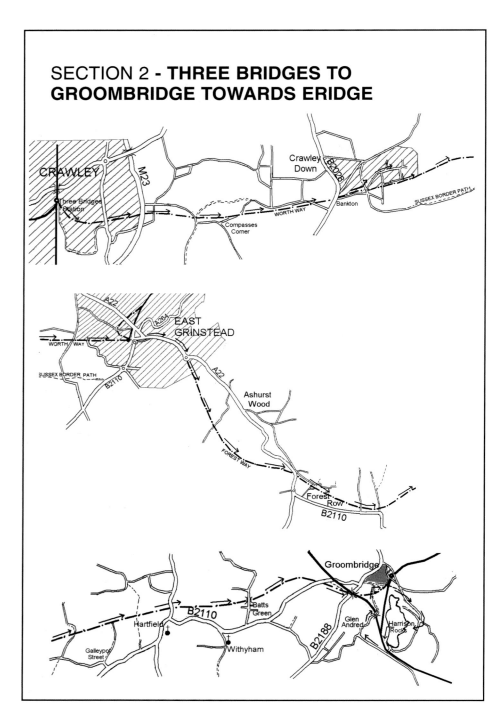

SECTION 2 - **THREE BRIDGES TO GROOMBRIDGE TOWARDS ERIDGE**

Distance:	17.5 miles. (1.5 additional miles from Groombridge towards Eridge)
Start:	Three Bridges railway station.
Finish:	Groombridge old railway station.
Public Transport:	Three Bridges is on the main London to Brighton railway. Regular buses from Groombridge to East Grinstead and Tunbridge Wells. Also trains from Groombridge to Tunbridge Wells on the preserved Spa Valley Railway.
Conditions:	This is an immensely satisfying walk, almost all of the old line from Three Bridges to Groombridge being available for walkers using the Worth Way and Forest Way footpaths.
Refreshments:	Pubs, cafes and shops in the Three Bridges/Crawley conurbation; pub and shop at Crawley Down; pubs, cafes and shops in East Grinstead; pubs, café and shops in Forest Row; pub and shop in Hartfield; pub and shops in Groombridge. RECOMMENDED PUBS: HARTFIELD - ANCHOR - 15th century olde-worlde pub, well-kept beers, decent bar food; WITHYHAM - DORSET ARMS - well-kept beer, decent local wine.

History

Although regular train services ran direct between Three Bridges and Tunbridge Wells for many years, the section between Three Bridges and East Grinstead opened some years before the East Grinstead-Tunbridge Wells section. The first section was built by the East Grinstead Railway Company and opened on 9th July 1855; the LBSCR operated it and duly acquired it from the East Grinstead Railway Company. It was again local enterprise, in the form of the East Grinstead, Groombridge and Tunbridge Wells Railway Company, that led to the extension to Tunbridge Wells which opened on 1st October 1866. There had been a number of delays in the opening of the line and the press eventually got so tired of waiting that they failed to report the actual opening!

The first station out of Three Bridges was Rowfant. Even now the site of the station seems quite remote, but it was opened in the days when land was given to a new railway company in return for the provision of a station on the estate. The land through which the line passed here was given by an American fur trader named Curtis Miranda Lampson and the station was given to Lampson in return, including a shelter for Lampson's coachmen! The second station was Grange Road, which was sited in what is now described on maps as Crawley Down, and which for a number of years had a rather longer name - Grange Road For Crawley Down And Turners Hill. It was opened in 1860. The third station, at East Grinstead, was initially a terminus, but following the opening of the Tunbridge Wells extension it became a two level station, the upper level - now the car park of the current station - being that used by the Three Bridges line, and the lower level used by trains coming from Lewes and going forward to London. The first station beyond East Grinstead was Forest Row, the busiest of the intermediate stations on the route; some trains from London to East Grinstead were in fact extended to terminate here, and in the final years of the line, a number of London commuters were using this station. The next station along the line was Hartfield, which despite the modest size of the community it served boasted a goods yard loop that could hold 13 wagons. Then came Withyham, with its unfussy slate roof and small goods yard; Groombridge with connections to Eridge and beyond; High Rocks Halt, opened in 1907 and designed to cater for visitors to the splendid rocky outcrops hereabouts; and Tunbridge Wells West, a splendid construction which with its clock tower and ornamental ceiling is now a listed building.

Bradshaw's 1890 timetable shows five direct services between Three Bridges and Tunbridge Wells each weekday, plus a couple of trains from Three Bridges to East Grinstead with the possibility of going forward to Tunbridge Wells on a train leaving 40-45 minutes later. There were two through trains on Sundays. The timing of the Sunday trains was curious: if you missed the 9.30am from Three Bridges, you would have to wait until 8.25pm for the only other eastbound train of the day. The line did grow in popularity and usage, and by 1955, the line west from East Grinstead to Three Bridges had 17 weekly and 10 Sunday return journeys. However, being a lateral cross-country connection, as opposed to a route in and out of London, it was especially vulnerable to Dr Beeching's axe, and closed on 1st January 1967. Ironically East Grinstead was Dr Beeching's home town for many years and on what was the old line there is now a street in East Grinstead called Beeching Way! With the vast majority of the still-defunct line now converted into two fine cycle/walkways, the Worth Way and the Forest Way, this is fertile terrain indeed for the old railway explorer.

The section of line between Groombridge and Eridge, a separate section from the Three Bridges-Tunbridge Wells line, was opened on 3rd August 1868 as part of a link line between Groombridge, on the East Grinstead-Tunbridge Wells line, and Uckfield which had been served by rail from Lewes since 1858. Notwithstanding the cessation, during the 1960's, of services between Tunbridge Wells and East Grinstead, trains

On the Worth Way section of the Three Bridges to Groombridge line, looking east.

continued to run from Tunbridge Wells via Groombridge to Eridge where passengers could pick up connecting services to Crowborough, Buxted and Uckfield to the south, and Edenbridge, and Oxted to the north. The Groombridge-Eridge line joined the Uckfield-Oxted line (which still survives) just a mile and a half or so south-west of Groombridge. Services between Tunbridge Wells and Eridge ceased in July 1985, but the section between Tunbridge Wells and Groombridge was subsequently turned into a preserved steam railway known as the Spa Valley Railway. It is hoped to extend the preserved section to Eridge in due course.

Walking the Railway

Your walk starts at Three Bridges railway station; there are excellent services to here from London, Brighton, Horsham and Chichester. Turn right out of the station and immediately right to pass under the existing railway, then turn immediately right again to follow Station Hill. In a few hundred yards look for the Worth Way signpost pointing along a footpath to the left; immediately to the right here you can see the point at which the old line left the existing one. Follow the Worth Way path and you will at once find yourself following the course of the old line. Initially the surroundings are distinctly suburban, but the going is very pleasant. Continue along the course of the old line, notwithstanding the signposting of the Worth Way away from the line, and follow it on until you reach an overbridge with a flight of steps built on to the side of it. You can continue a short way beyond, but your way forward is blocked by the M23 so retrace your steps to the bridge, climb up the steps, turn right and proceed southwards from the bridge along the footpath which soon emerges into Saxon Road on a modern housing estate. Turn shortly left into Harold Road and then almost immediately right into Alfred Close, soon arriving at the Worth Way again. Now turn left to follow what is an excellent footpath eastwards over the M23 then north-eastwards past Worth Lodge Farm. Near the farm buildings a lane leads off to the left and by following it you soon reach a pair of gates on either side. It is possible to turn left through the left-hand gate into the field and follow the course of the old line - obvious from the remains of the redbrick bridge just beyond the gates - back to the M23; having done that you could do the same beyond the right-hand gate, going forward to Turners Hill Road along the course of the old line as it skirts an area of vegetation. However there is no access into Turners Hill Road and you are forced to backtrack to the lane and return to the course of the Worth Way which proceeds eastwards, roughly parallel with and to the right of the old line, to the road. The sections of old line between the M23 and this point are not designated rights of way and you may prefer simply to stick to the Worth Way!

Having reached Turners Hill Road via the Worth Way, turn left and almost immediately right along the signed Worth Way path. You are now on the old line and will remain on it or immediately adjacent to it for a good couple of miles. You have left the housing behind and the going is delightfully rural. In less than a mile you cross Wallage Lane and pass the superbly preserved Rowfant Station, although there is no access inside the station building or on to the platform. From here to the B2028 overbridge, the going is straightforward and really delightful, the Worth Way running either on or immediately next to the course of the old line throughout. Beyond the B2028, you enter the built-up area known as Crawley Down and, as the course of the old line has now been built on, you are forced just to the south of the line to proceed to the centre of the village where there are ample refreshment opportunities. There is no trace whatsoever of Grange Road Station which was sited here.

The course of the old line is inaccessible for half a mile or so beyond the centre of Crawley Down, new housing having obliterated all traces of its course. Following the excellent Worth Way signposting, head north-eastwards into Burleigh Way, immediately opposite the small shopping parade. Proceed along Burleigh Way then turn right into Woodland Drive and shortly left into Hazel Way, still observing the Worth Way signposts. Follow Hazel Way then as it bends slightly left turn right into Cob Close; this leads to a footpath which goes forward to rejoin the course of the old line. Now it is a very easy and delightful two-mile walk to East Grinstead through unspoilt countryside with a mixture of woodland and open fields around you. You then enter East Grinstead and skirt the northern edge of the station car park, which is the site of the high level section of the old station. As you pass the car park, look out for a rather florid signpost with an arm pointing into the woods indicating St Margarets Loop. This was a loop line that was opened in 1884 and designed to link the Tunbridge Wells-Three Bridges line with the East Grinstead-Victoria line. It is worth detouring to have a look at this. Follow the path indicated by the signpost, accessible by crossing over a low metal bar at the edge of the trees and entering the woods, and immediately you will find yourself on the loop line. It is not a designated right of way, although it is marked on some street plans as such. The whole loop line is in a deep shady cutting, and there are a couple of fine tall brick overbridges. There is unfortunately no exit further up, the old line eventually merging in with the existing one, so you will be forced to retrace your steps all the way back. Progress is initially quite easy, but becomes very much tougher and more frustrating, with varying obstructions including thick undergrowth, fallen trees, accumulations of bricks and other debris, and often glutinous mud which almost claimed one of my shoes one June afternoon, in the middle of a heatwave! My advice is to turn back at the first overbridge, by which time you will have got a flavour of the loop line; you venture further at your own risk and I have to say it really isn't worth the effort.

Returning to the course of the old line, your journey along the Worth Way is now at an end and you must negotiate your way through East Grinstead. At the top end of the car park turn right and make your way over the footbridge across the existing railway, descending to the forecourt area of the present railway station. If you wished to stay absolutely faithful to the old line as it proceeded on towards Forest Row, you would need to turn left out of the station forecourt and then cross straight over the roundabout on to the A22 inner ring road heading just north of east, and follow this road. Ironically it is called Beeching Way after the man responsible for shutting the old line. There is no pavement and it is a potentially quite dangerous walk alongside what is an extremely busy road. In due course it arrives at a roundabout, and immediately across the roundabout you will see the signed Forest Way path. A much safer and pleasanter alternative, having crossed the roundabout beyond the East Grinstead station forecourt, is to enter Railway Approach (the next exit round from the A22 ring road heading east) and follow this road to its junction with London Road. Turn right into London Road, East Grinstead's principal shopping street, and follow it to a T-junction at the end. Turn left and follow the road past the church and a number of fine old houses and shops - really the nicest part of the town - eventually reaching the roundabout at the end of Beeching Way mentioned above. The Forest Way path is signposted immediately to your right, and you now proceed now along this path. You will be following the Forest Way from here all the way to Groombridge at the end of your walk.

Initially the path runs downhill and just to the right of the course of the old line, but soon finds itself following the old line. Soon you leave the suburbs of East Grinstead behind and head south-eastwards into open countryside. There are really excellent views, particularly to the right, where woodland dominates the skyline, and the walking is easy and very enjoyable. In two and a half miles from East Grinstead you arrive at the crossing of the A22, just a quarter of a mile from Forest Row. By detouring right and following the A22 you will soon reach the centre of this sizeable and quite sprawling village, with its good range of shops and refreshment opportunities including, at the time of writing, a café and pizzeria, though sadly the noise of the A22 London-Eastbourne road, which cuts through the village, does little to add to its charm. Forest Row is the closest you get to Ashdown Forest, with its plethora of footpaths and tracks which are a paradise for the woodland walker. Returning to the course of the old line, use the pelican crossing to negotiate your way across the A22 and continue your walk. To begin with you follow a driveway parallel with and immediately to the left of the old line, which follows an embankment above you to your right. It is possible to gain access to the embankment but it's hardly worth the effort as the undergrowth and vegetation along the embankment make progress either way impracticable. In any case, as you continue along the driveway, you will notice that the course of the old line to the right soon leaves the embankment behind and proceeds through the middle of an industrial estate, passing the site of the former

Forest Row Station. Its course through the estate is fairly obvious. Having followed the driveway, Forest Way walkers are then directed on to a track that forks to the right, the way straight ahead leading to what at the time of writing was an organic farm. The Forest Way having passed just to the left of the far end of the industrial estate, soon finds itself back on the course of the old line, heading for Hartfield.

The walk to Hartfield is quite delightful; it is four miles of disused railway walking at its very best, the Forest Way path sticking to the old line throughout. To begin with there is housing beside the route, but once clear of Forest Row you find yourself out in really charming countryside, with woodland to your right and meadows bordering the infant River Medway to your left. Initially you continue south-eastwards, but having shaken off the built-up area

Another glimpse of the Worth Way section of the Three Bridges to Groombridge line at Rowfant.

at the eastern edge of Forest Row, you begin to head north-eastwards. There are excellent views to the fine Ashdown House which lies on the left (north) side of the old line. This section of route is particularly popular with cyclists and walkers, so do not expect to be on your own! Four miles from Forest Row you pass underneath the B2026 Maresfield-Edenbridge road, with clear signposting leading you on to the road which takes you to the village of Hartfield just a quarter of a mile to the south. Hartfield is a beautiful village, attracting many visitors because it is in this area that the Winnie The Pooh books of A.A. Milne were set, and there is a shop in the village which sells a variety of Pooh merchandise. The village boasts a good food shop and pub, and a fine church with a magnificent spire which you can clearly see from the old line even if you decide not to visit the village. Directly beyond the access path for the B2026 you will see the old station building of Hartfield. It is now in private ownership and inaccessible, but with its distinctive red brick looks very similar to how it would have looked when trains ran along the old line. The Forest Way proceeds round the left hand edge of the old station area, allowing quite beautiful views to the adjoining meadows, and shortly rejoins the course of the old line.

Another lovely stretch of old line follows, and there is the additional delight of views to the rather wider Medway to your left. In just under 2 miles you cross a metalled road and pass the rather inelegantly-named hamlet of Balls Green, at which the old Withyham station building was situated. Withyham, with its picturesque church and pub - but not much else - lies about half a mile to the south-west. Beyond Balls Green the Forest Way, remaining faithful to the old line, hugs right up to the Medway and the going is still very pleasant. The first sign that you are nearing the end of your walk along the course of the old line comes when, just before Ham Bridge where the old line crossed over the B2110 Forest Row-Tunbridge Wells road, the Forest Way path leaves the old line and drops down to the B2110 to circumvent the former bridge crossing. It is open to you to follow the old line and then descend quite steeply to meet the road, but that option is perhaps best left to the purist! Cross the road and rejoin the Forest Way immediately opposite. You soon return to the course of the old line but your stay on it is short-lived, as very soon the Forest Way follows a course parallel with the old line but immediately to the right of it. It is here that the old line is united briefly with the still operational Edenbridge-Uckfield line coming in from the left. Proceed along the Forest Way parallel with this line and arrive at a crossing with the B2188 Groombridge-Maresfield road. Cross over the road and continue along the Forest Way. Initially it runs parallel with the Edenbridge-Uckfield line, but shortly swings left to pass underneath it; this is just beyond the point at which the Three Bridges-Tunbridge Wells line leaves the Edenbridge-Uckfield line, going off to the left. The Forest Way now runs parallel with the Three Bridges-Tunbridge Wells line as far as the next road junction just a few hundred yards ahead. The old line is completely inaccessible, and no more of it is in fact walkable. When you reach the road, turn left to follow it, passing underneath the old line, now on the outskirts of Groombridge. The road goes uphill and swings round to the right. It shortly bends left, and on the bend there is a footpath leading off to the right which passes over the old Groombridge-Eridge line (see below) immediately north of the point where the line comes in from Three Bridges and East Grinstead. At the time of writing this footbridge was declared unsafe and access across it was prohibited, but if it reopens, it is worth detouring to the bridge and back.

Continue from here along the road, now heading north along what is a residential street. You pass a little church and, heading downhill, reach a crossroads at which you turn right. Follow the road which narrows to a path and arrives at Station Road that links Groombridge and High Rocks, the old Groombridge railway station now straight ahead of you over the road. Cross over Station Road and go down the steps to arrive at the fine old redbrick station building which is now in private ownership and has been converted into offices. You may however proceed on to the old station platform and by following it towards its southern end, passing under the road you just crossed, you will reach the "new" station building which serves the Spa Valley Railway that links Groombridge with Tunbridge Wells West. It is not therefore possible to walk this part of the Three Bridges-Tunbridge Wells line, which crosses the border into Kent near High Rocks Station, the only intermediate station on the Spa Valley Railway. Since scheduled British Rail services only ceased to run between Groombridge and Tunbridge Wells in July 1985, many readers may recall travelling on the line before closure. The section between Tunbridge Wells West and Tunbridge Wells Central, as far as the point where it joins the line coming from Hastings, has fallen into disuse but since it is wholly within the county of Kent it is outside the scope of this book.

Although Groombridge Station brings your walk along the course of the old Three Bridges to Tunbridge Wells line to an end, it provides a base for exploration of the small section of disused railway from Groombridge towards Eridge. Return to Station Road via the old station and the steps, and turn left to cross over the railway, then proceed uphill along the road, reaching a right fork after a few hundred yards with a signpost for Eridge. Fork right here into Eridge Road, and shortly you will see a driveway with footpath sign leading off to your right. This is the approach road for Harrisons Rocks, which like High Rocks is a grouping of impressive rocky outcrops in attractive wooded countryside. Look out almost immediately for a path leading off to your left with a signpost for the High Weald Landscape Trail, and follow this path downhill through woodland to the valley bottom. Still following the High Weald Landscape Trail, bear left and head southwards. You now have the old Groombridge to Eridge line for company immediately to your right, and you can continue to walk alongside it while enjoying the view to Harrisons Rocks to your left. Keep walking beside the line - surely one of the most scenic stretches of country railway in Southern England - until it reaches its junction with the surviving Victoria-Uckfield line. At the time of writing there was a large gate across the old line, clearly visible from the path, just before the junction. From here you have a choice. You could go forward along the path to Forge Farm, turning right past the farm buildings and a lovely waterfall and crossing the Victoria-Uckfield line to reach Forge Road and, turning left here, proceed to Eridge Station which lies about a mile away. Alternatively, you could simply retrace your steps to Groombridge.

Instead of the walk from Groombridge described above, there is another possibility that may occur to you, which is to attempt to walk along the currently disused line between Groombridge Station and the gate at the junction with the surviving Uckfield line. The trackbed and tracks are still in place, and there are even one or two trucks on the line for added interest. I can only say that if you do attempt this, you do so at your own risk. It was made clear to me by the Spa Valley line ticket clerk at Groombridge Station that there is no public right to walk along the track, and you should expect to be challenged if you were seen to be attempting to do so. Moreover, it is likely that the Spa Valley line will be extended along this entire section in the not too distant future. If you are really longing to walk this lovely piece of line legitimately, you might consider becoming a volunteer helper for the Spa Valley Railway; the company is keen to attract more volunteers!

SECTION 2 - **LEWES TO EAST GRINSTEAD / HAYWARDS HEATH TO HORSTED KEYNES**

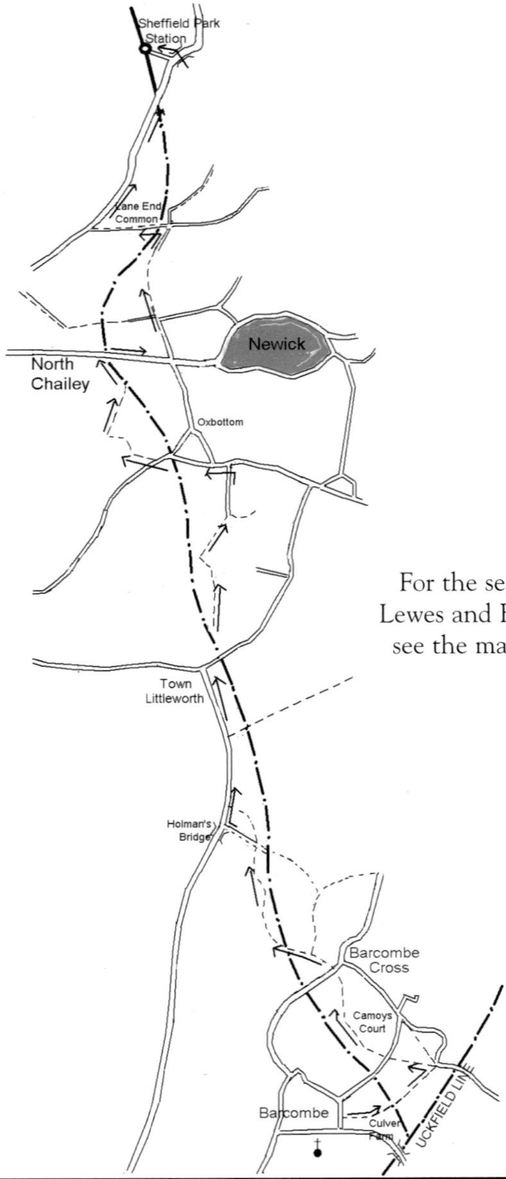

Sheffield Park
Station

Fane End
Common

Newick

North
Chailey

Oxbottom

For the section between
Lewes and Barcombe please
see the map on page 122.

Town
Littleworth

Holman's
Bridge

Barcombe
Cross

Camoys
Court

Barcombe

Culver
Farm

UCKFIELD LINE

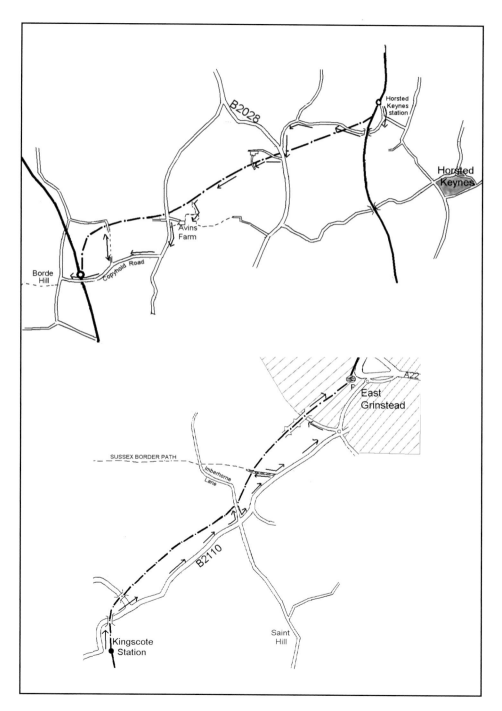

SECTION 2 - LEWES TO EAST GRINSTEAD / HAYWARDS HEATH TO HORSTED KEYNES

Distance:	Approximately 11 miles of walking in total.
Start:	Lewes railway station.
Finish:	East Grinstead railway station.
Public Transport:	Regular trains to Lewes from London Victoria, Brighton, Seaford, Eastbourne and Hastings. Trains from East Grinstead to East Croydon and London Victoria.
Conditions:	Sadly very little of the Lewes to East Grinstead line is available for walkers and much of the walk consists of frustrating road and footpath walking close to the route. There is however an excellent section of the Haywards Heath to Horsted Keynes line that is available to be walked. None of the available sections follow designated rights of way, save one tiny section on the Haywards Heath branch.
Refreshments:	Pubs, cafes and shops at Lewes; shop and pub at Barcombe Cross; refreshments available at Sheffield Park station; pub, café and shop at Ardingly; café at Borde Hill Gardens; pubs, cafes and shops at East Grinstead. RECOMMENDED PUBS: LEWES - BREWER'S ARMS, 91 High Street - Harvey's Best (brewed in town), real ales and real ciders; SHEFFIELD PARK - BESSEMER ARMS(on station platform) - good beer; ARDINGLY - OAK - good reasonably priced menu, magnificent old fireplace; HORSTED KEYNES - CROWN - comfortable congenial "local" on the green.

History

It was in 1877 that Parliamentary approval was given to construct a rail link between the two important Sussex towns of Lewes and East Grinstead, using part of the Lewes to Uckfield line (fully described in a separate chapter in this book) which had opened nineteen years previously. A company known as the Lewes & East Grinstead Railway Company, formed in 1875, had masterminded the plans for the new route, and once Royal assent was given, the LBSCR took it over and oversaw the construction of the line which opened in August 1882. Meanwhile, in July 1880, the LBSCR obtained permission to open a link line between Horsted Keynes, on the new Lewes to East Grinstead line, and Haywards Heath on the main London to Brighton line. This opened in 1883.

The Lewes to East Grinstead line followed the course of the Lewes to Uckfield line as far as Culver Farm, just short of Barcombe station; the point at which the "new" line left the Uckfield line was known unsurprisingly as Culver Junction. The first station on the East Grinstead branch was opened a mile or so north of Culver Junction at the village of Barcombe Cross and known as New Barcombe, but then changed to Barcombe, while Barcombe station further up the Uckfield line became Barcombe Mills! A pleasant cross-country journey through a very sparsely-populated area brought the line to its next halt, Newick & Chailey, and thence to Fletching & Sheffield Park although the station was renamed simply Sheffield Park just a year after opening. Beyond Sheffield Park, as Bluebell Railway enthusiasts will know, came Horsted Keynes. This was a remarkable station; it was the junction for trains to and from Haywards Heath, and was well-appointed and sizeable with a sturdy red-brick station building and platforms that benefited from canopies. Yet save for the small nearby village of the same name, there was no apparent source of passenger traffic. Beyond Horsted Keynes was West Hoathly, these two stations being separated by the 731-yard West Hoathly Tunnel. After West Hoathly the line descended to Kingscote, and just over a mile beyond that, East Grinstead was reached. Immediately before East Grinstead there was arguably the most impressive feature of the old line, namely the ten-arch red-brick Imberhorne Viaduct, and even today, surrounded by modern housing, this magnificent feat of engineering dominates the landscape. The only station on the link line to Haywards Heath from Horsted Keynes was at Ardingly, and thankfully the station building still survives. Interestingly this branch was electrified in July 1935 but the intervention of the Second World War caused electrification of the line to East Grinstead to be put on hold, and, steam trans continued to ply the East Grinstead line right up until closure.

The Lewes to East Grinstead line soon became extremely popular. By the beginning of the 20th century some twenty trains worked the line each day, carrying not only passengers but freight which included fruit, corn and milk. However traffic began to decline as the 20th century progressed, and it was decided to close the Lewes to East Grinstead line on 17th June 1955. The closure provoked a good deal of protest, and much to British Railways' embarrassment it was found that closure could only be brought about by Parliamentary authority, and not by the unilateral say-so of the railway company. The line therefore re-opened in 1956. During the brief period of its revival it was known as the "sulky service," with trains run during the middle of the day when they would have been of little use to anybody, and not stopping at certain stations that were not mentioned in the Act. This farcical situation could not continue indefinitely, and in due course a fresh Act of Parliament enabled the line to close legally in March 1958 although the line north of Horsted Keynes remained open on a "care and maintenance" basis for two more years. However, in 1960 a society for the preservation of the railway was formed, and the result was one of the best-loved preserved railways in the country Known as the Bluebell Railway, it initially ran trains between Sheffield Park and Horsted Keynes but subsequently was able to extend to Kingscote and it is hoped to continue right into East Grinstead to link with the main rail network. The link between Horsted Keynes and Haywards Heath survived until October 1963. It is hoped that this might also be restored and there has even been talk of electrifying it again!

Walking The Railway

This is a curious walk in that it is interrupted by the preserved section of Bluebell Railway, and obviously access to this is strictly forbidden for walkers. It is recommended that you spread your walk over two days, and take care to coincide it with the days the Bluebell Railway is running. On day one, you could walk from Lewes to Sheffield Park, where on Bluebell Railway operating days buses are available to Haywards Heath. On day two, you can return to Sheffield Park and take the morning train to Horsted Keynes, walk to Copyhold Junction (where the Haywards Heath branch met the main line), return to Horsted Keynes and pick up an afternoon train to Kingscote, from where it is a short walk to East Grinstead.

The section between Lewes and Culver Junction is fully described in the chapter devoted to the Lewes to Uckfield line. That chapter refers to the green embankment coming in from your right just north-east of Culver Farm; this is the southernmost part of the East Grinstead line following its branching off at Culver Junction. You can follow the embankment almost all the way back to where it left the Uckfield line, the course of which is very obvious. But annoyingly, once you have returned to the point where you joined it, further access northwards is impossible and you will need to continue along the course of the Lewes to Uckfield walk towards the road at Barcombe Mills, climbing through the field on the approach to the road. However, before you reach the road a signed footpath goes off hard left, at quite an acute angle - racing drivers might call it a hairpin bend - and drops down to a metalled road. Turn left on to the road and very soon you arrive at an elegant red-brick bridge with the old line going underneath. There is no possibility of access to the old line here - although you can see most of its course from the point where you had to leave it earlier - so proceed along the road and in a hundred yards or so you reach a signed footpath going off to the right. Turn right on to the path and follow it as directed across the field, entering a strip of woodland and descending quite steeply to arrive on the old line. It is possible to follow the old line back to the elegant bridge, in the shade of cuttings that are quite thick with vegetation, but you are unable to go under the bridge. Return to the point at which you joined the old line and you are now able to proceed along the old line for a few hundred yards towards Barcombe Cross. Sadly further progress becomes impossible, the crude path along the course of the old line veering left and downhill to a footbridge over a stream. You need to bear right, over a stile, to rejoin the official right of way that now proceeds across fields to the village of Barcombe Cross. When you reach the main village street, turn left and proceed down towards another fine railway bridge; the course of the old line coming up from the south is obvious but the line itself is inaccessible. Just before the bridge, turn right down a cul-de-sac and you will soon reach the old Barcombe station building. It has been beautifully restored and maintained, but is strictly private. The old line too is inaccessible hereabouts and you will need to return to the village centre to progress.

Go back up the village street - there is a pub and a general store on the right-hand side of the road - and turn left into the narrow Grange

The fine Imberhorne viaduct on the Lewes to East Grinstead line.

Road, which is virtually opposite the village general store. Follow Grange Road which emerges on to the village recreation ground, and continue in the same direction on the grass, now proceeding downhill. Shortly you hit a footpath which is also a scrambling track, and still in the same direction you drop quite steeply to cross a narrow stream. The path now bends slightly left and proceeds gently uphill through an open field to arrive back at the old line. Access to the old line to the left, back towards Barcombe station, is impossible, although you can readily see the nature of the surrounding terrain from the adjacent field. However at this point you can get on to the old line to proceed northwards towards Newick. There is a good path that follows the old line for a few hundred yards - a line of pylons also marks the course of the old line! - but sadly the path swings away from the line to the left, and further progress along the line is impossible. Keep to the path which continues north-westwards and passes just to the left of a sewage works. Proceed past the works and on into the next field from which it is possible to detour right and gain access to about 200 yards of old line, part in a northerly and part in a southerly direction, but the thickness of the vegetation will sadly beat you back and you are forced to return to the access point without being able to progress. Go back to the point where you began your detour and now head westwards to pick up the Barcombe Cross-Newick road at Harelands Farm. Turn right on to the road and follow it for just over half a mile to a T-junction.

Bear right at the T-junction, meeting the old line almost immediately; access to the line is, however, impossible, so just a few yards beyond, turn left on to a signed footpath known as Cockfield Lane. This proceeds most pleasantly northwards, offering good views to the embankment carrying the old line. To begin with the path runs parallel with the embankment then veers away from it, heading northwards. A gentle climb brings you to a crossroads of paths; turning left here brings you to a bridge over the old line, but again the line is inaccessible. Return to the main path and follow it downhill to a delightful river crossing, the footbridge known as Cockfield Bridge, then continue uphill to reach a metalled road. Turn left on to this road and follow it for roughly a quarter of a mile to a T-junction with the Chailey-Newick road. Again turn left and immediately you find yourself looking down on the old line again, both to the north and the south; sadly it is still impossible to get on to it in either direction! It is necessary to follow the road briefly south-westwards towards Chailey, but after about a hundred yards turn right on to a signed footpath which proceeds through a field and into a wooded area, arriving at a crossroads of paths as the trees are reached. Turn right on to the path which almost immediately bends sharp left, and heads just north of west towards the buildings of the picturesquely-named Vixengrove Farm. There is an open field to the right, inclining quite steeply downhill. Just before the buildings, you re-enter woodland and very shortly turn right on to a signed and well-defined footpath which heads north-eastwards and drops downhill through woodland. It is lovely walking, even though there is no old railway in sight! The path exits from the woodland briefly by means of a stile but continues to run parallel with the woodland edge, heading in the same direction, and another stile further down the hill returns you to the wood. An excellent path provides good walking on through the wood, which is particularly attractive in the spring with its profusion of bluebells. The path, having followed a straight line for a few hundred yards, now bends from north-eastwards to north-westwards, and follows just to the left of the backs of houses. At the bend you at last pick up the old line again; it is possible to make out the embankment and its course through what is now the back gardens of the houses. You continue immediately parallel with the course of the old line and arrive at the A272.

Once again you are forced to leave the course of the old line here, and indeed you will see precious little more of it until you reach Sheffield Park. Turn right on to the A272 and follow it for just over a quarter of a mile - fortunately there is a pavement! - then take the first road turning on the left. Follow the road just west of north to a ninety-degree bend then leave the road and join a path heading in the same direction as you have just been following, ie just west of north. The path is a well-defined bridleway that drops to a stream then ascends through woodland that forms part of Fletching

Common and having passed some buildings arrives at the Newick-Fletching Common road. Turn left and almost immediately you will cross the old line again, as disappointingly impenetrable as ever! Now follow the road for roughly a quarter of a mile westwards to the junction with the A275, and turn right to follow the A275 north-eastwards to Sheffield Park station. (It is possible to take a short cut across Fletching Common from the old line crossing referred to just now to a point a little north of the road junction with the A275, but the amount of time saved is negligible.) The walk alongside the A275 is just over a mile and is frustrating, there being no pavement but a great deal of traffic. Eventually, however, you see the old line coming in from the right (south) and can actually detour on to the embankment to view it, although there is no means of making progress southwards along it. Return to the roadside, and shortly turn left along the station approach road to Sheffield Park station. A charge is made for viewing the platforms as well as travel on the trains, but having bought your platform ticket you can easily see the course of the old line immediately south of the station to the A275 crossing.

Sheffield Park station, being the principal joining point for the Bluebell Railway, is a fascinating place for connoisseurs of old railways, and offers refreshments for weary walkers as well as would-be passengers. Assuming you are incorporating a ride on the railway into your itinerary, you need to catch a train initially to Horsted Keynes. If you have chosen a day when neither trains nor connecting buses are running, you will somehow have to find your way to Horsted Keynes station by other means; the shortest road route is along the A275 north-eastwards to Sheffield Green and then westwards via Ketche's Lane and northwards via Treemans Road. But it really is not to be recommended.

Alighting from Horsted Keynes, follow the station approach road to the first road junction and turn right to follow the road that soon passes underneath the Bluebell Railway. The road bends to the right and almost immediately beyond the bend you can see clearly to your left the embankment of the old line that formed the branch between Horsted Keynes and Haywards Heath. The continuation to your right, linking up with the Bluebell Railway at Horsted Keynes a few hundred yards away, is a lot less easy to make out amongst the thick vegetation. Follow the road on past Lower Sheriff Farm to a T-junction with Hammingden Lane, turning left and walking up to another road junction with the busy B2028 Haywards Heath-Ardingly road. Turn left on to this road and in about 100 yards turn left along a signed footpath which takes you past a private house and on into a yard. Aim for the right-hand corner of the yard as you enter it, to join a path which descends quite steeply through a wooded area, and which after wet weather can be extremely muddy. However at the bottom of the incline you arrive on the course of the old line, and although it is not a designated right of way it can be walked. You can first turn right on to the old line to head back towards Horsted Keynes; although the walking is not very interesting - there are no views to speak of - it is still pleasant, and you are able to go right back to the road coming down from

Horsted Keynes station. Retrace your steps but this time continue on along the old line, soon passing through an impressive road tunnel. At the time of writing this was perfectly safe (though it is always advisable, in case of doubt, to seek the owner's permission to pass through it) but do take care as it is quite dark in the middle of the tunnel and you may get wet from water dropping from the top of the tunnel to the ground below. As so many disused railway tunnels are boarded up, even on lines that are generally open to walkers, it is a great thrill to go through this one.

You emerge from the tunnel and continue. The going soon becomes exceedingly muddy but fortunately conditions underfoot quickly improve and you can enjoy a very easy and pleasant woodland walk along the old line, interrupted only by a collapsed bridge where you have to descend steeply to the track below and then climb steps to return to the course of the line. For less than a quarter of a mile beyond the bridge you are now on what is a permissive footpath where access is officially allowed, but all too soon you are instructed by a signboard to leave the old line using the next flight of steps going down to your left. Although it is necessary to descend these steps to progress further, you can in fact detour on along the old line for some distance until your way is barred at an overbridge crossing. With some regret, return to the steps and descend them, then follow the path. Shortly you reach a junction of footpaths; take the path signposted to the right, which leads round Avins Farm and forward to the Haywards Heath-Ardingly road. By turning right and following the road briefly you will arrive at the superbly-preserved old Ardingly station, the only station on the Horsted Keynes-Haywards Heath branch. You can see the old line either side of the road here, but the line itself is inaccessible.

Sadly there is no more walking available on the Haywards Heath branch. However you can get two further glimpses of it as you proceed towards Haywards Heath. Follow the Haywards Heath-Ardingly road southwards, back past Avins Farm, and in just under half a mile turn right into Copyhold Lane, with a signpost for the Borde Hill Gardens. Another half-mile walk along this road brings you to a signed footpath leading off to the right, and this clearly-defined path takes you to River's Farm where there is a bridge over the old line. There is no access to the old line but, most unusually for a disused railway in Sussex, the single track remains and the trackbed is completely uncluttered. It would indeed be grand to think that trains might once more ply this route! Return to Copyhold Lane and follow it on, south-westwards, to reach a bridge over the main London to Brighton line. You can see the old line running parallel with it and then, north of the bridge at what is known as Copyhold Junction, branching off towards Ardingly. One wonders how many regular users of what is one of the busiest stretches of railway line in the South are aware of this little branch line leaving the main line here. That is the end of your walk along the Haywards Heath branch, although garden enthusiasts may want to continue the short distance to the splendid Borde Hill Gardens, easily reached by walking beyond the bridge to the T-junction and turning left; the gardens are a short walk along the road on the right, and thirsty walkers may

A delightful section of the Horsted Keynes to Haywards Heath branch near Ardingly.

welcome the refreshment facilities offered in the garden complex when it is open. If you follow this road beyond the gardens you will reach Haywards Heath in just over a mile.

The final section of disused railway walking begins at Kingscote, just over a mile from East Grinstead. If the Bluebell Railway is operational, it is suggested you return to Horsted Keynes by the same route used to get to Copyhold Junction - omitting, obviously, the detours! You can then enjoy the Bluebell Railway as it passes via West Hoathly to Kingscote, where for now the trains terminate. If there is no Bluebell Railway service running your best option is to walk on from Copyhold Junction past Borde Hill Gardens to Haywards Heath and then use public transport to East Grinstead, walking from East Grinstead to Kingscote via the B2110.

Unfortunately, none of the old line whatsoever is available to walkers between Kingscote and East Grinstead. Leaving the immaculately-kept station at Kingscote by the front entrance, turn right on to the road and follow it under the railway, going forward to a T-junction with the B2110. Here you could detour left to see the fine bridge taken by the old line across that road, but otherwise turn right and follow the B2110. The surrounding countryside is pleasant enough but the road is very busy and there is no pavement. Just over half a mile after joining the B2110 you reach a crossroads, and a detour left along Imberhorne Lane offers, very shortly, another opportunity to view the old line as it passes under the lane. Return to the B2110 and follow it north-eastwards, initially uphill and then downhill. There is at least a pavement provided beyond the junction with Imberhorne Lane. Look out, in a quarter of a mile, for a signed footpath going off to the left, and follow this path to another bridge over the old line. Continue on beyond the bridge and almost immediately turn right to follow the right-hand edge of the field which descends to and then runs parallel with the old line. Please note that there is no designated right of way through this field. Your way forward is soon halted by woodland, but by turning right at the edge of the wood you are able (although you have no designated right of way) to pass back to the south-eastern side of the old line and look up to admire the quite magnificent redbrick Imberhorne Viaduct, one of the finest pieces of railway engineering of any disused line in Sussex. From here you can see the old line as it proceeds into the suburbs of East Grinstead. Disappointingly there is no way forward to the town centre from here and it is necessary to retrace your steps all the way back to the B2110. Follow the B2110 downhill to the roundabout, at which you turn left and then immediately left again along Garden Wood Road that soon passes underneath the viaduct. As soon as you have passed under the viaduct turn right on to a concrete path that goes steeply uphill, rising to the level of the old line and then above it, so you can actually look down on the old line as it crosses the viaduct. There is no access to the old line but you stay parallel with it. Shortly the old line is seen to reach East Grinstead station and the existing London line. The path skirts the right-hand edge of the station car park and arrives at a footbridge over the railway, which you can use to gain access to the existing station. The chapter devoted to the Three Bridges-Groombridge line gives directions to the town centre from here.

SECTION 2 - **SHOREHAM TO CHRIST'S HOSPITAL / CHRIST'S HOSPITAL TO SHALFORD**

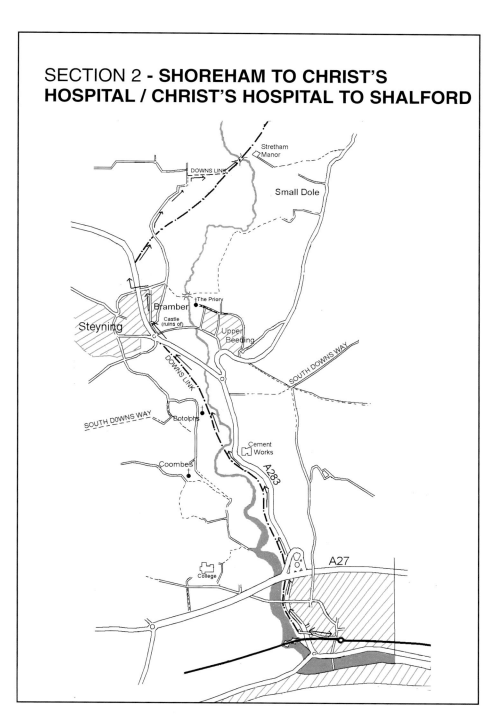

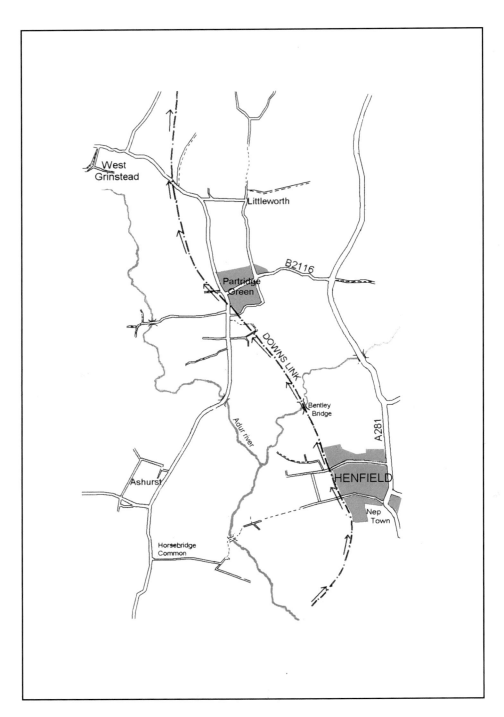

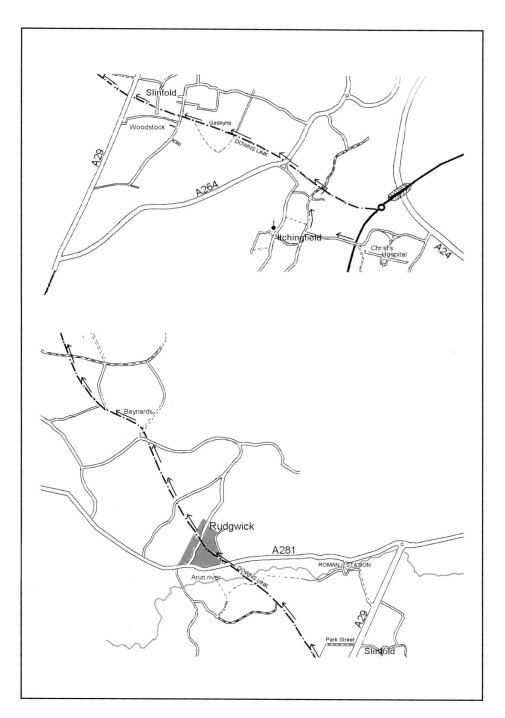

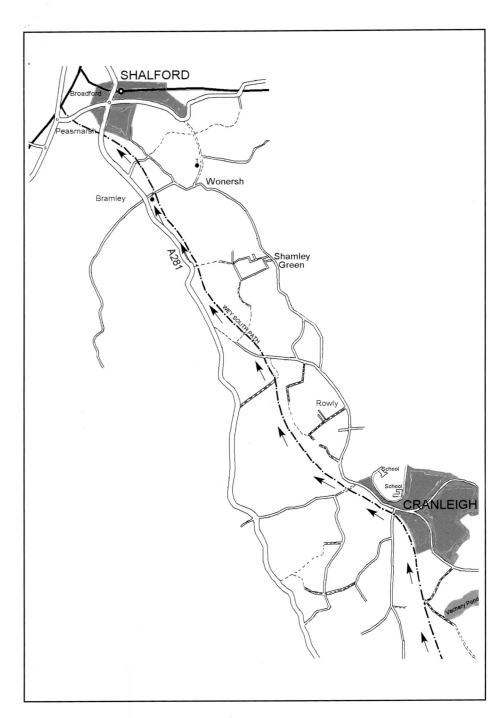

SHALFORD

Broadford

Peasmarsh

Bramley

Wonersh

A281

Shamley
Green

WEY SOUTH PATH

Rowly

School

School

CRANLEIGH

Vachery Pond

SECTION 2 - **SHOREHAM TO CHRIST'S HOSP'**
CHRIST'S HOSPITAL TO SHALFORD

Distance:	32 miles.
Start:	Shoreham railway station.
Finish:	Shalford railway station.
Public Transport:	Regular trains to Shoreham from Brighton, Hove and London Victoria to the east, and Worthing, Chichester and Portsmouth to the west. Regular trains also serve Christ's Hospital about halfway along the walk. Regular trains from Shalford to Guildford and Redhill.
Conditions:	For most of your route you are able to follow the Downs Link footpath which overlaps with large sections of the disused railway lines linking Shoreham with Christ's Hospital, and Christ's Hospital with Shalford. The signposting is excellent and the terrain very friendly not only for walkers but also cyclists and push-chairs.
Refreshments:	Shops, pubs and cafes at Shoreham; shops, pubs and cafes at Steyning; shops, pubs and cafes at Henfield; shop and pub at Partridge Green; café at West Grinstead; pub at Copsale; shops, pub and café at Southwater; shop and pub at Slinfold; shops and pub at Rudgwick; pub at Baynards; shops, pubs and cafes at Cranleigh; shops and pubs at Bramley; shops and pubs at Shalford. RECOMMENDED PUBS: SHOREHAM - MARLIPINS - good choice of bar food and well-kept beers; STEYNING - CHEQUER - timber-framed Tudor pub with good range of beers and wide choice of food; PARTRIDGE GREEN - GREEN MAN - good, well-presented food with Mediterranean influence; RUDGWICK - BLUE SHIP - small, unspoilt pub with traditional ales and inglenook fireplace; BAYNARDS - THURLOW ARMS - traditional bar snacks, fresh fish, pub's own-brewed beer.

History

The walk described in this chapter, although being reasonably faithful to the Downs Link throughout, in fact incorporates two completely separate lines with separate histories. It was in the mid-1850's that real interest was shown in constructing a through rail route between Shoreham and Horsham via Steyning, and two separate railway companies, the LBSCR and SHDR(Shoreham, Horsham and Dorking Railway) put in rival bids to build the route. The LBSCR route was authorised in July 1858 and opened in September 1861, linking Shoreham with Itchingfield Junction just to the south-west of Christ's Hospital where the route joined with the so-called Arun Valley line linking Horsham with Pulborough and subsequently Arundel. The line between Christ's Hospital and Guildford was authorised in August 1860 to be built by a company called the Horsham and Guildford Direct Railway , but the LBSCR took over the line in 1864 following the bankruptcy of the contractor, and it was not until October 1865 that services finally commenced.

The Shoreham to Christ's Hospital section was initially provided with five trains each way, most of them starting or finishing at Brighton, using the section of line linking Brighton and Shoreham that still exists today. Gradually the service increased to eleven journeys in each direction, with a much reduced service on Sundays. The summer 1948 timetable shows eleven trains starting at Brighton and working the line, although the last of these, the 9.57 from Brighton, terminated at Steyning. The first station stop out of Shoreham was Bramber, followed by Steyning, Henfield, Partridge Green, West Grinstead, Southwater and Christ's Hospital, with all trains going forward from Christ's Hospital to Horsham using the stretch of line between Horsham and Christ's Hospital on the London-Arundel line that still exists today. Train times between Shoreham and Christ's Hospital in 1948 were about forty-five minutes: the 9.44, for instance, got into Christ's Hospital at 10.26 and the 4.12 from Shoreham reached Christ's Hospital at 4.54.

The service between Christ's Hospital and Guildford consisted initially of four trains each way every weekday, although this had doubled to eight by 1948. All trains in fact originated at Horsham and then branched off at Christ's Hospital, the first station beyond which was Slinfold, followed by Rudgwick, Baynards, Cranleigh, Bramley & Wonersh, and Guildford. Just beyond Bramley & Wonersh, on the edge of the village of Shalford, the line joined the still-extant London-Portsmouth line for the remaining miles to Guildford. Bramley & Wonersh was the scene of the line's worst tragedy, on 16th December 1942, when a two-coach train carrying Christmas shoppers was strafed by a German Dornier 217 and as a result seven people were killed including the guard and the driver. The station at Rudgwick was particularly unusual: it was built on a gradient of 1 in 80 but the Board of Trade would not allow trains to stop on this incline. To achieve the prescribed 1 in 130 gradient the engineers had to raise the embankments and also the crossing of the river Arun, and this resulted in the construction of a girder bridge over the original brick arch, creating effectively a double bridge. Baynards was splendidly rural in character and was used as the setting

Full steam ahead - looking south on the Shoreham to Christ's Hospital line near Partridge Green.

for a 1950's dramatisation of the film *The Railway Children*; Baynards Tunnel, stretching for 381 yards, was also the "summit" of the line, at 250ft above sea level. Journey times for the 17 mile journey from Guildford to Christ's Hospital were very similar for the journey from Shoreham to the same destination. According to the 1948 timetable, it was theoretically possible to get a reasonable connection at Christ's Hospital if you had in mind a journey from Guildford to the coast; leaving Guildford at 10.34 you could arrive at Christ's Hospital at 11.15 and then have to wait only 8 minutes for a Shoreham-bound train. But if you missed the 10.34 the next did not leave Guildford until 1.42 and with an hour's wait at Christ's Hospital you would not make it to Shoreham until nine minutes past four!

Both lines were victims of the Beeching axe. Most freight services were withdrawn in 1962/63, and the final passenger services ran on the Guildford portion in June 1965 and the Shoreham section in March 1966. Although attempts have been made to restore sections of the line following closure, these have come to nothing. However, by way of compensation, both old lines are available for walking for virtually their entire lengths.

Walking The Railway

From Shoreham station cross straight over Brunswick Road into Hebe Road and follow this to its junction with Victoria Road. Cross straight over into Swiss Gardens and then turn second left into Freehold Street, going forward to a T-junction with Old Shoreham Road, just north of the point where the existing Brighton-Worthing line crosses Old Shoreham Road. Turn right into Old Shoreham Road, cross over and follow the road north-westwards past a row of houses, then beyond the houses turn left to gain access to the old line. Although your route along the old line will proceed northwards towards the massive A27 flyover, it is possible to follow the old line almost all the way back to the point at which it left the still extant Brighton-Worthing line. Assuming you wish to do this, turn left on to the old line, and follow it southwards; even though it is right of way throughout, it becomes less well defined and eventually reaches a dead end, but at least from the dead end you can see exactly where and how the Christ's Hospital line branched off from the Worthing line. Return to where you joined the old line, and now proceed northwards along the course of the old line with confidence. Immediately to your left is the Adur estuary, with views across to the magnificent Lancing College chapel, while ahead of you is the A27 flyover, and although some might regard this as an eyesore it is a magnificent piece of road engineering nonetheless. Follow the old line under the flyover, now leaving the buildings of Shoreham behind, and continue on through pleasant but unspectacular countryside to the old Beeding cement works. You arrive at the river and although you can clearly see the course of the old line across the river, you are now forced away from the old line, the bridge crossing having ceased to exist. Follow the right bank of the river upstream, and after a few hundred yards cross the river by the bridge. You are now on the South Downs Way and your arrival here signifies the start of the Downs Link, a waymarked footpath linking the South Downs Way and North Downs Way national trails. Your route will follow the Downs Link for almost all of its course. Having crossed the bridge, continue briefly up the left bank but soon arrive at a junction of paths, where you turn left to follow the South Downs Way away from the river. The picturesque church of Botolphs can be seen close by, and indeed the old line, the course of which you can clearly see coming in from the left, passed just to the east of it. Just before reaching the road beside which Botolphs Church is situated, you reach a junction of paths; you leave the South Downs Way here and turn right to rejoin the old line, using the Downs Link. You now follow the old line briefly, the Downs Link then taking you on to a path that runs parallel with it up to the A283. The old line then proceeded to follow a route round the edge of Bramber and Steyning using the same course that is now taken by the A283 Steyning bypass. The new road has obliterated all traces of the old line and there is no remnant of the old stations at Bramber or Steyning either. Cross this very busy road, bear left, and follow the Downs Link path that runs parallel with the road as far as the roundabout with roads leading off to Bramber (right) and Steyning (left).

The purist, wishing to remain faithful to the old line, could simply follow the A283, turning right at the footpath sign just beyond the second of two overbridges (Pick up the narrative at * below). However, there is no pavement and as cars pass along here at a tremendous speed, it can be quite dangerous. It is therefore suggested that from the roundabout you do not proceed along the A283, nor indeed turn right along the Street, but take the road between these two, Castle Lane, which initially runs immediately to the right(east)of the A283, and parallel with it. You continue along the Downs Link initially, staying on the same road which then swings in a more northerly direction and proceeds in a dead straight line (appropriately enough this stretch is called Roman Road!). The Downs Link turns right into King's Stone Avenue but I recommend that, in order to see another section of the old line that the Downs Link misses, and to give you the opportunity to visit Steyning, you continue all the way along Roman Road to the T-junction with Jarvis Lane. Turn left and cross over the A283 then take the first right into Cripps Lane and continue downhill to the magnificent parish church. (If you wish to visit the lovely town of Steyning, just carry on past the church into the town centre.) Immediately before the church turn right into Vicarage Lane and then bear right at the end of Vicarage Lane along a path. Follow this path very briefly, then where the path widens into a road, turn left along a path which brings you past an area of modern housing and a children's play area to the A283 again. Cross straight over this road* and descend the steps to follow a footpath that runs parallel with and to the right of the old railway embankment, carrying the old line towards Henfield. You soon arrive at a junction with a track; bear left here to continue along the path, heading northwards then swinging north-eastwards, crossing a footbridge and then proceeding through a field, heading uphill. Aim just to the right of the bridge where the old line passed underneath Kings Barn Lane, and go forward to reach the lane; now reunited with the Downs Link, you turn left into the lane and cross the bridge. Having crossed the bridge, you can detour down on to the old line and follow it briefly south-westwards back towards Steyning but are soon forced back on yourself and indeed the old line cannot be walked for the next mile or so. Return to the lane and follow it until you arrive at Wyckham Farm; turn right here, off the Downs Link, on to a signed footpath that takes you across a field to the old line, and when you reach the course of the old line, turn left on to a path that runs parallel with and to the left of it, heading north-eastwards. After a few hundred yards, you are reunited not only with the Downs Link but also the old line which you can now follow all the way to Christ's Hospital with only small breaks at Henfield, Partridge Green and Southwater. The going is now really enjoyable as you follow the old line to Henfield. The surrounding scenery is not spectacular but it is most attractive with beautiful meadows bordering the old line and fine views to the South Downs; there is one particularly scenic spot, at the point where the old line goes over the River Adur, with the beautiful grounds of Stretham Manor immediately beyond. Gradually the surroundings become more built up and you find yourself in the outskirts of Henfield. You are forced downhill off the course of the old line to arrive at Lower Station Road, and looking straight ahead, you can in fact see that the course of the old line is completely obliterated by new housing development. Turn right on to the road then, continuing to follow the Downs Link, turn left on to Station Road, following it uphill - noting a road named Beechings leading off to the left! - to a T-junction with Upper Station Road. A useful pub is situated just across the road here. To continue along the Downs Link, turn left and shortly right on to a signed Downs Link path that immediately takes

The splendidly restored station at West Grinstead on the Shoreham to Christ's Hospital line.

you back on to the old line, heading now for Partridge Green. However if you detour right at the T-junction by the pub, you can follow Upper Station Road, which leads into Church Street, which in turn brings you to the attractive centre of Henfield. There are ample amenities here including buses to Partridge Green and Horsham to the north, and Brighton to the south, and there are at least two cafes as well as shops and pubs.

Back on the old line beyond Upper Station Road, the walking is easy as you proceed from Henfield towards Partridge Green. Initially the path is in the shade of vegetation, but moves into open country and crosses the Adur once more at Betley Bridge. As you approach Partridge Green, a signpost points the Downs Link away from the old line, heading off to the left, but it is perfectly possible for you to remain on the old line for another couple of hundred yards (this is not a designated right of way) and then, when it is impossible to proceed further along the old line, you can turn left on to a signed footpath which snakes around to the left of an industrial estate and emerges by the Steyning-Partridge Green road. Turn right on to this road and then just before the bridge over the old line (the course of which to your right is obliterated by new development) follow the signed Downs Link path to the left to return to the old line. Partridge Green is just a few minutes' walk beyond the bridge crossing; there is a shop and a pub here, as well as a good bus service to Horsham and Brighton.

The going is now extremely easy all the way to Christ's Hospital, with only very minor deviations from the old line. The section between Partridge Green and West Grinstead is delightfully rural and unspoilt, with pleasant pasture on both sides and, as you approach West Grinstead, there is the very pretty Furzefield Wood to the right.

West Grinstead station, with its signal and station board, has been restored to look very much as it would have done when the old line was still functioning. There is easy access here to the A272, which goes over the old line here, and your reward for climbing up to the road is nearby refreshment availability at the handy Little Chef restaurant, just along the road to the right! Beyond West Grinstead the surroundings remain very rural and attractive, with rather more woodland than previously; it is necessary to drop down to the road at Copsale, where the bridge over the road no longer exists, but there is the compensation of a lineside pub. Returning to the line, you then enjoy a quite beautiful stretch which is best seen in the spring when the surrounding woodland is crammed with bluebells and wild garlic. Slight anticlimax follows with the negotiation of the A24, a modern underpass taking you very briefly away from the old line, and then a section with a more suburban feel as you proceed into Southwater, effectively a dormitory of Horsham. As you arrive at Southwater Country Park, a pleasant rather than an outstandingly attractive amenity, you again have to drop down to a road crossing where a bridge once was, and there is quite a scramble up the other side. You continue past modern development to reach the old station platform at Southwater, but immediately before the platform there is easy access to Southwater's modern shopping precinct. This does contain a useful café although at the time of writing it was shutting quite early in the afternoon on weekdays and at midday on Saturdays.

Though some OS maps show the Downs Link as leaving the old line hereabouts, a right of way does exist along the course of the old line as it proceeds on to Christ's Hospital; changes of land use do however mean that it is almost impossible at times to guess that you are following an old railway line until you are some way out of Southwater. It is good to return to "normal" railway walking, but almost too soon you will be aware of the existing Arundel-Horsham line coming in from the left. The Downs Link stays faithful to the old line right up to Itchingfield Junction, the point at which the old and existing lines met, and then runs parallel with the existing line to the road bridge crossing just a few hundred yards short of Christ's Hospital Station. The Downs Link, and your route, turns left on to the road and crosses the railway using the bridge; to get to the station, simply turn right on to the road and proceed along it, passing the buildings of Christ's Hospital School. The road bends right, but by continuing straight on along a more minor road you arrive at the station buildings, with hourly trains to Horsham and London in one direction and to Arundel and Chichester in the other. This then completes the Shoreham-Christ's Hospital line. Assuming you are not attempting the whole walk in one day this may be an appropriate point at which to break your journey.

To continue on along the Christ's Hospital-Guildford line, follow the road just north of west beyond the bridge until you reach a T-junction of roads in the vicinity of Itchingfield. Turn right here and follow the road past Weston's Farm, shortly beyond which the road bends sharp left. Turn right here on to a narrow road, continuing along the Downs Link, and head towards the bridge crossing of the old line. Just before the road bridge crossing, there is a gated track leading off to the right. If you are fortunate and the gate is open, you can follow this track which will allow you to see some sections of the old line that ran from Christ's Hospital to this point, although virtually none of these sections themselves are accessible. Initially the track runs parallel with the old line, then after a few hundred yards swings left, crosses the course of the old line and then goes away from it, although you can continue walking through the field on the south side of the old line. As you walk through the field, you will see that the vegetation under which most of this stretch of old line is submerged does relent to enable you to inspect and walk a few paces of the old line, and by passing to the north side of the old line you can clearly see the course taken by the old line from Christ's Hospital. Further progress back towards Christ's Hospital is impracticable and you will need to retrace your steps to the road bridge. Now cross over the bridge; beyond it, turn left along a signed Downs Link path that soon reunites you with the old line and enables you to proceed on towards Slinfold.

It is now plain sailing for several miles, as you continue along or immediately adjacent to the old line by means of an excellent well-signposted path via Slinfold and Rudgwick to Baynards Tunnel. Initially the surroundings are pleasantly rural, but even when after a mile and a half you pass the housing and industrial development of Slinfold the walking remains agreeable and very easy. The old line passes a little to the south of the centre of Slinfold but there is straightforward road access to the village. The section between Slinfold and Rudgwick is in my opinion the most beautiful of the entire walk, passing lovely unspoilt woodland interspersed with fine stretches of open pasture, and including a most impressive crossing of the river Arun. It is disused railway walking at its very best. Sadly the timeless atmosphere is broken with the crossing of the busy A281, beyond which the surroundings become more suburban as you approach Rudgwick. The large overbridge you reach a few hundred yards beyond the A281 carries the village street. There is very easy access to Rudgwick from the old line: look out for the Medical Centre car park to your right just beyond the overbridge, and follow the road leading from the car park up to the village street. There are two convenience stores very close by.

Immediately beyond Rudgwick the walking is predominantly wooded and initially straightforward, but soon the marked Downs Link path is seen to fork left and go steeply uphill. The purpose of this detour from the old line is to get round Baynards Tunnel. It is possible to follow the old line to the southern mouth of the tunnel, but the tunnel itself is firmly boarded up so you will have to go back and follow the Downs Link. It is quite a shock to have such a steep climb, but the woodland walking is delightful and the reward is a lovely view to the surrounding countryside as the woodland relents. Once on the hilltop, you pass a signpost marking the border of Sussex and Surrey, and are given the choice between Downs Link footpath and bridleway route; the footpath route, which it will be assumed you wish to follow, is signposted left into the woodland, and then shortly right. You emerge into an open area of long grass between two areas of woodland, and now have the course of the old line for company immediately to your left, it having emerged from the tunnel. Shortly your path goes under a bridge, and proceeds easily to a road crossing, immediately beyond which are forbidding gates; turn left on to the road and then very shortly right, following the Downs Link route. The reason for this little diversion is to get round Baynards Station, which is privately owned and not open to the public. However as you pass you will enjoy excellent views to the station, named after the nearby Baynards Park; it is splendidly preserved, its buildings and advertising hoardings looking very much as they would have done when the line was last operational in June 1965, and the gardens on the platform, at the time of my visit, were quite beautifully kept. In a way it is frustrating not to be allowed entry, but those disappointed at being denied access can console themselves with the thought that there is a welcoming pub immediately adjacent!

The next three and a half miles to Cranleigh along the Downs Link are very straightforward and wholly faithful to the old line. Though the beautiful woodland around Rudgwick has been left behind, the countryside remains unspoilt and attractive, with pleasant wooded walking in Lodge Copse, some particularly fine parkland in the vicinity of Vachery House and Vachery Pond, and an impressive backdrop of wooded hills visible to your right. A build-up of housing on one side and playing fields on the other signifies your approach to Cranleigh, and beyond the playing fields you arrive at Knowle Lane, the first road crossing since Baynards. By turning right into Knowle Lane and following it for a hundred yards or so you reach Cranleigh's charming main street; it boasts a number of attractive houses and a good range of shops and eateries, and there are regular buses to Guildford and Horsham.

Returning down Knowle Lane to rejoin the Downs Link, you will find that progress on to Bramley along the old line is just as straightforward as it was to here from Baynards, and you have the pleasant prospect of just under 5 miles' very easy walking. It takes a while, as you might expect, to escape from the built-up area on the western outskirts of Cranleigh, but having done so you will enjoy a very pretty walk indeed, enlivened not only by the variety of scenery but by the proximity of the Wey & Arun Junction Canal, a reminder that the old railway is not the only defunct form of communication in this part of Surrey. Beside the path there was, at the time of writing, a useful notice board giving information about the canal. It is ironic that the one thing that spoils the final mile and a half or so into Bramley is the incessant noise of traffic from the A281 to your left, and indeed as you enter the built-up area this road is just a few yards away. The final half mile is rather uninspiring as you pass the backs of houses, and if you have walked non-stop from Cranleigh, you may feel you deserve a break when you finally reach the road crossing that gives access to the centre of Bramley. If you wish to detour to the village centre, with its good range of amenities, turn left down the road and then left again at the mini-roundabout. Buses run to Guildford, Cranleigh and Horsham, although note that Horsham-bound buses don't enter the village centre but follow the road crossed by the Downs Link.

To continue along the old line, cross straight over the road then proceed past the old

Lengthening shadows on the Shoreham to Christ's Hospital line near West Grinstead.

Bramley & Wonersh station platform and on along the obvious path through attractive woodland scenery. It is on this section that you say farewell to the Downs Link which now leaves the old line and proceeds in an easterly direction to join the North Downs around St Martha's Hill. Remaining on the old line, you will find that the sound of traffic again becomes intrusive as you approach and finally reach the A281 crossing, where things get a little more complicated. Pass straight over the A281 and, following a straight line, pick up a narrow path that proceeds along the course of the old line on an embankment. You are now not only off the Downs Link but are not in fact on a designated right of way. In many ways, however, this is one of the loveliest sections of the walk; it is totally unspoilt and very rural, with thick vegetation all around you. In due course you arrive at the River Wey, only to find that the bridge which used to convey the old line has been largely demolished. Having therefore admired what is left of the bridge, and the most attractive riverside surroundings, you are forced back to the A281 by the same route. When you return to the A281, turn left, follow the road for a few yards, then just across the other side of the bridge over the Wey & Arun Junction Canal turn left on to a signed footpath. Initially this runs parallel with the water, then deviates slightly from it. Now following the Wey South Path, close to the point where the canal meets the River Wey, you return to the waterside and enjoy a pleasant walk to Broadford Bridge where you meet the A248 Godalming-Shalford road. Turn left to cross the bridge, then immediately left again to follow the opposite (west) bank of the River Wey; in a few hundred yards you arrive back at the remains of the bridge which conveyed the old line across the river, but now on the other side of the water. It is possible to ascend from the riverside path on to the old line and follow it on towards Guildford, on what is a permissive footpath.

The going is now very straightforward. Follow the old line, soon passing under a bridge which carries the A248, continue through a wooded area, and very shortly you reach the site of the junction with the existing main line between Guildford and Portsmouth. You could now retrace your steps to the A248 which can easily be accessed from the old line, turn left on to it, and follow it via Broadford Bridge to Shalford where there are buses to Guildford and Horsham and trains to Guildford and Dorking. However, there is a more interesting route back to the A248 at Broadford Bridge. Rather than retracing your steps, simply continue along the footpath beyond the site of the junction, the path now in fact following the loop line that linked the main Guildford-Portsmouth line with the Guildford-Redhill line. You proceed pleasantly on an embankment above the meadows, then after passing a World War 2 pillbox you descend to the river. (The last tiny section of the loop line, beyond the river which was crossed by a bridge, is inaccessible; note how close the Redhill line is by the river bridge crossing of that line to the left.) After descending to the river, turn right to walk along the Wey South Path back to Broadford Bridge, and there turn left on to the A248 which you follow to reach Shalford.

SECTION 3 - **RYE TO CAMBER SANDS (THE RYE AND CAMBER TRAMWAY)**

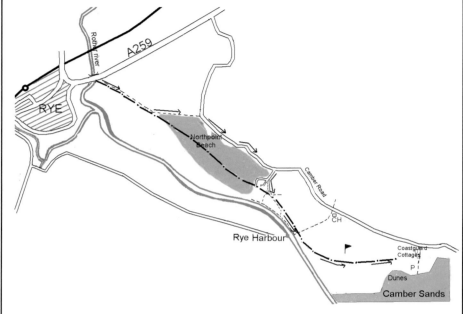

Golf Links Halt on the Rye to Camber Sands line.

SECTION 3 - **RYE TO CAMBER SANDS (THE RYE AND CAMBER TRAMWAY)**

Length:	3 miles each way.
Start and finish:	Rye town centre.
Public transport:	Regular trains to Rye from Hastings to the west and Ashford International to the north-east. Regular buses to Rye from Hastings, Brighton and Folkestone.
Conditions:	This is a delightful walk. It is extremely easy, the surroundings are very attractive, much of the old line is available for walking, and Rye with its wealth of beautiful buildings and refreshment opportunities makes an ideal base.
Refreshments:	Pubs, cafes and shops in Rye. RECOMMENDED PUB: RYE - MERMAID - black and white timbered building, good beers and wine list.

History

Like the Selsey Tramway, the Rye & Camber Tramway was not a true tramway at all, but a light railway which was in fact opened just two years before the Selsey line, in 1895. It was another of the Colonel Stephens railways, run with an eye to economy, and like the Selsey route it linked a place of immense historical interest with a more modest but still bustling seaside community. At the time of the opening, on 13 July 1895, it simply linked the town of Rye with the famous golf links of the same name, and during the first six months of operation of the line, a total of 18,000 tickets were sold for the eight and a half minute journey of a mile and three quarters, with most of the customers being golfers, paying 4d return for the privilege. With the extension to Camber Sands, opened exactly 13 years after the opening of the Rye-Golf Links section, the line also became attractive to holidaymakers bound for the superb sands and sandhills around Camber. There were just three stations on the line. The first of these, Rye, was a completely different station from the one that still exists, on the Hastings-Ashford line, and there was no rail link between the two stations. The Rye terminus on the Camber line was hardly palatial, but its sturdy corrugated iron structure boasted a waiting room and an office, and there were two sets of engine sheds. Golf Links Halt, the single intermediate station, was much more modest, consisting simply of a corrugated iron shed and single platform within sight of the Rye golf clubhouse; until the extension to Camber Sands station was constructed, it was

The Rye to Camber Sands line near Golf Links Halt, note the rails still in place.

described on maps as Camber. One curiosity about the station was that it had a urinal for males wishing to answer the call of nature but Colonel Stephens, a bachelor, made no equivalent provision for the ladies! The station building still survives today as a storehouse for the golf club and the exterior looks in very respectable condition. Camber Sands, the eastern terminus, was the most basic of all, with no ticket office - tickets had to be issued by the guard or the driver - nor any shelter for passengers; a photograph of the station in 1938 shows simply a generous-sized platform and a rather feeble tea-hut. At the time of opening, the line had just one locomotive and one carriage, but later two more locomotives were added, one being petrol powered, and the Tramway also acquired a second carriage and a small quantity of goods wagons for the conveyance of shingle from the nearby beach for ballast.

Following the outbreak of the Second World War in 1939, the Tramway was abandoned (services in fact ceased the day after war broke out) and Camber was evacuated because of invasion fears. The line was requisitioned by the Navy in 1943 to link a training establishment set up near Rye Station with the harbour, and areas of the track were concreted over for the benefit of road vehicles. The Tramway was also used by the Navy to transport shingle from the Camber Sands area to supply dumps in the Rye area. When the war came to an end, the cost of properly re-laying the track proved to be too great and the line never reopened. Rye station was demolished in 1947 but as stated above, Golf Links Halt still survives as do some fragments of the concreted Tramway.

Walking the Railway

From the centre of Rye, make your way down to Fishmarket Road which runs below the town to its east, and proceed northwards to the roundabout, turning right here on to the A259 New Road, signposted Folkestone. Very soon you cross a bridge over the Rother, and almost immediately beyond the bridge turn right on to a signed footpath signposted for Camber. This was the site of the old Rye station and terminus of the Tramway. Do not turn hard right here on to the riverside embankment path but follow the signed footpath south-eastwards in a straight line, now actually on the course of the old line. Keep to the footpath, continuing to follow the course of the old line, all the way to a sizeable lake. The old line proceeded on in the same direction across land which has now been completely submerged by this lake, and you therefore need to bear left. Proceed along the footpath, hugging the north shore of the lake and, you soon arrive at Camber Road; turn right on to the road and walk beside it, keeping the lake immediately to your right. In less than half a mile you reach the south-eastern end of the lake, and immediately beyond this point you turn right on to a metalled road which is signposted as a private road. Shortly the road swings from southwards to south-eastwards, a footpath coming in from the right at this point,* and you now find yourself back on the course of the old line with evidence of the old tracks beneath your feet. Continue to follow the track south-eastwards, now passing Rye golf course - take care as the twelfth hole actually crosses this track - and go on in more or less a straight line to arrive at the splendidly-preserved hut which was once Golf Links Halt station. You can see how convenient this would have been for golfers! At this point there is a useful signboard with information about the Tramway. Continue along the path indicated by the signboard, sticking to the course of the old line; shortly you are directed over a stile and swing in a more easterly direction to follow the course of the old line along an embankment. This really is lovely walking with Rye golf course immediately beside you and fine views back to the cliffs around Fairlight just east of Hastings.

The excellently signposted path continues, passing a sturdy shelter with seats - welcome on a wet windy day - and now heads towards the sand dunes, keeping a ridge of sandhills to the left and another golf course, the Jubilee course, to the right. There is no trace whatsoever of the old Tramway or the Camber Sands terminus which was sited not far beyond the shelter referred to above, but for the sake of completeness, and to re-enact what would have been an obvious journey for beachbound rail travellers, I suggest you follow the path eastwards to the Tramway signpost by the fence where you reach a T-junction with a sandy track. Here you must either turn left to the Coastguard Cottages and Camber village, or right up a steep sandhill to enjoy a splendid view to Camber Sands themselves. When I walked this on a Monday in November I was completely on my own but in the summer this sandy path is very popular indeed with holidaymakers and day trippers.

It is possible to return to Rye by bus from Camber, utilising the excellent bus service, but you may prefer simply to retrace your steps, following the same route as before. You could in fact choose to vary the route by turning left on to the footpath referred to at * above, at the point where the metalled track proceeding from the old Golf Links Halt station leaves the course of the old line and swings from north-westwards to northwards. Take this path which briefly follows the course of the old line but then swings to the left, away from the old line (the course of which ahead of you is submerged by the lake) to head towards the bank of the Rother. Continue on this embankment path which on reaching the waterside swings to the right, and provides a pleasant waterside stroll all the way back to the A259 New Road, with fine views initially to Rye Harbour on the other side of the river and then subsequently to the town of Rye itself. There are ample refreshment opportunities in Rye where you can celebrate completion of your walk.

The Rye to Camber Sands line as it passes Rye golf course on its way to the terminus at Camber.

SECTION 3 - **POLEGATE TO ERIDGE**
(THE CUCKOO TRAIL)

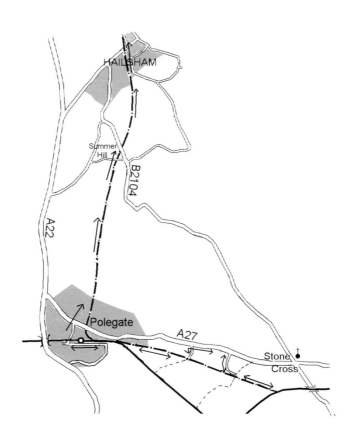

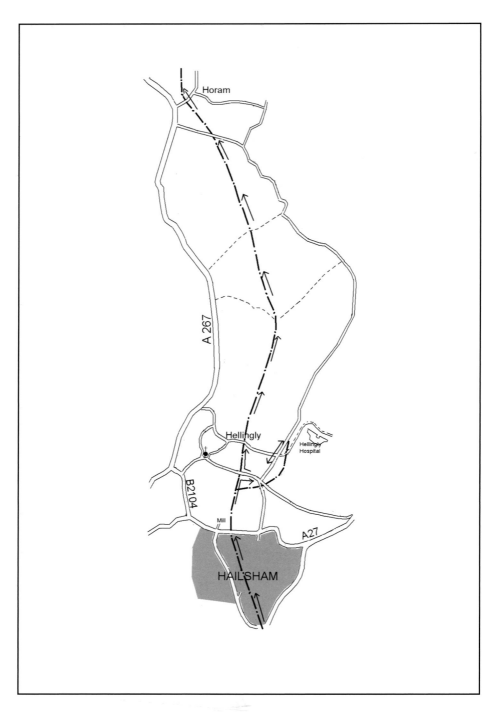

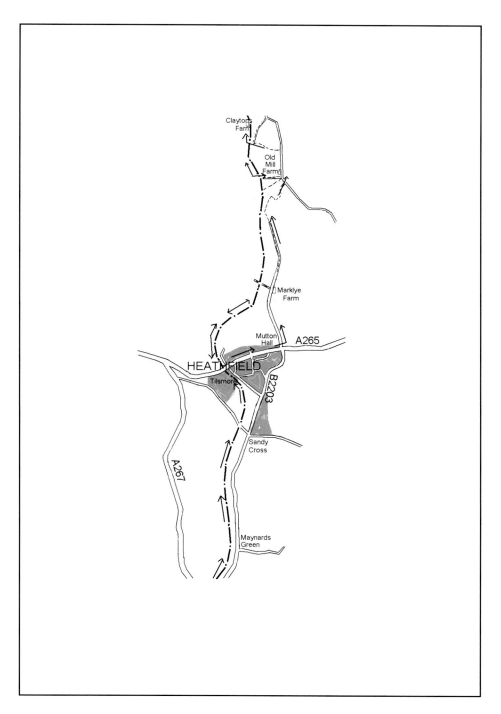

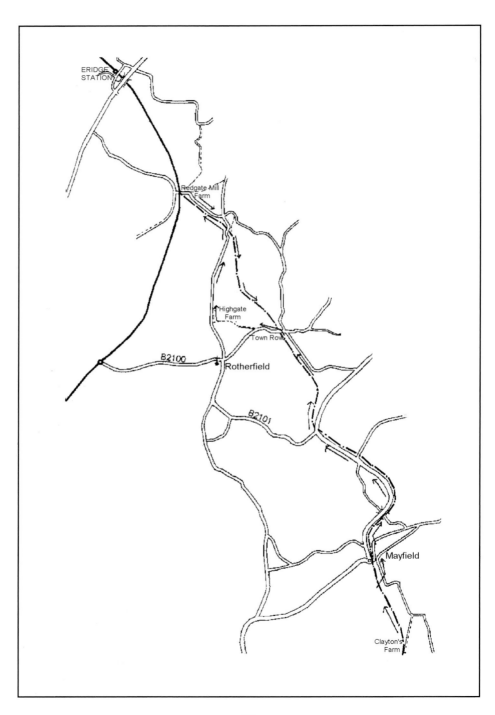

SECTION 3 - **POLEGATE TO ERIDGE** (THE CUCKOO TRAIL)

Length:	Approximately 20 miles.
Start:	Polegate railway station.
Finish:	Rotherfield village.
Public transport:	Regular trains to Polegate from London Victoria, Brighton and Lewes to the west, Eastbourne to the south, and Hastings to the east. Regular buses from Rotherfield back to Polegate and northwards to Tunbridge Wells.
Conditions:	This is a superbly rewarding walk. Over half of it, between Polegate and Heathfield, has been turned into a walkway/cycleway known as the Cuckoo Trail. The remaining section contains a number of walkable sections and the scenery is delightful throughout.
Refreshments:	Pubs and shops at Polegate; pubs, cafes and shops at Hailsham; pub at Hellingly; pub, café and shop at Horam; pubs, café and shops at Heathfield; pubs, café and shops at Mayfield; shop at Town Row; pub, café and shop at Rotherfield. RECOMMENDED PUBS: OLD HEATHFIELD - STAR - "smashing old place" with good choice of beers and malt whiskies; MAYFIELD - MIDDLE HOUSE - massive fireplace, local cider, generously-served and popular food; ROTHERFIELD - KING'S ARMS - generous food; ERIDGE STATION - HUNTSMAN - well-kept beers, interesting wines.

History

It was during the mid-1840's that a rail link was completed between London and Polegate via Lewes, and 14th May 1849 saw branches opened between Polegate and Eastbourne to the south, and between Polegate and Hailsham to the north. The branch to Hailsham was extended northwards to Heathfield, this extension opening on 5th April 1880, and on 1st September of the same year there opened a further extension via Eridge and Groombridge. This enabled trains to run direct from Eastbourne to Tunbridge Wells and back, using stretches of line that had been built between East Grinstead and Tunbridge Wells in 1866 and between Uckfield and Groombridge via Eridge in 1868. A 1924 timetable shows nine trains a day doing the full journey in both directions on weekdays, and three on Sundays; a number of other trains made shorter journeys which might start or finish at Hailsham or Heathfield, the two principal intermediate stations. The journey from Eastbourne to Tunbridge Wells was exceedingly slow. Despite the distance being less than 30 miles from end to end, the average journey time was about an hour and a half and some journeys were a good deal longer; the 4.34pm from Eastbourne, for instance, did not arrive in Tunbridge Wells West until 6.21pm. Virtually all services were operated by the LBSCR prior to the formation of the Southern Railway in 1923. The line became known as the Cuckoo Line, not because cuckoos were particularly abundant in the vicinity of the line, but because of the Cuckoo Fair held at Heathfield on 14th April each year; the line would have conveyed many passengers to the fair from other parts of Sussex.

Although subsequent to nationalisation British Railways streamlined operations and improved frequency of services, the line became a victim of Dr Beeching, with the section between Hailsham and Redgate Mill Junction (where the line met the Uckfield-Eridge-Edenbridge line) shutting on 13th June 1965, the Polegate-Hailsham section closing on 8th September 1968, and the section between Eridge and Tunbridge Wells via Groombridge (covered more fully in walk III of Section 2 of this book) closing on 6th July 1985. The section between Polegate and Eastbourne still survives, as incidentally does the line linking Uckfield and Edenbridge via Eridge. Fortunately a magnificent initiative by East Sussex County Council saw the whole section between Polegate and Heathfield, including the Heathfield Tunnel, converted into a walkway and cycleway during the 1990's; the remainder is, however, still in private hands and having regard to its current usage it seems unlikely that it will become generally available for public access.

There were six intermediate stations between Polegate and Eridge. The first was Hailsham, a sizeable station with a goods yard and shed which were enlarged towards the end of the 19th century. The next was Hellingly, a rural station which until 1899 served the needs of what was a small village and the agricultural community surrounding it. However in that year, construction work started on the huge East Sussex Asylum, as it was known at that time (later to be known as the Hellingly Mental Hospital), and to facilitate the building of the asylum a branch line of a mile and a quarter was built from the station. When the asylum opened in 1903, the branch line was acquired and subsequently electrified by the local council; the line was used to transport not only patients but also coal for the boilers and generators that were used by the institution and which in turn provided power for the electric locomotive. Notwithstanding the line's closure, Hellingly Station building has been magnificently preserved. The third station was Horam, initially known as Horeham Road for Waldron, then Horeham Road & Waldron, then Waldron & Horeham Road, and finally Horam; considering the small size of the community it served, it was another impressive construction with tile-hung exterior and much ornamental plasterwork. The fourth station, Heathfield, was lavishly built, boasting a goods yard and fully glazed footbridge, and just north of the station was the longest tunnel on the line, running to 266 yards and still accessible today. It was a couple of miles north of Heathfield that there was a serious derailment in September 1897, resulting in the death of the driver and a number of injuries. The penultimate station was Mayfield, much of the building of which is still standing today, and again an elegant building with gables and tile-hanging. The final station was Rotherfield, three quarters of a mile from the village of that name and in fact built in the smaller village of Town Row. Set in a beautiful rural location amongst rolling hills and coniferous woodland, the station was advertised on sign boards as Rotherfield And Mark Cross (Mark Cross being a mile or so to the east) and boasted a goods yard that handled a considerable amount of merchandise, notably coal. It has since been splendidly restored into a private dwelling and makes a delightful spectacle for the railway rambler.

Walking the Railway

Your walk begins at the existing station at Polegate, which was built as recently as 1986 and which replaced the old station that lay a few hundred yards to the east. It was from that old station that trains proceeded, heading initially westwards out of the station and then parting company from the Lewes-bound line almost immediately and swinging northwards. It is possible to view this "parting of the ways" by turning right out of the ticket office on the north side of the station and heading eastwards through the station car park. Towards the far north-east corner of the car park there is on the left a metalled gate, beyond which is an area of vegetation and a crude path which follows the course of the old line as it proceeded out of Polegate. Shortly, however, the path is lost in impenetrable undergrowth and you will be forced back to the station car park; now retrace your steps through the car park and carry on past the station ticket office to the main village street, turning right on to the street and following it to its end. Turn right at the T-junction on to Station Road then bear shortly left into School Lane. (By continuing along Station Road you will shortly see on your right the northern end of the area of vegetation marking the course of the old line which actually went underneath Station Road; new development has obliterated all traces of the course of the old line on the other side of Station Road. Return to School Lane to continue.) Follow School Lane initially, but as it curves to approach the school buildings, you continue on in a straight line to join the walkway/cycleway known as the Cuckoo Trail which will convey you all the way to Heathfield, using the course of the old line virtually throughout. Almost at once you can see how much time and effort has been invested into the project by the local council, and all the way along the Cuckoo Trail you will enjoy excellent signposting, firm concrete surfacing, and ingeniously carved lineside sculptures and benches. Follow the Cuckoo Trail out of Polegate and into open country, soon crossing the new A27 Polegate bypass. Although the noise of the traffic from the bypass will stay with you for some time, the walking becomes pleasantly rural with tall vegetation bordering each side of the path and a signboard telling you of some of the bird life and wildlife in the vicinity. You pass a welcome tearoom within a mill complex just to the right of the path, then rise to cross Summerhill Lane; road junctions and bridges are all signed, using a green motif that is reminiscent of old station signboards in times past. A pedestrian crossing is provided at the next road junction (note the crossing-keeper's cottage to your left, just across the road) and it is not far beyond the crossing to the next built-up area, Hailsham. The path widens into Freshfield Close and you are then directed right into Lindfield Drive and left into Station Road, with an attractive lake to your right. Continue up Station Road, passing the Railway Tavern, then just before reaching the top end of the road turn left, as indicated, off the road, descend briefly and bear right to enter the underpass just to the right of the skateboard park. You are now back on the course of the old line and you can see roughly the course it would have followed to reach this point from what is now Freshfield Close. If you wish to visit Hailsham, with its good range of amenities, simply carry on to the end of Station Road and cross over into North Street, which in turn leads to the High Street.

Returning to the line, proceed through the underpass and enjoy some more straightforward railway walking, passing under the impressive Teinicks Bridge, a fine piece of brickwork, then the rather less inspiring Eastwell Place Bridge and the singularly unappealing London Road Bridge. You are then faced with a large modern housing estate; initially the Cuckoo Trail skirts the right-hand edge of it, but you are then forced through the middle of it, following a path that is provided for walkers. You emerge from the estate, passing under the Hawks Road Bridge which feels more like a small tunnel than a bridge, but the suburban feel remains as you continue to the very busy Upper Horsebridge Road where a pelican pedestrian crossing is provided. Cross over the road and proceed towards Hellingly, having left Hailsham behind; shortly you reach the magnificently preserved old Hellingly station building, complete with canopy, and just under the ensuing road bridge you will get easy access to the village with its pub.

At Hellingly it is possible to make a detour to inspect the old hospital line referred to above. Just before the old Hellingly station there is a children's play area to the left, and opposite this area a footpath leads off to the right, providing a view to the course of the old hospital line as it left the Cuckoo Line. Return to the Cuckoo Trail and follow it almost to the road bridge beyond the old station, then just before the bridge turn right on to a path giving access to the road. Turn right on to the road and follow it to a crossroads, here turning right again and looking out for a gated grassy track leading off to the right almost immediately; this is the course of the old line and is not a right of way although I had no difficulty gaining access. You reach a dead end almost within sight of the old Hellingly station so return to the crossroads and now take the road signposted for Hellingly hospital. You are now walking parallel with the course of

The northern mouth of the Heathfield tunnel on the Polegate to Eridge line.

the old hospital line which runs through a field to your right, the course of the line clearly marked by a green strip through the field quite close to the road. Fork right on to the hospital approach road and very soon you reach Rosslyn House; by turning right on to the drive for Rosslyn House and immediately right again you can follow a track which leads straight on to the course of the old line and the green strip mentioned above. Although this is not a right of way it can be followed down to a locked gate beyond which is the road leading eastwards from the crossroads. Return to the hospital approach road and continue to follow it, now on the course of the old line, very soon reaching the old hospital buildings where the line finished. Simply retrace your steps from here along the road to the old Hellingly station.

Beyond Hellingly station you drop down to cross Mill Lane, and shortly cross over the Cuckmere River, which is still relatively narrow hereabouts. Glorious walking follows, ranking amongst the best of all railway walking in Sussex, with fields and woodland on both sides and a real sense of tranquillity. You pass under Shawpits Bridge and the fine triple-arched Woodhams Bridge, and over the quaintly-named Cattle Creep Bridge, the path now in the refreshing shade of woodland which seems to thicken as you near Horam. You have to negotiate your way through another modern housing estate - simply follow the Cuckoo Trail signposts - but soon return to the course of the old line and pass the site of Horam station, of which there is now no trace. Clear signposting points the way into Horam, which boasts a good range of amenities and also the Merrydown cider press.

As you continue up the Cuckoo Trail along the old line beyond Horam, your walk remains very straightforward. There is a contrasting scene between left and right: to the left, delightful rolling fields and woods, and to the right, the busy B2203 road, the noise from which can seem quite intrusive. You drop to Tubwell Lane, then continue over Maynards Green Bridge and Runts Farm Bridge, the path getting a little further away from the traffic noise. Some steps have been created in the small cutting to your left hereabouts, giving access to a picnic area with a fine viewpoint. Shortly you arrive at New Ghyll Road which you cross, and proceed to plain Ghyll Road, descending to cross this road and now entering the sprawling outer reaches of Heathfield. Keep following the Cuckoo Trail signposts, your path proceeding in determined fashion through the seemingly endless modern development, but then rather petering out as it reaches the junction with Newnham Way. Ahead of you is an industrial estate; although if you enter the estate you can see how the old line progressed towards Heathfield Tunnel, you will not be able to follow the old line all the way along to the tunnel. You are instead forced to retrace your steps through the industrial estate and turn north-eastwards (i.e. left out of the industrial estate) into Newnham Way and then left on to Station Road. You proceed north-westwards up Station Road, bearing left into Station Approach and very shortly right on to a path that gives access back to the course of the old line, the access path leading to a children's play area and then forward to the mouth of Heathfield Tunnel. You now walk through the tunnel - it is reassuringly well lit - and, emerging from it, you enter a small country park known as Millennium Green. You initially continue along the course of the old line, and although you are no longer on the Cuckoo Trail you may in fact follow the old line northwards for the best part of a mile, through beautiful woodland scenery. However, you then come to a fence which bars further progress; there is no way round it, and you are forced back to the country park. An obvious footpath conveys you away from the old line to the left shortly before returning to the tunnel, and up through the carpark of a superstore (handy for provisions!) to Heathfield's main street. Turn left (eastwards) on to the street and follow it to continue your railway walk. Heathfield is a pleasant rather than especially attractive place, but it contains the best range of amenities on your walk.

Continue eastwards along the main street and then stay on the same road which becomes Mutton Hall Hill. Pulling away from the town centre, ascend the hill to arrive at a crossroads, with the B2203 Tower Street going off to the right, and Marklye Lane, with a sign indicating a cycle track to Mayfield, to the left. Turn left and follow Marklye Lane, going downhill and reaching Marklye Farm. A signed footpath going off to the left provides a detour to Orchard House; just short of Orchard House you can see a section of the old line, but it is wholly inaccessible. Return to Marklye Farm and continue along the signposted Mayfield cycle track in a northerly direction, the track narrowing significantly and becoming a footpath which now enters an area of woodland. In about half a mile the woodland to the left relents and the path passes beside a field which is to your left; at this point you may leave the track and enter the field which at its western end provides views through the trees to the course of the old line. Keep on along the track which soon swings eastwards and then heads in a more north-easterly direction, emerging from the woods and proceeding through fields to arrive at the metalled Newick Lane. Turn left into Newick Lane, cross a stream then immediately turn left on to a signed footpath. Almost at once the path forks; take the left fork and proceed south-westwards, now heading for a splendid bridge carrying the old line. You can easily regain the old line here by turning left just before the bridge on to a path which brings you up on to the line. It is possible to follow the old line a little way to the left(south) and rather further to the right(north) but rather frustratingly in both cases you are forced back to where you started. The walking, although not on designated rights of way, is extremely pleasant, particularly in the northerly direction where you will pass through some beautiful woodland, but eventually you come to a dead end and you are forced to go all the way back to Newick Lane the way you came. Turn left to follow Newick Lane northwards, and soon you arrive at another river bridge crossing; almost immediately beyond that there is a signed footpath leading off to the left. Follow this footpath which takes you westwards through fields, swinging more sharply north-westwards and arriving at a track that has come south-westwards from Clayton's Farm. Turn left and continue south-westwards on this track, soon passing under the old line, although it is impossible to follow or access the old line to the south of this point. However having passed under the bridge, you may turn immediately right on to a path that runs parallel with the old line heading north, ascending to the same level as the old line, and in a couple of hundred yards it is possible to access the old line and follow it northwards, although it is not a designated right of way. In a quarter of a mile you will see some buildings at the top of the cutting on your left, shortly before the line enters an area of woodland. (It is possible to follow the old line on into the woods, now just a short distance from Mayfield, but you are forced back by the density of the undergrowth and must backtrack to the buildings.) To your right here is a gate which at the time of writing was unlocked; by passing through the gate and turning left it is possible to walk uphill along left-hand field edges, keeping the old line below you to the left, to another gate which if unlocked brings you to the metalled Knowle Hill just on the edge of Mayfield. Follow Knowle Hill downhill towards Mayfield. If this gate, and/or the gate leading off the old line, is locked, you will have to retrace your steps all the way back to the Clayton's Farm track and follow this track north-east to Clayton's Farm where it rejoins Newick Lane. Turn left on to Newick Lane and follow it; in due course it becomes Knowle Hill, and you simply continue downhill along it towards Mayfield. There is one brief detour, left along a signed path, enabling you to see a little of the old line as you proceed down Knowle Hill, but the path passes high above the old line in thick woodland and there is no possibility of access.

At the end of Knowle Hill you reach a junction; the way forward is by going on into Station Road (not hard right into West Street), but by turning left towards the roundabout you will see the course of the old railway embankment both to your right and left. You can access the left embankment heading back in the direction you have just come, but you cannot follow it for long, and it is necessary to return and follow Station Road briefly. By continuing along this road you would reach the delightful centre of Mayfield, but you do in fact need to turn left almost at once off Station Road down Fir Toll Close and go forward on to the path leading to the A267, beside which you proceed to continue your journey. Just beyond Fir Toll Close is Station Approach which gives access to the old Mayfield station building, but you cannot enter the building, nor can you access the old line hereabouts, so return to Fir Toll Close and drop down along the footpath to the A267 Mayfield bypass. Turn right and walk along the verge beside the A267 heading north-eastwards and then swinging north-westwards; the old line ran immediately parallel with this road, and just to the right of it.

Pass the right-hand turn into Tunbridge Wells Road which gives access from the north of Mayfield into the village centre, and shortly you will be able to access a small section of old line on your right, running parallel with the A267. It is not actually a designated right of way, and it isn't possible to follow the old line very far, the route soon becoming blocked by impenetrable vegetation. You are forced back to the A267 which you now follow to Argos Hill; Bassetts Lane, a right turn just a short way beyond the accessible stretch of old line, does give access to a bridge over the line but there is no means of getting on to the line from the bridge. Return to the A267 and go on to the little village of Argos Hill, taking care as this is a very busy road and for much of this section there is no pavement. At the centre of Argos Hill is the junction with the B2101 where there was once a pub, the Bicycle Arms; at the time of writing the pub had closed and it appeared to have become a private residence. Very shortly beyond the junction you reach a bridge over the old line, but just before the bridge you will see an opening and a steep path leading downhill off the road on to the old line. It is possible to follow the old line south-eastwards back towards Mayfield, but you are soon beaten back by the vegetation, so retrace your steps and continue walking into the tunnel under the A267. It is a most impressive construction and although it is not nearly as long as the Heathfield Tunnel it certainly seems darker and somehow more of an adventure. Emerge from the tunnel and now keep walking along the old line; neither this, nor the section of old line on the Mayfield side of the tunnel, nor the walk through the tunnel itself, is a designated right of way but access north of the tunnel is not a problem and there follows a quite delightful section of old line in the shade of trees. After about half a mile, shortly beyond the point where the woodland on the left opens out into a field, further progress becomes impossible. Fortunately, you do not need to go all the way back to Argos Hill; simply return to the southern field boundary and you will see to your left a path heading away north-eastwards and following the left-hand edge of a lake. Take this path which runs pleasantly through woodland and beside the lake, arriving at the metalled Yewtree Lane. Turn left on to this lane (a path going off to the left just before the junction takes you to a bridge carrying the old line but access to the line is impossible) and follow it. You can see the course of the old line clearly visible to your left and by taking the signed path leading off to the left in a couple of hundred yards, shortly before Sheriff's Lane comes in from the left, you can cross the old line, continuing forward to Sheriff's Lane. Turn right into Sheriff's Lane and almost immediately left back into Yewtree Lane, passing under the course of the old line again. Now follow Yewtree Lane, keeping sight of the old line which runs parallel with this lane to your left; theoretically you could get on to the old line hereabouts but there is little point in doing so, as there is no forward access and its course is obvious in any event. Simply now follow Yewtree Lane to the little village of Town Row where there is a useful shop, and on arrival at the B2100 Mark Cross-Rotherfield road turn left.

Though your route passes under the course of the old line, it is possible to detour up the road to the right just before the site of the bridge crossing to inspect Rotherfield Station, which has been magnificently restored and is now a very impressive private dwelling. Return to the B2100 and follow it just north of west towards the village of Rotherfield which is almost a mile from here; you begin climbing and in a few hundred yards pass the Rotherfield Methodist church, just beyond which you turn right into Chant Lane and then immediately right on to a signed path that goes steeply downhill. You cross a stream then climb again, soon reaching the course of the old line. Looking to your right towards Rotherfield Station building you will see there is no access, but it is possible to follow the course of the old line to your left, through

The Polegate to Eridge line just north of Heathfield.

pleasant countryside with fields immediately around you and woodland beyond. In due course you reach the edge of the woods* and further progress is impossible, meaning that you are forced all the way back to Chant Lane. Note that this stretch of old line is not a designated right of way. Once back at Chant Lane, follow it just north of west then just south of west to the Rotherfield-Eridge Green road. Turn right and follow this road which passes Highgate Farm and enters what is one of the most thickly wooded areas of the High Weald. Just under a mile from the point at which you joined the road, look out for a signed public footpath leading off to your right**(if you find you have emerged from the wood and are still looking, you have gone too far) and follow the path through the woods; it soon swings to the left, at the time of writing being marked with a signpost saying 49. You then descend quite steeply and as you near the foot of the hill you will see the old line clearly to your right. Although it is not a designated right of way there is no difficulty of access to the old line simply by leaving the path before the foot of the hill is reached and cutting across through the woods. It is then possible to turn right, southwards, and follow the old line back to the point marked with the single star above. Frustratingly, having enjoyed a most pleasant walk and then retraced your steps to the point at which you joined the line, you then find further northward progress obstructed, so you then need to go all the way back to the Rotherfield-Eridge Green road at the point marked ** above. Turn right and follow the road down to the point where it crosses the old line$, the road bending sharply to cross it. It is here possible to access the old line and follow it south-westwards to the obstruction referred to above. Effectively, therefore, you have managed to follow the progress of the old line all the way from Rotherfield Station, albeit that none of it is along designated rights of way.

Return to the road and turn right on to it, following it to a crossroads a matter of yards away, then turn left and follow the road uphill towards Redgate Mill Farm. From the road you can see the course of the old line as it proceeds towards its junction with the still surviving Uckfield-Eridge line. A gate leading into the field to the left, just before the road descends to the farm, does allow access to the old line which you can follow almost all the way back to the crossing marked $ above, but yet again you will need to retrace your steps and return to the Redgate Mill Farm road. It is just a short walk from here along the road past the farm to two bridge crossings, the first carrying the old line and the second carrying the Uckfield-Eridge line. The two lines united just a short way to the right of these crossings. Although it is possible, having passed under the bridges, to turn right on to Sandhill Lane and follow this to the A26 with Eridge Station a further three quarters of a mile to the right along this busy road, it is definitely preferable to go back along the roads you have just come, but this time passing the end of Chant Lane and continuing on to Rotherfield. There are buses from here to Tunbridge Wells, Heathfield and Polegate.

On returning to Polegate, or even before you leave it to start your walk up the Cuckoo Line, it is worth spending an hour and a half or so following the course of the old link line between Polegate and Stone Cross to the east. Trains running from Polegate to Hastings must now dip southwards into Eastbourne and then reverse to continue, passing through Stone Cross lying just two miles east of Polegate. The link line, which effectively bypassed Eastbourne and allowed the possibilities of quicker rail journeys east of Polegate, opened in June 1846 and shut in January 1969. To follow this line, proceed to the far end of the station car park on the north side of Polegate station and proceed directly into Porters Way which runs roughly parallel with the existing line. Keep going along Porters Way which runs into Station Road; turn right into Station Road and immediately note the old Polegate station building on your right which at the time of writing was a popular pub and restaurant. Proceed along the road, running parallel with the course of the old link line along the embankment to your right (the existing Eastbourne line having now parted company), then bear first right into Lynholm Road and follow it, the course of the old line to your right masked now by new housing development (though note the old bridge crossing very soon after joining the road). Continue along the road for about a quarter of a mile and go uphill slightly. As you rise, look out for the cycle path signpost leading off the road to the right, and take this signed cycle path route; this shortly swings left and now follows the course of the old link line, providing lovely walking with beautiful views to the South Downs. Soon you reach a flight of steps leading down to a crossing of the busy and noisy A22, and you leave the cycle track to take these steps. Cross the A22 with immense care, then ascend the steps; having reached the top you now find yourself back on the course of the old line. Almost immediately a footpath sign directs you left, but it is possible to follow the old line for a couple of hundred yards - not a designated right of way - before the surrounding vegetation makes further progress impossible. Return to the footpath sign and follow the path northwards, soon arriving at the Polegate-Stone Cross road. Turn right to follow it briefly, but then turn right again southwards down the next track on your right; a signed footpath leads away northwards from the road at this point, so it should be easy enough to identify the track. Follow the track, in due course passing a pond and children's play area which lies to your left. Just beyond the pond, the track bends left to enter an area of new housing, and immediately after the left bend there is a track leading off to the right. Follow this track which passes under the old line and goes forward to a gate which you pass through - there is a public right of access beyond the gate - to enter a pleasant area of open rolling fields. It is very easy to turn left here to follow parallel with the course of the old line through the fields, right up to the point where the line coming up from Eastbourne meets it just west of Stone Cross. You can also follow parallel with the course of the old line back towards Polegate, again through open fields, but are then blocked by the fencing round the A22. The quickest and pleasantest way back to Polegate is simply to return exactly the same way you came, minus the detours.

SECTION 3 - **CROWHURST TO BEXHILL**

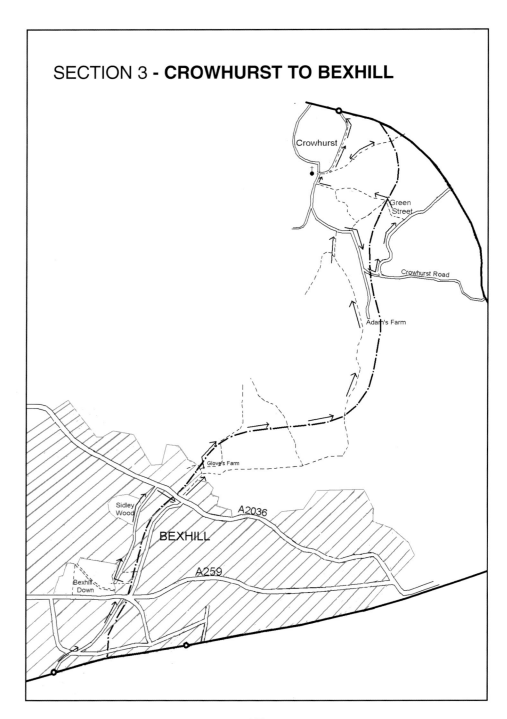

SECTION 3 - **CROWHURST TO BEXHILL**

Length:	5 miles.
Start:	Collington railway station, Bexhill.
Finish:	Crowhurst railway station.
Public transport:	Collington is on the main Eastbourne-Hastings line with frequent trains calling at the station. Crowhurst is on the main London Charing Cross-Hastings line with an hourly service in both directions.
Conditions:	This is a very rewarding walk with some good sections of disused line for viewing and walking (although none of the walking is on designated rights of way), and fine scenery once you have left the sprawl of Bexhill behind.
Refreshments:	Pubs, shops and cafes at Bexhill; pubs and shops in and around Sidley; pub at Crowhurst. RECOMMENDED PUB: BEXHILL - ROSE AND CROWN(Turkey Road) - good beers.

History

The Crowhurst, Sidley & Bexhill Railway Company was formed to build a four and a half mile branch from the London-Hastings line at Crowhurst, providing a "short cut" from this line to the popular seaside resort of Bexhill. The line, authorised by an Act dated 15th July 1897, was opened on 1 June 1902. There was just one intermediate station, at Sidley, an inland suburb of Bexhill, and two most impressive features, namely the Combe Haven viaduct, and the terminus, which became known as Bexhill West. The Combe Haven viaduct was a brick-built construction reaching a height of 70 ft across the Crowhurst Valley; Bexhill West station, as distinct from Bexhill station on the main Eastbourne-Hastings line (with which the Crowhurst-Bexhill line did not link, being separated simply by the width of a road!) was a huge station with a substantial concourse, a long two-faced platform, extensive sidings and a large goods depot.

The line became popular and in 1925 there were eighteen weekday departures from Crowhurst to Bexhill. However, traffic declined with the electrification of the Eastbourne-Hastings line which made it less immediately attractive to cut across from this line to the Hastings-Charing Cross line via Sidley and Crowhurst. The line did come back briefly into its own in late 1949 and early 1950 when extensive engineering

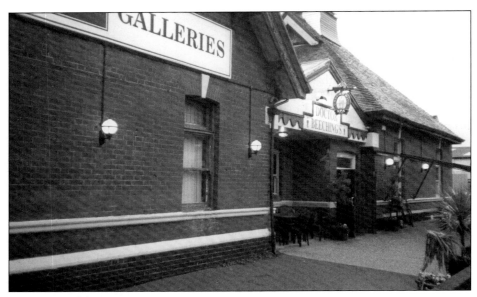

The former Bexhill West station building on the Crowhurst to Bexhill line.
Doctor Beeching extends a welcome!

work in the tunnel between West St Leonards and Warrior Square on the London-Hastings line just outside Hastings caused Hastings trains to be diverted to Bexhill West. However, the line continued to lose money thereafter, finally closing to goods traffic on 9th September 1963 and to passengers on 15th June 1964. No efforts have been made to preserve the line either by means of reviving it or converting any of it into a walkway, and the old redbrick station at Bexhill West is the only really impressive feature of the branch line that has survived.

Walking the Railway

Leave Collington Station by the footpath leading from the eastbound platform, and proceed to Terminus Avenue, turning right into this road and following it eastwards, crossing where convenient. Very shortly you pass a parade of shops, where you can stock up with supplies for the journey, then shortly beyond that, now in Terminus Road, you pass the splendid redbrick building that used to be Bexhill West Station. Note the particularly aptly named Dr Beeching's Restaurant! It isn't possible to follow the course of the old line for the initial section north-eastwards from Bexhill West, as it is now occupied by the Beeching Park industrial estate. Therefore continue briefly along Terminus Road then turn left into Beeching Road - you can't escape Beeching references hereabouts! - and follow it to its end. You can if you wish detour off Beeching Road into the industrial estate in places and see the course that would have been taken by the old line, at the point at which the far northwestern end of the estate meets the backs of the houses in Colebrooke Road and Downlands Avenue. At the end of Beeching Road, turn left and almost immediately arrive at a crossroads with the A259 Little Common Road, noting the embankment used by the old line which can clearly be seen on the south-west segment of this crossroads. Cross over into the A269 London Road, signposted Sidley, and follow this north-westwards; school buildings obliterate the course of the old line which runs parallel with this road just to the left. Just before number 167 London Road, turn left to arrive almost immediately at a mini roundabout at the bottom end of Barncroft Road; crossing the course of the old line between London Road and the mini-roundabout you will see the impossibility of accessing it! Turn right on to Barncroft Road and follow it, going forward into Buxton Drive which in turn takes you uphill into the suburb of Sidley. The old line runs parallel with this road and to the right, and glimpses of it can be obtained but access is for now impossible. At the end of Buxton Drive you turn right on to the main road (A269 again) and almost immediately arrive at a bridge crossing of the old line; just before the bridge, you can turn right on to sliproad which goes downhill and into a small industrial estate. You will note that the old line, just south of the A269 overbridge crossing, has been converted into a motorcycle training area and access is notionally possible when the gates to this area are open, but it is prudent as well as polite to seek permission before entering. There is little difficulty in gaining access to the rough grassy area south of the motorcycle training area that is also on the course of the old line, but you cannot backtrack much further, and the area is in any case not one to which the general public has a right of access. Even when the motorcycle training area is open, you cannot pass under the A269 on the old line, so return to that road along the sliproad and cross over.

Having crossed the A269 turn right, go over the bridge and take the first left turn into Wrestwood Road then turn immediately left on to a signed public footpath. This path goes parallel with, above and to the right of the old line, which again is inaccessible here. Don't be tempted on to the metal of St James Crescent but continue behind the backs of the houses of the crescent and on through a field along a clearly marked path to arrive at a T-junction with Glovers Lane. Turn left into Glovers Lane and cross back over the old line almost at once. As soon as you've crossed the old line, turn right on to a narrow path that drops down to arrive at the old line, and you are now able to follow the old line for about a mile. It is quite delightful walking through open country which contrasts magnificently with the suburban housing of Sidley. Keep walking, enjoying the surroundings, until you reach a junction with a footpath with signs indicating the course of the waymarked 1066 Bexhill Trail. You will see that the course of the old line, delightfully clear and unobstructed to this point, is almost impenetrable beyond this junction, so turn left on to the 1066 walk and follow the path through the field, heading north-eastwards and downhill. As you descend, aim just to the right of the accumulation of trees you can see just east of north at this point, but just to the left of the fence you can see to the right of the trees! As you reach the fence the course of the path will be obvious. Heading northwards now, go forward to cross a stream by a footbridge, then head north-eastwards again along an obvious path, a sign pointing the correct direction, aiming for a wooded area and the buildings of Adam's Farm. The countryside hereabouts is delightfully quiet and unspoilt. You can see initially the course of the old line, shrouded in trees, but then as you head for Adam's Farm the course of the old line - running roughly parallel with your route to the right but beyond Adam's Farm - becomes impossible to follow. Keep to the path as indicated, and you now have a very easy footpath walk to the south edge of Crowhurst, keeping a stream to your right all the way along. In due course you arrive at a road with a most convenient pub just to your left!

Turn right on to the road and follow it uphill; as you near the top of the hill you approach a bridge crossing over the old line, half hidden by the vegetation. There is an opening in the trees just short of the bridge (coming from the pub) which gives access to a small section of the old line immediately north of(not under) the bridge, but you cannot go far. Retrace your steps and continue towards the bridge; a right turn down a track just before the bridge leads back towards Adam's Farm, but although the course of the old line can be seen briefly to your left, it is soon lost. However there are wonderful views from here across the valley you have just followed. Return once more to the road, cross the bridge and turn first left into Swainham Lane which heads north-

A rather overgrown section of the Crowhurst to Bexhill line at Sidley.

eastwards, then swings left and shortly right, swinging left and then right again to pass a stables. Just beyond the stables there is a very inconspicuous plinth indicating a footpath which you follow downhill in a north-westerly direction, and which at the time of writing was extremely overgrown. Continuing in the same direction, you pass over a bridge going over the old line, but the line is so overgrown that there is no possibility of access to it. Just before the bridge you could detour right on to a path which goes briefly uphill and into a field which if followed along its left edge provides glimpses of the old line, but again you cannot access the line and you are forced back to the bridge just mentioned. Beyond the bridge, the going is even narrower and harder to negotiate but soon you arrive at a drive. Cross over the drive and it is now much easier more open walking along an obvious signed path through fields, proceeding north-westwards and aiming for the unmistakable landmark of Crowhurst Church. You descend to a footbridge, and ignoring a path heading left here, cross the bridge and continue towards the church, soon arriving at the road. Turn right on to the road and at the next road junction, just beside the church, turn right into Station Road.

If you're in a hurry, you could simply follow the road to the station, about half a mile up the road, but there is a very worthwhile detour you should make if you have time. Almost as soon as you've entered Station Road, turn right along a signed path, heading for farm buildings; footpath walkers are then directed left just before the buildings, so follow this leftward path, proceeding most pleasantly just east of north through a landscape of mixed field and woodland and past an attractive area of water. In about half a mile after leaving Station Road you will see ahead of you a splendid redbrick arch, formerly a bridge which conveyed the old line and now looking somewhat incongruous! It is possible to climb on to the top of the arch and follow the old line back towards Adam's Farm, but you are soon beaten back by the sheer volume of vegetation and therefore you must retrace your steps, descending from the top of the arch. Now keep going in a straight line over the field to view, in the trees beyond, the embankment which conveyed the old line to its junction with the Charing Cross-Hastings line just south-east of Crowhurst station. You can probably hear trains on the existing line as you walk this. Now simply retrace your steps towards Crowhurst Church, and turn right up Station Road to Crowhurst Station for the train home. To return to Collington by train requires you to travel along the Hastings line to St Leonard's Warrior Square, changing here for Collington via Bexhill.

SECTION 3 - **ROBERTSBRIDGE TO BODIAM**

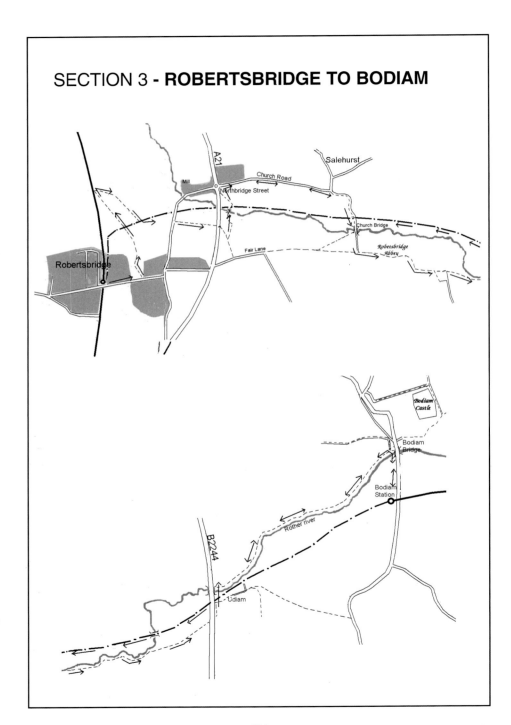

SECTION 3 - **ROBERTSBRIDGE TO BODIAM**

Length:	approximately 4 miles each way.
Start and finish:	Robertsbridge railway station.
Public transport:	Hourly services to and from Robertsbridge station on the London Charing Cross-Tunbridge Wells-Hastings line; connections at Hastings for Ashford, Eastbourne, Lewes and Brighton, and connections at Tonbridge for Redhill and Gatwick.
Conditions:	Very little of the line itself is walkable, but most of it can at least be followed, much of it using agreeable riverside paths.
	Refreshments: Pubs and shops at Robertsbridge; pub at Salehurst; pub and café at Bodiam.
Recommended Pubs:	ROBERTSBRIDGE - STAR - early medieval, good range of beers; BODIAM - CURLEW - several real ales.

History

The line linking Robertsbridge and Bodiam was part of a line which linked Robertsbridge, on the London-Hastings main line, with Headcorn on the London-Dover main line. Following application by the Rother Valley Railway Company, it was in 1896 that an Act was passed allowing the construction of a branch line between Robertsbridge and Tenterden, but in fact when the Light Railways Act received Royal assent in the same year, it was decided by the company to construct the line under the provisions of that Act which meant that construction costs were able to be reduced. The line opened to goods traffic on 26th March 1900 and to passengers exactly a week later. Initially trains ran only as far as Rolvenden, over a mile short of Tenterden, but a new station much closer to the town was opened on 16th March 1903. Anticipating that a number of extensions would be built, the company changed its name to the Kent & East Sussex Railway Company, but in fact despite proposals for extensions south-eastwards from Northiam to Rye, south-eastwards from Tenterden to Appledore, and westwards from Tenterden to Cranbrook, the only extension was north-westwards to Headcorn and this opened on 15th May 1905. At its peak, there were six daily return journeys on weekdays along the full length of the line, although by the early 1950's the level of services had greatly reduced. There were a number of intermediate stations and halts between Robertsbridge and Headcorn; the section of interest to us, between Robertsbridge and Bodiam, boasted stations at these locations and also two intermediate halts, Salehurst and Junction Road, although these two halts had no buildings. Bodiam station, popular for visitors to the nearby castle, did have a building although its design was somewhat rudimentary. The journey time for the four mile ride from Robertsbridge to Bodiam averaged 10 minutes.

For many years the line was managed by H.F. Stephens, who also managed the Selsey Tramway and Rye & Camber Tramway described elsewhere in this book. Stephens was noted for his zest for economy and his tendency to swap locomotives between various lines under his control; as on the Selsey Tram, the railway saw the deployment of primitive petrol railbuses in place of steam locomotives. It was Stephens' refusal to allow the line to become incorporated into one of the four new companies during the 1923 amalgamation that meant that the line kept its independence right up until 1948 when it came under the control of British Railways. Nevertheless, since 1932 the line had become unprofitable and just six years after becoming part of BR the line closed, the final passenger service running on 2nd January 1954 although goods services south from Tenterden continued until 1961. However, a preservation society was subsequently formed and on 3rd February 1974 weekend passenger services were resumed between Tenterden and Rolvenden; gradually the operation extended south-westwards, and by 2000 trains were running all the way from Tenterden to Bodiam. The section of disused line between Tenterden and Headcorn is wholly in Kent and outside the scope of this book. The section to Robertsbridge from Bodiam, wholly in Sussex and subject of the description below, also remains disused although it is hoped that one day it will be fully restored. At the time of writing, having regard to the amount of work still to do, that day seems still very far off.

Walking the Railway

From Robertsbridge Station proceed to the station car park adjacent to the station building. Here you can view what are now the headquarters of the Rother Valley railway, and you can inspect the terminus of the old line, some of the rolling stock acquired by the company, and the line itself as it set out on its journey eastwards. It is impossible to follow it, so walk down to Station Road and turn left, following Station Road towards the village centre. You descend gently, and just past the Gray Nicholls buildings on the left you bear left along a public footpath; at the time of writing the right of way initially passed through some construction works and it is possible that the path may be re-routed in future. You leave the buildings behind and proceed along a clear path, soon passing underneath the old line, although access on to it is impossible. Continue just west of north, keeping a barbed wire fence to your right and heading for the still extant line between Robertsbridge and Etchingham. As you come near this line, look out for a stile in the fence to the right; bear right to cross over the stile and now follow a footpath heading south-eastwards, crossing over a footbridge and passing

The Robertsbridge to Bodiam line at Northbridge.

through a field, continuing to a kissing gate at the corner. Pass through this gate and cross the old line again, then immediately you have crossed it turn left and walk parallel with it until you reach the road. At the time of writing it is possible to climb on to the old line and walk along it for about a hundred yards, but there is no right of way along it and no guarantee you will be able to follow it as restoration work proceeds. As you reach the road at Northbridge, you can look back towards Robertsbridge and discern the course of the old line quite easily, but looking ahead, it is difficult if not impossible to see any evidence of it. The simplest way to proceed from here is to turn left and follow the road to the roundabout with the busy A21, crossing straight over and following the minor road towards Salehurst. Alternatively, turn right and bear almost immediately left on to a signed footpath which follows a pleasant meadow; it affords a slightly better view to the course of the old line than the road route does. Aim for a stile just short of the main road you can see immediately ahead, proceed over the stile and go forward to the road, crossing with extreme care. Beyond the road, continue briefly in the same direction then bear left as indicated and follow a path through a field, crossing over the course of the old line, to arrive at the roundabout mentioned above. Turn right on to the Salehurst road to be reunited with the shorter route already stated.

It is a pleasant road walk to Salehurst less than a mile away; the course of the old line is completely obscured in the flat fields below you to the right and there is no realistic possibility of access through the fields. Salehurst has two distinguishing features, namely a church with a splendid and very conspicuous tower, and a pub right on the route, called Salehurst Halt after the railway halt of the same name that stood close by. Just beyond the pub the road bends sharp left, but you keep straight ahead along a bridlepath which soon bends south-eastwards and descends, crossing the course of the old line which hereabouts is a great deal clearer but is still inaccessible. Go forward along the track to cross over the Rother at Church Bridge, and, keeping to the established right of way beyond it, you soon arrive at a T-junction with the access road for Robertsbridge Abbey. Turn left here and proceed along the access road which beyond the abbey bends round to the right and then bends sharp left, proceeding in a straight line. A signpost then indicates a bridleway going off to the right and a footpath going straight on; keep to the footpath, heading straight ahead and now proceeding as signposted in an easterly direction, with the river Rother immediately to your left. Using the Rother as your guide, you now simply keep to the path, using the left-hand field edges, all the way to the deceptively busy Cripps Corner-Hawkhurst road, then turn left to follow the road, taking great care. In a couple of hundred yards, having crossed over the old line at the site of Junction Road Halt, you cross over the Rother, and immediately turn right on to a riverside path which you can follow all the way to Bodiam, just a mile away. The course of the old line is inaccessible and impossible even to view east of the Cripps Corner-Hawkhurst road.

The riverside walk to Bodiam is extremely pleasant, with good views to Bodiam Castle throughout the walk. In one mile you reach Bodiam, arriving at a road with a pub to your left and the castle, including a popular tea-room (it is not necessary to pay the castle admission fee to patronise it) immediately across the road. By turning right and following the road for a quarter of a mile you will reach Bodiam Station, which at present is the western terminus of the Kent & East Sussex Railway; facilities here are extremely limited but trains are available to take you to Tenterden on the preserved line. Looking back the other way, towards Robertsbridge, you can see the line still in place, disappearing off in the direction you have just come, but signs warn you against trespassing on to the railway. With reluctance you will have to retrace your steps and follow the riverside path back to the Cripps Corner-Hawkhurst road.

On arrival at the road, turn left and walk the short distance to the course of the old line which will be obvious from the surrounding vegetation. Immediately beyond it, turn right into the field, and follow the right-hand field edge immediately parallel with the old line, the course of which is shrouded in trees and bushes and will continue to be so much of the way back to Salehurst. In a few hundred yards you will arrive at the Rother, and you will be able to cross the river using the old railway bridge. Immediately beyond the bridge there was, at the time of writing, an accumulation of wire which one supposes was once intended to bar further progress. However the obstruction, such as it is, is easily surmounted (although it is suggested that you seek the owner's permission before venturing beyond it) and by crossing over a shallow gully you can return to your field-edge walk, proceeding immediately parallel with the old line. It really isn't worth trying to follow the old line itself, as progress will be hampered by overhanging branches and undergrowth. Soon you arrive at a barbed wire fence but a convenient stile in the fence a bit further to the left allows you to continue. Shortly afterwards the Rother swings in from the left and in order to make progress along the path that squeezes between the river bank on one side and the course of the old line on the other, you will need to cross two fences using the wooden constructions provided. (One hesitates to call them stiles.) Beyond them, the going is easier, and you can now enjoy lovely views to the church tower at Salehurst. You enter a field, at which point the course of the old line again becomes impossible to discern, although from the line of trees you have just passed you can guess the course it took. Follow the left-hand field edge until you arrive at a narrow tributary stream of the Rother, crossed by an extremely narrow plank bridge which although rather fragile-looking did take my daughter's and my combined weight of roughly 15 stone! Assuming you have made it safely, proceed to the next field and continue along it to arrive back at Church Bridge. It must be emphasized that NONE of the walk I have described to get you back from the Cripps Corner-Hawkhurst road to Church Bridge is along designated rights of way and one cannot rule out the possibility of obstructions being erected which will bar progress along some or all of this walk. You will in that case be forced back to the road and will have to retrace your steps taken for the outward journey.

At Church Bridge, turn right to rejoin the track which takes you back to Salehurst, and very soon you will be crossing back over the course of the old line. Continue to Salehurst the way you came, then proceed along the road back to the roundabout and go forward into Robertsbridge beyond the roundabout. The station is reached by turning right into Station Road in the middle of the village.

Trespassers on the Robertsbridge to Bodiam line be warned!

SECTION 3 - **LEWES TO UCKFIELD**

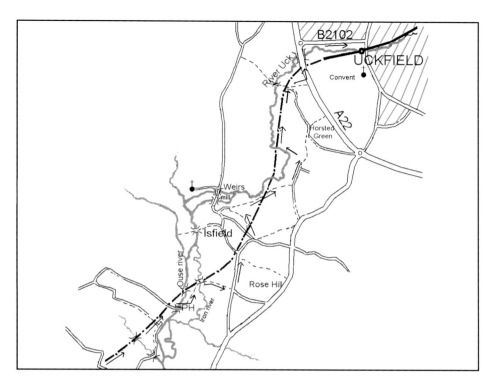

A relic of the Lewes to Uckfield line near Barcombe.

SECTION 3 - **LEWES TO UCKFIELD**

Length:	9 miles along the old line, but about 12 miles of walking will be required.
Start:	Lewes railway station.
Finish:	Uckfield railway station.
Public Transport:	Excellent rail services to Lewes from London Victoria, Brighton, Eastbourne and Hastings; very good bus service back to Lewes from Uckfield; regular trains from Uckfield on to Oxted and London Victoria.
Conditions:	Some good sections of the old line are available to walkers and where access is impossible there are footpaths to make the necessary links. The walking is pleasant rather than especially scenic, mostly through farmland in the valleys of the Ouse and Uck with good views to the South Downs.
Refreshments:	Pubs, shops and cafes at Lewes; pub at Barcombe; pub at end of Anchor Lane a mile beyond Barcombe; pub at Isfield; pubs, shops and cafes at Uckfield. RECOMMENDED PUB - BARCOMBE - ANCHOR - lovely riverside setting on the route.

History

The LBSCR had arrived at Lewes, the county town of Sussex, in the mid-1840's, and as early as 1844 there were suggestions for a link between Lewes and Uckfield, then an important agricultural centre. The Lewes & Uckfield Railway Company was established and, with the support of the LBSCR, opened the branch line from Lewes to Uckfield in 1858; services commencing on 11th October of that year and ownership of the line passed LBSCR during the following year. For its first ten years the line initially followed the line for Wivelsfield and Haywards Heath, heading north-westwards, before branching off at Uckfield Junction a short distance out of Lewes and then striking out north-eastwards. That was to change in 1868 (see below). There being no significant centres of population between Lewes and Uckfield, there were just two intermediate stations, serving relatively small villages. The first station on the line out of Lewes towards Uckfield was Barcombe, serving as it did the nearby village of

Barcombe of that name, but the station was renamed Barcombe Mills when another station was built at Barcombe on the Lewes-East Grinstead line (see chapter devoted to that line). Barcombe Mills station proved extremely popular with anglers, and during the 1920's upwards of a thousand train tickets were collected at Barcombe Mills from anglers on Bank Holidays. The second station was Isfield, virtually identical in construction to the one at Barcombe Mills and extended at the same time. During the First World War Isfield saw considerable deliveries of milk churns, and the station was also an unloading point for prisoners of war who were doing forestry work in the area. The flatness of the terrain meant that no tunnels were necessary but there were several road and path crossings, and a number of bridges had to be built over the Ouse or its tributary the Uck; just beyond Barcombe Mills two bridges in quick succession were needed to take the line across the two channels into which the Ouse divided at this point, one being known as the River Ouse Bridge, and the other known as Iron Bridge. Much of the line was in fact barely above the river level, and flooding occurred from time to time.

Ten years after the line opened, and nine years after the LBSCR takeover, there were two important events in the history of the line in quick succession. On 3rd August 1868 a line linking Uckfield with Tunbridge Wells came into being, allowing direct trains between Brighton and Tunbridge Wells via Falmer, Lewes, Uckfield, Crowborough and Eridge, and indeed it became theoretically possible to travel from London to Brighton using the Lewes-Uckfield portion. Then on 1st October of the same year a new stretch of line was opened between Lewes and Hamsey, a short way east of Uckfield Junction, heading eastwards out of Lewes station and then proceeding more directly towards Barcombe Mills past Hamsey Church. Not only did this allow a faster more direct journey, but it meant that trains that had started their journey from Brighton did not have to reverse back out of Lewes to continue towards Uckfield. This new section of line was from August 1882 to be shared with another branch line which left the Uckfield line at Culver Junction, just before Barcombe Mills, and proceeded northwards to East Grinstead via Chailey, Sheffield Park, Horsted Keynes and Kingscote.The Lewes-East Grinstead line is described elsewhere in this book.

In 1869 there were six weekday trains (two on Sundays) going from Lewes to Uckfield and on to Tunbridge Wells via Crowborough and Eridge, while an 1890 timetable shows weekday trains leaving Lewes for Uckfield at 7.32am, 8.32am, 9.55am, 12.18pm, 2.05pm, 4.53pm, 6.02pm, 6.21pm, 7.38pm and 9.32pm, with many although not all of these trains going on to Tunbridge Wells. In 1912 some ten weekday trains were still plying the Lewes to Uckfield line each way, the first train of the day leaving Tunbridge Wells at 7am, and arriving at Uckfield at 7.43am, Isfield at 7.49am, Barcombe Mills at 7.56am and Lewes at 8.05am. During the late 1930's daily through trains existed between Brighton and Chatham and also between Brighton and Reading, using the Uckfield line in each case.

The Lewes-Uckfield line was to be a victim of the Beeching axe; following a steady reduction in the number of services, the last train ran on 23rd February 1969. The line north of Uckfield was spared, leaving Uckfield effectively as a terminus. Ironically it is the station buildings of Barcombe Mills and Isfield that survive today, whilst Uckfield, which still boasts a railway service northwards towards Crowborough and Eridge, lost its original station comparatively recently and a brand new building has been constructed in its stead. In recent years there has been considerable pressure for the Lewes-Uckfield line to be reinstated, allowing for a link between the Victoria-Uckfield line and the network of routes that go out of Lewes towards Eastbourne, Hastings, Seaford, Brighton and Haywards Heath. So far attempts at reinstatement have not met with success, with considerable sums needing to be spent on restoring the river crossings. However, following the purchase of Isfield station by the Milham family in 1983, this station was restored and the track nearby was relaid to allow trains to ply a small section of the old line to the north-east of Isfield. This small section became known as the Lavender Line, not because of the surrounding vegetation but after the coal merchants A.E. Lavender who used to operate from the station yard. Since then a Lavender Line preservation society has been established and it is possible to enjoy journeys from Isfield along this section of line on coaches hauled by old steam locomotives.

Walking The Railway

Beginning at the existing railway station at Lewes, turn right out of the station forecourt and head along Station Road towards the town centre, soon reaching a road junction with Southover Road and Lansdown Place. Turn hard right, effectively doubling back on yourself, down Pinwell Road which drops to the railway level, then just before the yellow barrier bear left and shortly fork right along a footpath running parallel with the existing line. Soon you approach a footbridge over the railway, and a signboard indicating "Lewes Railway Land." Fork left here on to a path that enters an area quite dense with vegetation and with a semi-rural feel. After a few yards you will see ahead of you a strip of water, just before which is a "hump" across the path; shortly before the hump turn left on to a path that heads northwards, away from the existing line, and soon climbs up on to an embankment. You are now on the course of the old Lewes-Uckfield line, using the section that was added in October 1868. You remain on the embankment briefly then descend again, following the path to its end on the corner of Court Road. Enter Court Road, continuing in the same direction, and follow it to Friars Walk just east of which ran the old line, the street running immediately east of the old line hereabouts appropriately being known as Railway Walk. Turn right into Friars Walk and follow it, continuing on into Eastgate Street past Safeways; the old line proceeded northwards between Eastgate Street and the river Ouse. Swing right on to Phoenix Causeway and soon cross the Ouse, noting a small fragment of railway embankment, covered with vegetation, which still exists just to the left before the Ouse crossing. Pause here before the crossing and look north-east across the river to the Tesco superstore; a bridge used to carry the old line across the river from where you are standing to the spot now occupied by the store.

Cross the river and immediately turn left to follow the riverside path along the east bank. Pass the Tesco store and you will see a large area of green ahead of you; follow this area of green north-westwards, keeping parallel with the river - this is the course of the old line - and aim for a green embankment at the end. Climb on to the embankment, which carried the old line, and walk along what is a good track with deep cuttings to your right and left, and the suburban village of South Malling just above you to the right. You pass under two bridges, and emerge from the cuttings at a fence with a stile which you cross to enter open countryside. There are lovely views ahead of you including Hamsey Church, delightfully

A wet afternoon on the Lewes to Uckfield line near Barcombe.

positioned on the hilltop. Soon you reach the Ouse again, but although you can see the course taken by the old line to cross it and continue on past Hamsey Church, there is sadly no way over the river here today. You will have to retrace your steps all the way back to the large green area I mentioned at the start of this paragraph. Descend to the green area then bear hard right to join an obvious path; don't turn right to go underneath the embankment, but turn left and follow the path to a footbridge over the Ouse. Immediately after crossing the footbridge, turn right on to a riverside path that keeps the river to the right and the railway across fields to the left. You proceed north-westwards but in just under a mile from the bridge, the river and riverside path swing north-eastwards. Looking north-westwards at this point, you can identify where the old line left the still extant main line during the first ten years of its life. Shortly the river divides, your path continuing along the left bank of the narrower straighter channel, and by Hamsey Place you reach a metalled road at which you turn right, then immediately cross a bridge and follow the road uphill towards Hamsey Church. Just before reaching the church you see the remains of a bridge over the old line and can now look southwards to the spot where you had to backtrack. You can also look north-eastwards to follow (sadly with your eyes only) the course of the old line along a grassy embankment, and you may see how the line crossed the water and proceeded resolutely north-eastwards towards Barcombe.

Retrace your steps to Hamsey Place but now head straight on along Ivors Lane, heading north-westwards and very soon crossing the course of the pre-1868 old line, immediately beyond which is a signed path going off to the right. Follow this path, which runs parallel with and immediately adjacent to the course of the pre-1868 old line, then squeezes past the garden of a private house to arrive at another metalled road in the tiny village of Hamsey. Across the road, the old line can clearly be identified leading away in a north-easterly direction towards Barcombe Mills (the post-1868 section meeting up with the pre-1868 section just east of Hamsey) but unfortunately there is no public access. You are forced to turn left and follow the metalled road briefly, soon arriving at a signed footpath leading off to the right, which you take. This path is well-defined and as it is set slightly above the course of the old line, you get an excellent view to the course of the old line to your right as you walk.

Your path from Hamsey proceeds pleasantly enough, continuing north-eastwards past Cowlease Farm and on towards the village of Barcombe, dominated by its church. Beyond Cowlease Farm there are two footbridge crossings in quick succession; at the second a path forks left to the church. Do not take this but continue in the same direction and shortly come to a broad track linking Barcombe with Culver Farm. Cross straight over on a well-defined albeit narrow path which after skirting some private housing turns sharply right and descends gently across a field to a footbridge. You can still make out the course of the old line, still to your right, quite easily, and the footbridge is as close as you will get to Culver Junction, where the East Grinstead branch left the Uckfield line. At the footbridge you swing in a more north-easterly direction again, crossing the East Grinstead branch (covered more fully elsewhere in this book)Shortly there is another footbridge crossing and then a gentle ascent to the road linking Barcombe Mills and Barcombe Cross. Turn right to follow the road downhill to a pub, immediately behind which are the old station buildings of Barcombe Mills. Until a few years ago, the old station served as a café, but this has now closed, and at the time of writing the buildings are private and inaccessible to walkers. The good news, however, is that you can now join the old line for the next mile, heading north-eastwards; the going is very straightforward through pleasant unspoilt countryside, and it is a shame when you reach Anchor Lane and discover the way ahead is blocked off. Turn right on to Anchor Lane and very shortly reach the deservedly popular Anchor Inn with its delightful garden that backs on to the Ouse.

Much of the next mile of old line, between here and Isfield, is accessible to walkers although this section of old line is not a designated right of way. After passing the Anchor, use the footbridge to cross the river, then bear left and follow the right bank of the river. Soon you reach the course of the old line again, and it is possible to climb up on to the line (attacking it from the far side) and follow it north-eastwards. This is not a designated right of way but there is no difficulty of access. There is shortly a bridge crossing which at the time of writing is quite secure; should access become impossible or prohibited, there is a public path running north-eastwards parallel with, and to the right of the old line, and easily and obviously followable from beyond the bridge crossing at the Anchor. Sadly it is necessary in any event to leave the old line beside a small pond barely half a mile from the Anchor, for although at the time of writing it was possible to follow the old line a little further, major building/excavation works on the old line immediately south-west of Isfield, which are obliterating remaining traces of the old line, will force you to retrace your steps. Bear right off the old line round to the south tip of the pond to pick up a path which now runs just south of east to arrive at a metalled road. Turn left to follow the metalled road northwards to Isfield which boasts a beautifully preserved station and a handy pub that is situated nearby.

If time allows, you should certainly explore the station, with its wonderful reminders of a time when through trains between Lewes and Uckfield did exist, and travel on one of the steam trains that ply the very small stretch of preserved line that runs north-eastwards from here. The station is on a road junction, and to continue on foot you need to take the road running to the south-east of the line, marked on maps as Horsted Lane. The road bends right and then right again; at the second bend turn left on to a signed path which heads north-westwards and very soon crosses the preserved line. Your path runs all too briefly parallel with the line but almost at once goes off left, north-westwards, and then swings left again, going downhill towards the buildings of Tile Barn Farm. As you reach the farm you need to turn right on to a public footpath that heads north-eastwards; this right turn was not properly signposted at the time of writing and could very easily be missed. Continue north-eastwards through fields to arrive at the River Uck, then briefly follow the right (south) bank of the Uck, before using a footbridge to cross over the river. Follow the left bank, keeping to the path and heading north-eastwards. You temporarily lose the river at a meander round a small patch of woodland but are soon reunited with it and now swing in an easterly direction, shortly meeting the old line just north of the point where the preserved section ends, and passing under the bridge which carried the old line. It is possible to detour immediately left after crossing the bridge, following the field edge parallel with the old line, and it may be possible to access the line itself (though it is not a designated right of way), but your way forward is soon barred by the Uck and thick vegetation, so you must return to the bridge.

Proceed away from the old line, heading eastwards, along the path which soon crosses the Uck and carries on across grassland, skirting the southern edge of an area of woodland, and arriving at a road on to which you turn left. Very shortly turn left again on to a delightful green track (not a designated right of way), which skirts the right hand edge of an area of woodland and then runs parallel with and immediately to the right of the River Uck. You pass a weir and an inaccessible footbridge then climb gently to be reunited with the old line on the Uckfield side of the river. Though again it is not a designated right of way, there is no difficulty in obtaining access to it. Proceed in a north-easterly direction along the old line towards Uckfield; it is a delightful walk, staying roughly parallel with the Uck which is to your left, and offering very pleasant views across the surrounding meadows. The sound of traffic on the very busy A22 Uckfield by-pass becomes more intrusive and as you get closer and closer to the A22, passing just to the left of the buildings of Owlsbury Farm, the going gets rather more difficult, with increasing amounts of vegetation and loose stones to negotiate. Maddeningly, a tantalising few yards from the A22 and barely half a mile from the centre of Uckfield as the crow flies, you reach a dead end and are forced back on yourself. There is now no possibility of following the old line any further.

Retrace your steps a couple of hundred yards to a junction with a farm track that leads directly to the buildings of Owlsbury Farm. Turn left on to the track and follow it past the buildings then, just beyond them, look for a footpath going off to the left, heading just north of east and proceeding down to the A22. It seems there is no way forward, but by turning right and following the field edge parallel with the road you soon reach a stile to your left which you cross, then walk along a narrow path that takes you up to the A22. Cross the road then turn left to follow alongside this extremely busy road for about half a mile; there is no pavement, so you will need to keep to the verge. Soon you will see the section of old line you walked a short while ago coming in from the left. To complete the walk into Uckfield, continue past a large industrial estate beside the A22 to the roundabout where you turn right along the B2102. In just over half a mile you reach the bus station on your right, from which there are frequent buses back to Lewes, and just beyond the bus station is a T-junction with the High Street. By turning right into the High Street you soon arrive at the railway station which is on the left, noting that the course of the old line to the right is neither clear nor accessible. Trains leave the station for Eridge, Edenbridge and Oxted; to get back to Lewes by train would involve a complicated journey with changes either at Oxted and East Croydon or Edenbridge and Gatwick Airport, and a journey time of up to three hours!

POSTSCRIPT - FURTHER INFORMATION

If your exploration of the disused railways of Sussex has whetted your appetite for further old railway walking, or has fuelled your interest in making more of the disused railway network available for public access, there are two organisations that will be of particular interest to you.

The RAILWAY RAMBLERS provide a nationwide programme of organised walks along stretches of disused railways and publish regular newsletters packed with information about disused railway lines throughout the country. For more information contact its Chairman, Jeff Vinter, 1 Victoria Road, Chichester, West Sussex. Their website is www.railwayramblers.org.uk

SUSTRANS, an abbreviation for "Sustainable Transport," is an organisation which promotes the creation of walkways and cycleways to provide a more environmentally friendly means of getting around. The conversion of disused railways is a key aspect of their strategy. You can visit SUSTRANS on its website which is www.sustrans.org.uk

S.B. Publications publish a wide range of local interest books on Sussex.
For a free catalogue please write to:
S.B. Publications, 14 Bishopstone Road, Seaford, East Sussex.
or access our website on
www.sbpublications.co.uk